NEXT OF KIN

Sharon Sala

CHIVERS

> **British Library Cataloguing in Publication Data available**

This Large Print edition published by AudioGO Ltd, Bath, 2012.
Published by arrangement with Harlequin Enterprises II B.V./S. à r.l.

U.K. Hardcover   ISBN   978 1 4713 1886 3
U.K. Softcover   ISBN   978 1 4713 1887 0

Copyright © 2012 by Sharon Sala
A Rebel Ridge Novel No 1

Printed and bound in Great Britain by
MPG Books Group Limited

I'm dedicating this book to my families, because "When life gets rough — when you need a friend — you can't go wrong with your next of kin."

If that statement wasn't so long, I'd have it made into a bumper sticker.

Family is everything to me. I often talk about the people who I've lost, and what holes they leave in my life. I don't talk enough about the ones who are still here, who make my days brighter and my life worth living, so I'm naming them now. Listen up, my sweet babies, 'cause I'm bragging on you.

My mother, Iris, is and always has been the perfect example for me of how a life should be lived — in the service of others. She was a teacher.

My son, Chris, and his wife, Kristie, are the perfect example of how a marriage should work. Their daughters, Chelsea, Logan and Leslie, have been taught from an early age to respect their elders, appreciate what they've been given and love each other.

My daughter, Kathy, and her husband, Ashley, are an A+ example of making a blended marriage work. Each has a son, and the boys not only get along but really love each other. Even though the boys don't live together full-time, they are still brothers of the heart, if not by blood.

My niece, Crissy, and her husband, Andy, work hard every day to make sure they're giving their three girls everything they need to succeed in life. The girls, Destiny, Devyn and Courtney, know they are treasured in every way.

I come from a long line of people — the Shero family and the Smith family — who love and protect their own.

I am blessed.

ONE

Rebel Ridge, Kentucky

Ryal Walker couldn't sleep. He'd fought the bed until the covers were in a mess before he finally gave up, thinking maybe a little fresh air would help clear his mind. It was nearly 2:00 a.m. when he pulled on a pair of sweatpants, then walked barefoot through the darkened rooms of his home and out onto the front porch. Upon his arrival, an owl took flight from a nearby pine.

"Sorry about that," he said softly, aware that he'd trespassed by disturbing the status quo around the house.

A slight breeze quickly cooled the sweat from his body as he sat down on the porch steps and rested his elbows on his knees. He couldn't figure out what was bugging him. He hated to admit it, but he knew something bad was going to happen. He'd had the same feeling ten years ago when he learned Beth's parents had moved in the night, taking her away from him. He hadn't understood it then any more than he understood it now. Up on the mountain, it wasn't uncommon for distant cousins to marry. Her mother and his mother had been fourth cousins and not even close friends at that. And the difference in his and Beth's ages wasn't uncommon, either. He'd been twenty-five to her seventeen.

It was weeks later before he learned the move had nothing to do with their love for each other. Instead, he and Beth had been the victims of a much larger problem. Once he'd found out what had happened, he'd tried to contact her, but all his letters had been returned unopened.

None of the other Venables would talk to him or seemed willing to interfere with her family's decision to cut themselves off from Rebel Ridge. Today, people would call their unrequited love affair collateral damage, but back then it had been a tragedy, at least for him.

He put the thought of her back in his memory, where she belonged, as he gazed into the trees surrounding his home. He wasn't one to dwell on lost causes, but he couldn't help but wonder what their lives would have been like if her family had stayed.

Just then something rustled in the bushes beside the house. He turned to look just as a possum wandered out from beneath a lilac bush and ambled across the yard. Solitude was a good thing in daylight, but sometimes at night it could feel threatening. Tonight was one of those nights.

He kept scanning the tree line, looking for something that seemed out of place, but saw nothing at which he should feel alarmed. Still, it wasn't the first time he'd had a feeling like this, and he'd learned long ago not to ignore his instincts, so he waited, hoping for an answer.

Sound carried in the mountains, and he could hear someone running his dogs on the next ridge over. The animals' barks and yips were high-pitched and frantic, but when they suddenly shifted to baying howls, he knew they'd just treed whatever they'd been chasing.

At that moment the skin crawled on the back of his neck. That was exactly how he felt — treed — which made no sense. He wasn't trapped — in fact, far from it. There were few places on this earth more free than the vastness of the Appalachian Mountains. He liked his life, even though it was, despite his large extended family, sometimes a lonely one.

He liked building things, and over the years he had created a decent business building handcrafted, one-of-a-kind pieces of furniture. And, despite the persistence of various young women in the area, he'd never found one to replace the love he'd had for Beth.

As he listened to the hunting dogs' frenzy, he heard another sound — more poignant, more frantic. It was the death screams of the animal they had treed.

Ryal had heard that sound plenty of times over the thirty-five years of his life, but for some reason, hearing the creature's death throes in the midst of his uneasiness seemed like another omen of something bad.

He stood up, eyes carefully sweeping the darkened tree line around his home, then went back into the house, locking the door behind him.

Los Angeles, California

Some believe that the fate of every living thing hinges upon little more than chance.

For twenty-seven-year-old Beth Venable, it began with a gas leak in her Los Angeles apartment building, followed by a phone call to her friend Sarah Steinman, asking if she might spend the night at her place until the all clear was given for the residents to

10

go back. Pleased to get to spend a night with her friend, Sarah happily agreed, and Beth's dilemma was over.

That night, as Beth bedded down on Sarah's living room sofa, the unfamiliar surroundings and the huge bank of curtainless windows made it difficult for her to fall asleep. After tossing and turning for what seemed like hours, she got up to get a drink. Outside, the moon was full, the sky cloudless.

The night view of the city pulled her toward the windows with their bird's-eye view of the steady stream of traffic on the streets below. She watched the cars weaving in and out of line without really focusing. She was more worried about her apartment, hoping they got the leak repaired before the entire building blew up. Everything she owned was in it.

She glanced up at the sky, and not without a little bit of regret. This was definitely not the same view of the night sky that she remembered from where she'd lived as a child, although it had been ten years since she'd been back to Kentucky. There, heaven looked as if it were within reach — the unending array of stars so clear they looked like diamonds on black velvet. Here, the only stars anyone was interested in seeing walked on two legs, and heaven wasn't on their radar as often as it should have been.

She rarely let herself think about those years in Kentucky, because the memories brought back nothing but pain. She'd loved Ryal Walker with a passion far beyond her seventeen years, and when they were abruptly separated, she'd expected him to follow. For weeks she'd watched the streets and haunted the mailbox, certain he would find a way to contact her, but the weeks had turned to months and the months to a year. By that time she had learned how to hide her emotions and to live with a broken heart. Losing Ryal had taught her one thing: to never count on anyone but herself.

A phalanx of cop cars followed by a fire truck went flying past on the street below. She said a quiet prayer of safekeeping for whomever was in danger, then turned away from the window. As she did, she noticed a telescope in the corner. It was mounted on a tripod and aimed at the sky. She knew Sarah was into astrology but had not known that included stargazing, as well.

Curious, she pulled the telescope out of the corner, dragged it to the window and aimed it skyward. It took a couple of moments to adjust the focus to her eyesight, but then she was pleasantly surprised to discover how clearly she could see distant objects. After a couple of minutes of scanning the heavens, she turned the telescope to the view of the city, then, a couple of minutes later, to the apartment building directly across the street.

Most of the windows were darkened, like hers — except for one apartment. Not only were all the lights still on, but the curtains had also not been drawn. She could see a couple standing at the windows, and from their expressions, they were having an argument.

Before she had time to feel guilty for spying, they went from shouting to physical violence. The man suddenly shoved the woman against the back of a sofa. She reacted with a hard, vicious slap to his jaw. Beth saw rage sweep across his face, and then all of a sudden there was a knife in his hand. He slit the woman's throat so quickly that, had it not been for the arterial spray that abruptly splashed across the window, Beth would have thought she'd imagined it.

She let out a scream, and then started jumping up and down.

"Oh, my God, oh, my God! Sarah! Sarah! Help!"

Sarah burst into the room carrying a baseball bat, a frantic expression on her face. When she realized Beth was in the room alone, she shrieked, "What the hell's wrong?"

Beth was shaking so hard she felt ill. She kept pointing at the window and shouted, "He killed her. They were fighting, and then he just slashed her throat."

"What? Where?"

"There, in that apartment across the street — the one with all the lights still on."

Beth looked back into the telescope just as the man turned toward the windows. She gasped, then froze, suddenly afraid he could see her.

"I need lights," Sarah muttered, and reached for the switch.

"Don't!" Beth screamed. "No lights. Oh, my God, no lights!"

"Good grief, Beth. Are you sure you weren't dreaming?"

"I wish," Beth said. "Come here. See for yourself."

Even though the lights were still off, the man's studied focus gave her an eerie feeling. She feared he could see her silhouette at the window but resisted the urge to hide as she mentally mapped the contours of his features, the sharp beak of a nose set in a middle-aged face, olive complexion, low forehead and no hair. His eyes were dark

14

and deep-set, with equally dark bushy eye-brows.

She watched as he took a handkerchief from his pocket and methodically wiped the blood spray from his face. As he turned away, his movement reminded her of the moment's urgency — that he would be gone before they alerted the authorities.

"Let me see," Sarah said.

Beth stepped back as Sarah peered through the scope.

"I don't see anyone," Sarah said.

Beth shoved her aside. "Well, I did! Call the police. Hurry. Hurry! The apartment is on the same floor as this one, the corner unit."

Beth's anxiety seemed to be catching. Sarah made the call, her voice shaking as she rattled off the address of the apartment building where the murder had occurred, then gave them her name and address. As soon as she hung up, she ran back to where Beth was standing.

"Is he still there?"

"Yes," Beth said.

"Let me see," Sarah begged, but all she saw was the back of the man as he walked out the door.

"He's gone!"

Beth groaned. "Maybe he'll come out the

front door. You watch to see if a car comes out of the alley. I'll watch the front of the building."

Within a couple of minutes they heard sirens, just as a black sports car came shooting out of the alley beside the building and turned north, driving away from the approaching sirens.

Sarah groaned. "If that's him, he's getting away."

"Get back on the phone and tell the police about the car," Beth said, as she began pulling on her clothes.

"What are you doing?" Sarah asked.

"I'm getting dressed. You gave the police your name and address, didn't you?"

"Yes."

Beth reached for her slacks. "Then they'll be coming to talk to us."

"Oh, Beth, you can't . . ."

Beth yanked her shirt down over her head. "Sarah! He killed her. I can't ignore what I saw."

"I know, I know . . . it's just scary, that's all," Sarah said.

"Not as scary as it must have been to her," Beth said, as she began to look around the room. "Where did you put my briefcase? I need my briefcase."

"Why?"

"Because I saw his face and I'm an illustrator, that's why."

"Right. It's in the hall closet," Sarah said. She called 911 again, and quickly related the information about the black sports car and the direction it had gone. When she hung up, her hands were shaking. "I guess I'd better get dressed, too," she said, and left the room on the run.

Within twenty minutes there was a knock on the door. Beth was sitting at the dining room table with her head down, concentrating on her sketch pad.

Sarah peered through the security port and saw two men holding up their badges.

"It's them," she hissed, then opened the door to two plainclothes detectives flashing LAPD badges.

"Sarah Steinman?"

"Yes."

"I'm Detective Burroughs, and this is my partner, Detective Franklin. May we come in?"

Sarah stepped aside as they entered the apartment, then realized the sofa was still set up as Beth's makeshift bed. "Sorry for the mess," she said, as she hurried to move the bedding aside. "My friend Beth is spending the night."

Beth looked up briefly, as Sarah wrapped

her arms around her waist to keep from shaking and asked, "Was there really a murder?"

They nodded.

"Oh, my God," Sarah said. "Beth is the one who actually witnessed it. I just made the call."

Burroughs eyed Beth curiously. "You don't live here?"

Beth paused. "No, sir. I live about thirty minutes south. My apartment had a gas leak earlier today. They evacuated all the residents while it's being repaired. I begged a bed from Sarah for the night."

Detective Franklin had already spotted the telescope and was looking through it. "Is this how you witnessed the murder?"

Beth nodded. "I couldn't sleep." She got up from her chair and walked back to the window, then hugged herself to keep from shuddering. The memory of what she'd seen was horrifying. "I'd been up for a while when I saw the telescope and tried it out. That's when I saw the couple fighting in the apartment directly across the street."

She pointed to the brightly lit apartment across the way, where a large number of people were now moving about. "The man was older and bigger, but the woman was in his face screaming right back at him. He

18

pushed her. She slapped him. Then all of a sudden he pulled a knife and slit her throat so fast I wasn't sure what he'd done until I saw blood spray across the window. That's when I screamed."

"Her screams woke me up," Sarah said. "I nearly fell getting out of bed, I was so scared, and when I got in here, Beth was telling me to call 911, so I did."

"Did you see him, too?" Burroughs asked.

Sarah shook her head. "By the time I looked, he was walking out the door. All I saw was the back of a bald-headed man in a dark suit. But we both saw a black sports car come out of the alley a few minutes later and drive away really fast. It went south as the police came in from the north."

Both detectives were making notes as the women kept talking.

"Did either of you know the woman in the other apartment?" Burroughs asked.

"No," Beth said. "I've never been here before."

"I don't even know my neighbor across the hall," Sarah said.

Burroughs eyed Beth. "Do you think you could identify him if you saw him again?"

"Yes."

"Would you be willing to come down to

headquarters and go through some mug shots?"

"I can do better than that," Beth said, and hurried back to the table. She tore the top sheet off her sketch pad and gave it to Burroughs. "I'm an illustrator."

"This is amazing," Burroughs said. He was eyeing the drawing she'd made when a frown suddenly furrowed his forehead. "He looks familiar."

Franklin glanced over his partner's shoulder at the drawing Beth had made, his eyes widening at her attention to detail. She'd even added a small puckered scar between the man's nose and upper lip. "The LAPD could use someone as skilled as you."

Beth shook her head. "Thanks, but I'll stick to illustrating children's books."

Burroughs rolled up the drawing and dropped his notebook in his pocket. "We're going to need you to come down to headquarters to give an official statement."

And so it begins, Beth thought. Like it or not, she was now a witness in a murder investigation.

"Let me get my purse and jacket."

Sarah shivered. "Do I have to go, too?"

"No, ma'am. Your testimony would be secondhand, since you didn't actually witness anything."

The relief on Sarah's face was obvious. She gave Beth an apologetic look and then hugged her. "When you've finished there, come back. Tomorrow is my day off, so even if you're not back till morning, I'll still be here, and you'll need a place to shower before you go in for that meeting you said you had."

Beth hugged her. "I'm sorry for causing so much trouble for you."

"You didn't cause anything," Sarah said, and then ran to her hall table, opened a drawer and took out a key. "This is an extra key to the front door. I'll probably still be asleep."

"See you later," Beth said.

Sarah waved goodbye and locked the door behind them.

Ike Pappas had wasted no time as he strode out of the elevator into the underground parking of his ex-wife's apartment building. He'd glanced at the security cameras, confident that they were all still off, and jumped into his Aston Martin. As soon as he cleared the alley and got back in traffic, he'd looked up in the rearview mirror and flexed his jaw, which was still stinging.

His eyes narrowed angrily. He couldn't believe Lorena had flipped out like that.

Granted, he'd once been married to her, which he supposed gave her a sense of false security, but she'd been wrong — very wrong — to threaten him. He'd expected her to be pissed because he'd finally taken their son into the business, but he'd under-estimated her anger. She kept screaming that he'd reneged on his promise — the one he'd made to her years ago that he would keep their son, Adam, out of organized crime — and she was going to make him pay. She'd said she would rather see Adam in prison than turn into a killer like Ike.

What Lorena hadn't given him time to explain was that Adam had plans of his own. He had been grooming himself to step into his father's shoes and wouldn't be dis-suaded. Ike had to admit he was proud of his son's ambitions. What man wouldn't want his son to follow in his footsteps? In Ike's case, very lucrative footsteps.

He knew the law would be calling once her identity was known, and he knew they would find his DNA and prints all over the place, but he wasn't worried. He owned the building. Once Lorena was dead, he'd gone straight to the security room, killed the guard on duty, then scrubbed the past twelve hours of security footage before disabling all the cameras, making sure there was nothing to tie him to the scene.

He'd set her up in the apartment years ago, and he and Adam visited regularly, often for a meal. She was, after all, the mother of his only child, and family was important — to be revered. But after screaming at him that she was going to the Feds, she'd given him no choice.

It wasn't until Ike had driven back through the iron gates marking the entrance to his estate that he began to relax. The guard at the gates wasn't on duty at night. The gates automatically swung shut behind him as he drove onto the grounds.

The mansion in which he lived was more like a castle, minus the moat, standing three stories tall at the center, with two-story wings spreading out on either side and sprawled over three acres of land, with ten more acres surrounding it. It was built like a fortress for a reason. Ike Pappas had made many enemies during his rise through the ranks of organized crime. There was always someone interested in taking down the kingpin of a syndicate like his.

He turned off the headlights as he neared the house and quickly drove into the garage under cover of darkness. Once inside, he made a sweep through his own security footage and deleted the few minutes that showed him leaving in his car earlier, then reappearing later.

He took the back stairs up to his suite so he wouldn't pass Adam's bedroom to get to his own. Once inside, he stripped out of his clothes, underwear and shoes included, rolled them up and stuffed them into a garbage bag, then left the bag in the middle of his bedroom floor as he headed for the shower.

The hot water sluicing down his body washed away the last remnants of his ex-wife's blood in a swath of soap and heat. He scrubbed until his skin was stinging, then took a nailbrush to his fingers, making sure there was no evidence of her DNA left behind.

Once he was out, he dressed in a pair of navy silk pajamas and black Gucci lounge shoes, and carried the plastic bag down to the basement. He entered a closet housing a dozen electrical panels that controlled the entire property, turned on a light and walked in, closing the door behind him. Once inside, he pressed on a hidden panel. Another door opened, swinging inward on silent hinges. He tossed the bag inside, then quickly shut the door. It wasn't the first evidence that could send him to prison he'd stowed in there, and it probably wouldn't be the last, but it was as safe in there as anywhere on earth. No one — not even Adam — knew about the existence of the room he'd added to the house after he'd bought it, seeing as the man who'd designed and built it was no longer alive to tell the tale.

Ike exited the closet and went back to the main floor, then into the library, where he poured himself a stiff drink. If Adam caught him up at this hour of the morning, all he had to say was that he'd been unable to sleep and had gone down to get a drink. A little ouzo should serve his purposes and help him unwind.

He was pouring his second drink when the phone on the desk began to ring. It was a dedicated line and only rang in this room. The only people who had the number were his snitches. He emptied the glass, then answered on the second ring.

"Pappas."

"Mr. Pappas . . . this is Donny Franco."

Ike frowned. He had people everywhere, including the LAPD. Nothing happened in the city that he didn't know about — certainly nothing that mattered to him.

"It's late," he said shortly.

"They brought a woman into headquarters tonight who's claiming she witnessed the murder of your ex-wife."

Ike's heart skipped a beat. *How the hell?* But he wasn't giving himself away to anyone, especially to a cop on the take. He injected a note of incredulity into his voice.

"Is this true? Is my ex-wife really dead?"

"Yes, sir. A woman named Sarah Steinman, who lives in the building across the street, called the police. Apparently she witnessed it through a telescope from her apartment. Apartment 9B."

"I see. Thank you for the information."

"Uh . . . Mr. Pappas?"

"Yes?"

"That's not all. They have a sketch of the killer — a very good sketch. I thought you'd want to know."

"I always appreciate information and reward it accordingly."

"Yes, sir."

Ike ignored the excitement in Franco's voice and hung up. He went to his desk and pulled out a throwaway. There was only one number programmed into the phone, and once it had served its purpose, it would disappear like his clothes.

He made the connection, knowing Pacheco would answer by the second ring.

"Yes, sir?"

"Sarah Steinman. Brickman Apartments.

9B. Now."

"Yes, sir."

"Call me back on this number when it's done."

"Yes, sir."

The line went dead in his ear.

He went back up to his bedroom, then stretched out on the bed and closed his eyes. The police would be here within hours. Might as well get a little rest while Pacheco cleaned up.

Beth glanced up at the wall clock over Detective Burroughs's desk. It was after 3:00 a.m. Why was it taking so long? She'd given her statement, picked a man from a photo lineup even though she'd already furnished them with a sketch, and agreed to testify in court should he be brought to trial. What more could they possibly expect from her?

Her eyes were burning from lack of sleep, and she was in the process of getting a headache. There was no way she was going to be able to make it to that meeting tomorrow. She hoped people would understand. Deadlines were a big deal in the publishing world, and client approval was always the first order of the day, although in this case all her sketches were done and turned in.

27

The meeting was just a follow-up, in case any changes needed to be made.

All of a sudden the door to the captain's office swung open and Detective Burroughs came out. There was a strange expression on his face, but when he spoke, he was all apologies.

"I'm sorry to have kept you waiting," he said. "If you're ready, I'll take you back to Miss Steinman's apartment."

Finally. "I'm ready," she said, then gathered her things and followed him to the parking lot.

Once inside the car, the silence got to Beth. "So the man I picked out in the photo lineup . . . who was he?"

Burroughs hesitated. They didn't want to spook her, but on the other hand, they couldn't just let her go about her life without knowing how dangerous he was.

"He's associated with organized crime. Let's just say it would be best not to mention names at this point, not until we're able to gather more evidence against him."

Beth was shocked. "You mean you aren't going to arrest him right now?"

"He'll be questioned, but I can promise you, he'll have an airtight alibi. It will come down to your word against his, which won't hold up in court, and we don't want him to know there's a witness. We're still processing evidence from the scene. Finding his DNA on the victim's clothing would be a plus. It's complicated."

Beth frowned. "But I saw him push her, then cut her throat as calmly as if he were slicing a loaf of bread. Not even an expression on his face. What good does it do for a witness to come forward when this is all that happens?"

Burroughs knew how she felt. Sometimes the police felt just as helpless. The justice system was complicated, and quite often the people with the most money and power could get away with a lot. It was going to take an ironclad case against Ike Pappas to bring him to justice, and they didn't want to mess it up by jumping the gun.

After that, the drive was silent. Beth wasn't in the mood for conversation, and the detective seemed focused on the street traffic as well as the traffic on the police radio. When they finally reached the Brickman Apartments, she breathed a quick sigh of relief. The sooner she could put this behind her, the better.

"Here we are," Burroughs said as he pulled up to the curb. "I know there's a security guard on duty, but considering the hour, I'll walk you back in."

"Thank you," Beth said.

They entered the building in tandem. Beth stepped aside long enough for the detective to flash his badge and remind the guard that Miss Venable was a guest in 9B; then they got on the elevator together.

"You really don't have to walk me all the way to the door," Beth said.

Burroughs smiled. "It's not a problem."

There was nothing more she could say. The elevator stopped on the ninth floor with a jerk. As they neared the apartment, Beth began digging for the key Sarah had loaned her, and when they stopped at 9B, she slid the key into the lock.

She paused. "So here we are. Thank you for the escort."

"Yes, ma'am," Burroughs said, and stepped back as Beth opened the door, revealing a darkened interior.

"I guess she turned off the lights," she said, and fumbled for the switch just inside the door.

In seconds the interior lit up.

Beth walked inside. "I'll be okay from here."

Burroughs nodded as he turned and headed for the elevator.

The unfamiliar feel of a strange apartment was still with Beth as she walked toward the sofa, where her bed had been remade. She tossed her jacket on the arm and dropped her purse on the floor. She was just about to kick off her shoes when she glanced up, then stopped short. The door to Sarah's bedroom was ajar, and she could see flashes of light, probably from the television screen. Beth wasn't in the mood to talk, but if Sarah was awake, the least she could do was let her know she was back.

The moment the door swung inward her mind went blank. It took another second for her brain to register the scene.

The television was on, but muted. Sarah was lying in bed with two pillows propped up behind her and the remote in her hand. Her eyes were open. But it was the hole in the middle of her forehead and the blood-soaked pillows behind her head that made reality kick in.

Beth screamed, then covered her face and screamed again before it hit her that the killer might still be inside. With her heart in her throat, she bolted for the door.

Burroughs was halfway to the elevator when he heard the first scream. By the time she screamed again he had already pulled his weapon and was running back down the hall. Just as he reached the door, it flew open and Beth Venable fell into his arms.

"She's dead. Sarah's dead. Someone shot her. There's blood everywhere. Oh, my God. Oh, my God!"

Burroughs gave her a rough push. "Stay back," he ordered, and slipped inside with his gun still drawn. He quickly checked out the living room and kitchen, then moved toward the bedroom and the gaping door. He'd seen plenty of bodies during his career, but it was something he'd never gotten used to.

Beth Venable was right about one thing — Sarah Steinman was definitely dead. From the size of the hole in her forehead, he would guess a .38 caliber. The odd thing about the room was that nothing was out of place. There'd been no fight, no resistance. The muted television was odd, and he couldn't help but wonder if she'd heard something out of place and muted her program to listen closer. He could picture an intruder entering the apartment, pushing open the bedroom door and firing point-blank. She wouldn't have had a chance to scream or run, and since nothing had been reported, he suspected the killer had used a silencer.

A few hours ago this twentysomething woman had called in to report a murder, and now she was dead.

The whole setup stank.

He holstered his gun, got Beth Venable out of the hall and called in the murder. When he turned around, Beth was still standing where he'd put her, white-faced and shaking so hard he thought she might faint.

"Sit there," he said, pointing toward the sofa. "I've called it in. Police will be here shortly."

Her eyes were wide with shock. "Why did this happen?"

The first thought that went through his mind was that Pappas already knew there was a witness, which meant there was a snitch in the department. The possibility definitely existed. It made him sick.

"It's hard to say. Obviously someone took her by surprise. She didn't even have time to fight or run."

Beth wrapped her arms around herself, rocking back and forth where she sat, but the expression on her face was one of dazed disbelief. She kept remembering that moment in the dark when she'd felt as if the killer were staring straight into her eyes. Maybe he had seen her at the window. This was Sarah's apartment. He would have had no way of knowing Beth had been the witness — the *only* witness.

"It was the killer from across the street, wasn't it? There was a moment when I thought he saw me. He must have. That's why this happened. Oh, God. It's my fault. It's my fault Sarah's dead."

TWO

Rebel Ridge, Kentucky

Ryal was finishing his first cup of coffee as day broke in the east. He tossed the remaining dregs into the rosebush by the front steps and then set his cup on the porch railing. He needed to deliver a special-order hutch he'd made for a customer's wedding anniversary, but for some reason he didn't want to leave. That uneasy feeling he'd had last night was still with him, but business was business.

An hour later he was loaded and ready but continued to hang around the house, delaying the inevitable trip as long as he could. He kept thinking he was going to miss something important if he left, then reminded himself that if he were really needed, he would eventually be found.

Beth had cried until she was numb. Except for a throbbing headache, she felt nothing.

She hadn't moved since Detective Burroughs had set her down on the sofa other than to pull a blanket up around her shoulders. It wasn't because she was cold so much as a subconscious effort to hide from what was going on. Every time she closed her eyes, she saw Sarah's face and that blank, sightless expression — and the blood. Dear God, the blood.

Police were everywhere. The crew from the LAPD crime lab was still taking photos and fingerprints and bagging evidence, although the coroner had come and gone, taking what was left of Sarah Steinman to the morgue.

As Beth glanced toward the windows, she was shocked to see the faint rays of first light pushing over the horizon. A new day was about to dawn while she had yet to come to terms with the old one.

Startled by a flurry of activity at the doorway, she turned to look just as three men in dark suits entered the room. She saw Detective Burroughs glare, have a few words with them, then look her way. Her heart thumped hard against her chest as Burroughs started toward her with the three men at his heels. Something bad was happening.

"Beth, these men want to talk to you."

Beth drew the blanket tighter beneath her chin as the tallest of the three men flashed a badge.

"Miss Venable, I'm Special Agent Ames with the Federal Bureau of Investigation. These men are Special Agent Burke and Special Agent Charles. We'd like to talk to you."

Beth blinked. The FBI?

"About what?"

Ames sat down on the sofa beside her, then leaned forward, resting his elbows on his knees in what she supposed was a move to try and put her at ease, but that was never going to happen — not here.

"You know the man you picked out of a photo lineup at the police station . . . the one who matched your sketch and who you said committed the murder in the apartment across the street?"

She nodded.

"His name is Ike Pappas. He's the current head of a crime syndicate that reaches all the way to the other side of the country. The woman you saw him kill is his ex-wife, Lorena. We've been building a case against him — or trying to — for the past two years. Problem is, our witnesses keep recanting their statements or disappearing — or dying."

Horror was rising within Beth in creeping increments. Just when she thought things couldn't get worse.

"Have you arrested him?"

"Not yet. The police are still working the evidence from the crime scene. Lorena was going to testify against him. The fact that she's dead tells us he probably found out. And the fact that your friend is dead is obviously because he found out that there was a witness to the murder. With the intelligence he's able to gather, it won't take him long to find out he had the wrong woman killed."

Her fingers curled into fists to keep them from trembling.

"But wouldn't his fingerprints be all over the place? And his DNA must be on her. They were hitting each other before he cut her throat."

"Unfortunately, it's not that simple. Pappas owns the building. He set his ex-wife up in the apartment and visits regularly. His DNA and fingerprints are all over the place with good reason."

Beth's heart was pounding so fast it was difficult to breathe. "Are you saying he's going to get away with it?"

"Not if we can help it. Not if we can keep you safe until we go to court."

Beth glanced toward Sarah's bedroom.

"And you're sure that's why Sarah was killed."

"We think so."

Too shocked to cry, she kept trying to make sense of Sarah's death. "How did he find out about the phone call so fast?"

Ames glanced at Burroughs, who looked away.

"In this case, we believe someone from LAPD gave him a heads-up that there was a witness, so he did what he always does — eliminates the obstacles in his path. This is the first time that his information was faulty. Because the call that came in was from your friend and the crime was witnessed from this apartment, he made the assumption that she was also the witness. He and his informant don't know about you. Yet."

It was the "yet" that made the skin crawl on the back of Beth's neck.

"What are you saying?"

Ames glanced again at Detective Burroughs, who was trying not to glare. Ames knew the LAPD was angry that the Feds were commandeering their case. It was a territorial thing that had nothing to do with Beth Venable's situation. But the bottom line was that she had to be protected, and the FBI had the better chance of making that happen.

Ames turned his attention back to Beth.

"You've already agreed to testify, right?" he asked.

She nodded.

"Then we need to put you in protective custody until the case goes to trial."

Beth flinched. The blanket dropped from around her shoulders. "Because I'm next?"

"We know they'll try to eliminate you once they realize they killed the wrong person. We can protect you."

Her head was swimming. This couldn't be happening. And all because of a gas leak on the other side of the city.

"For how long? I have a life. I have a job. I can't just disappear. And doesn't it take months, sometimes years, for a case to go to trial?"

"Time will mean nothing to you if you're dead."

Beth slumped against the arm of the sofa and covered her face. Swamped with guilt for causing Sarah's death and fearing she would be next, she felt defeated.

"Ma'am?"

Beth made herself look up.

"You need to come with us."

A thousand thoughts ran through her mind in the few seconds that she sat there, but she kept going back to the hole in

40

Sarah's forehead. There was no escape.

"I'll get my things."

It was just after 6:00 a.m. when the detectives pulled up to the gates of the Pappas estate and rang the bell. A few seconds passed, and then someone answered.

"The Pappas family is not receiving visitors this early."

The detective pulled his badge and aimed it toward the security camera.

"LAPD. Open the gates."

A few moments later the gates swung inward and the detectives drove through. The arrival of the police was beyond the staff's area of responsibility. The housekeeper immediately rang Ike Pappas's room.

Ike hadn't been asleep more than a couple of hours, and hearing the phone ring was like fingernails on a chalkboard.

When he realized it was an in-house call, he was pissed.

"This better be good."

"The LAPD is on their way to the house, sir. I thought you'd want to know."

Ike shifted mental gears and apologized to his housekeeper. "Oh. Sorry for snapping at you, Beatrice. I'll be right down."

He rolled out of bed and made a quick trip to the bathroom before putting on a robe and house slippers, then headed down the stairs.

He met Adam coming up. He was wearing workout clothes and dripping with sweat.

"What's going on, Dad?"

"Beatrice just woke me. She said the police are on the way up the drive. On another note, you're up early."

"Working out, obviously," Adam said, turning to follow his father back downstairs.

At that point the doorbell rang. The housekeeper appeared in the hall and went to answer.

The door opened. He watched a couple of detectives flash their badges as they walked in. He called out as he continued down the stairs,

"Thank you, Beatrice. I'll take it from here. Make some coffee, please."

She scurried away as Ike moved toward the detectives with his son at his heels. He'd had a lifetime of dealing with confrontations and had already prepared himself for this moment. He pulled the sash of his robe a little tighter as he crossed the foyer.

"What the hell, guys? Don't you have enough to do without getting a man out of bed?"

One of the detectives stepped forward and

flashed his badge again. "Detective Samson, Homicide. This is my partner, Detective Phillips."

Ike frowned. "Homicide?"

"Yes, sir. We regret to inform you that your ex-wife, Lorena Pappas, was murdered in her apartment last night."

Ike had practiced the look of shock that he forced onto his face, along with his gasp of disbelief.

"What the hell?" He turned to Adam, who'd gone white as a sheet, and pulled him into his arms. Ike morphed his true concern for Adam's grief into a very passable imitation of rage. "What happened?"

"Someone entered her apartment and slit her throat."

Adam groaned, then began to sob, clinging to Ike even tighter.

Ike kept his arms around Adam's shoulders as he faced the cops. "Tell me you have the son of a bitch who did this." When the detective hesitated, he pushed his anger up another notch. "Certainly you at least have a suspect! I own the damn building. Security is topnotch. He would have been caught on camera!"

"The security system was disabled, and the guard on duty is dead," the detective said.

"Noooo," Adam wailed, and pushed out of his father's arms.

Ike saw the pain on his son's face changing swiftly into rage. An involuntary shudder swept through him, knowing how close he was to having his carefully constructed world rip apart. It was time to point opinions in the right direction.

He ran a hand over his bald head, as if in frustration. "I'm sure you know I have enemies."

Samson nodded, took a quick breath as if gearing up for the question, then blurted it out.

"We need to know where you and Adam were last night."

Ike shifted from concern to indignation. "You ask such a question of *us*? What the fuck's the matter with you people? We have no reason to want Lorena dead. I was on good terms with my ex, and Adam adores his mother."

"It's protocol, and you know it," Samson said, and stood his ground.

Ike cursed softly, then shook his head as if trying to gain some control. "I had a late meeting. Got home around nine p.m. Then Adam and I had a late dinner together. We watched ESPN until after eleven, when I finally called it a day. Adam was still awake

44

when I went upstairs."

Adam's eyes were red-rimmed and still swimming in tears, but his head was up and his shoulders back. When the detective turned to him, he pointed.

"Watch what you say to me," he said. "Don't you defile my mother's name by insinuating that she would raise a child who would be capable of taking her life. She was a saint, you bastards. She was a *saint!*"

Ike continued to play a saddened man supporting his son's grief at such a tragic time. He put a hand on Adam's shoulder.

"Take it easy, son. They're just doing their job."

Adam was cursing and crying all over again, ignoring his father and still seething at the cops. "I loved my mother. She was everything to me. You don't come in here and tell me she's dead, and then tell me I need a fucking alibi for the time of her death! We were home last night! Both of us! All night! Now get the hell out of our house and go find who killed my mother or I'll do it for you."

The detectives had barely opened the door to leave when Adam slammed it shut behind them, then turned around. He was so angry he was shaking.

"Who did this? You have to have a suspicion. Who did you piss off who would be stupid enough to put a hit on Mom to get back at you?"

Ike frowned. "I know you're hurting. I'm sick at heart myself, but everyone knew she was my *ex*. As crass as this will sound, killing her wouldn't send any kind of a message to me. I have nothing invested in that relationship anymore, remember?"

Adam flinched. "What are you saying?"

"You tell me. Of the two of us, who had the most to lose with her death? Who have *you* pissed off?"

Adam reeled as if he'd been punched. His face paled, but he wasn't his father's son for nothing. He jabbed a finger in Ike's chest, punctuating every word as he spoke.

"I don't know. But I will find out who did this, and when I do, I will kill him myself."

Ike shuddered slightly, then gathered himself. "Get dressed. I'll call Moreno and have him find out when we can claim your mother's body. There's family to notify and services to plan."

At the mention of the family lawyer, Adam spun on his heel and took the stairs two at a time.

Ike's eyes narrowed thoughtfully. Adam was proving to be a formidable enemy. That was good. He was going to have to be tough to survive the family business.

As the day progressed, Ike moved with a sense of purpose, confident that the loose ends left behind after his deed had been tied up. But that only lasted until he got a call while he and Adam were at the mortuary picking out a coffin.

The undertaker was pointing out a hand-carved detail on a cherrywood casket when Ike's phone rang. He glanced at the caller ID, then frowned.

"Sorry, but I need to take this. This casket is a nice choice, but ultimately it's Adam's decision." He nodded at his son, then left the room with the phone at his ear.

"Yes?"

"There's a problem."

He recognized Pacheco's voice. "Is your line secure?"

"Yes, sir."

"Talk to me."

"There was another woman in the apartment last night. She was at the police station when I arrived. She was the real witness, and the Feds have her in protective custody."

Ike's gut knotted.

"Can you find her?"

"It might take a couple of days."

47

"Do it as fast as you can and finish the job."

"Yes, sir."

Ike cursed silently as he dropped the phone back in his pocket. An unforeseen hitch, and he didn't like surprises.

Ryal made the furniture delivery but decided to stop off in Mount Sterling before he went home. He needed to go by the lumberyard and pick up some cherrywood to make a pair of end tables for another customer. Once there, he scanned the lumber racks until he found what he wanted, and marked the pieces, and was watching them being loaded into the bed of his pickup truck when his cell phone rang.

Even as he was pulling it out of his pocket he was wondering if this was it — if this would be the call that explained why he was so unsettled.

"Hello?"

"Ryal, it's me, James. Hey, I stopped by your place and you were gone. By any chance are you in Mount Sterling?"

"Yes, what do you need?"

"A couple of bags of cattle cubes. My milk cow's fresh, and you know Julie, she wants to milk her."

Just the mention of his brother's wife

made him smile. She wasn't the kind to waste anything, even time.

"You got it," Ryal said.

"Thanks, big brother. I owe you."

Ryal smiled. "How many times have I heard that? I should be home before four."

"See you then," James said, and disconnected.

Ryal pocketed his phone and went inside to pay.

Three days later

Beth was leafing through a magazine without seeing the text. There'd been a big fuss at the first safe house less than twenty-four hours after her arrival. It had prompted a sudden change of address after they'd received a tip that their location had been compromised. It unnerved her deeply and brought home the fact that she might never be safe again.

The enforced inactivity at the second safe house was driving her nuts. She wanted her laptop so she could work, but they'd confiscated both it and her cell phone with an explanation that she might be tempted to talk to friends, which could inadvertently reveal her location if someone were able to hack into her account.

Even though she'd assured them that she

would keep her online mouth shut, it didn't matter. They refused to trust her to keep her word.

The two agents on guard duty today were a man named Dewey and a woman named Andrea. They were playing poker at the kitchen table while waiting for a pizza delivery, and Andrea had just accused Dewey of cheating. Beth was still grieving for Sarah, as well as the life she'd carved out for herself and was in the process of losing, and was not amused by the agents or their squabbles. She glanced out the window, watching people going about their lives, and wondered what they would think if they knew she were here, hiding among them. The neighborhood seemed ordinary, close to shopping centers and schools, with a couple of churches not far away — the kind of place a family would choose to live. Would they be shocked by her presence, knowing it might put them at risk?

She thought about her parents' sudden decision to move away from Rebel Ridge, how they'd turned away from everything they knew without a satisfactory explanation. Despite everything she said, and all the crying and begging, nothing had changed. They'd come to L.A. — a place as different from rural Kentucky as it could possibly be — and then lived in quiet exile. When Ryal had turned away from her, never making an effort to contact her, she'd turned her grief inward and lived a life of quiet sadness.

Then, four years ago, she and her parents had been broadsided by a drunk driver on their way to church. They had died instantly. She was still fading in and out of consciousness in the hospital when her dad's brother, Will, came in from Kentucky and dealt with the business of shipping the bodies back home to be buried. She had brief memories of seeing him in her hospital room for days afterward. He was the one who broke the news to her about her parents' deaths, and when she was finally released, Will was the one who took her home and helped her pack up what she wanted to keep and sell the rest, then move into a smaller apartment of her own.

During all that time, she never asked about family back home other than her grandmother. Lou Venable was the only member of their family her parents had not abandoned.

Lou had sent Christmas and birthday cards and tiny messages of love to Beth throughout the years, but despite the connection Lou refused to give up, her family never went back. And then it had been too late.

Beth saw Will periodically after that, when he was coming through L.A. on a long haul, or when he brought birthday and Christmas gifts to her from Granny Lou. But it had never occurred to her to move back, not when it was her behavior that had driven them away and estranged them from the rest of the family.

Now here she was, holed up in some strange house with people she didn't know, hiding from a man who wanted to kill her and grieving for a friend she'd loved dearly. In the worst of times, her thoughts were turning more and more to family, to the people to whom she was kin.

As she sat, she noticed a car pulling up to the curb and realized it was the pizza delivery they'd been waiting on for their dinner.

"Pizza's here," she called out.

"About time. I'm starving," Dewey said. He tossed his cards onto the table and headed for the front door, pulling money out of his wallet as he went.

Andrea got up and opened the cabinet to get some glasses for the free Pepsi that would come with the order as Beth headed for the bathroom to wash up.

52

Halfway there, Beth heard a pop. She turned to look just as Dewey crumpled to the floor. All of a sudden Andrea was screaming at her to get down and running toward the living room with her gun drawn.

Beth took a dive behind the sofa as a barrage of bullets ripped through it just above her head. The gunman was still firing as Andrea entered the living room. He spun toward her, popping off a round that splintered the door facing beside Andrea's left ear, but she didn't flinch as she fired three rounds into his chest. The force propelled him backward. He landed faceup across the threshold with his feet on top of Dewey's lifeless body.

For Beth, the silence afterward was heartstopping. Who was still alive? Did she dare move? What if the killer was waiting to see if she got up? God, oh, God . . . what should she do? Then she heard Andrea's voice.

"Beth! Are you okay?"

Beth breathed a shaky sigh of relief. "Yes, I'm okay." She crawled to her feet, then saw Dewey's body and the blood spreading out onto the floor beneath it. "Oh, my God, is he okay?"

"No," Andrea said and turned away, her cell phone already at her ear.

THREE

As luck would have it, Special Agent Ames was one of the agents in the car with Beth. The other agents were silent and had been ever since they'd taken her from the crime scene, and she was tired of it. She wanted answers.

"Agent Ames?"

He looked over his shoulder from the front seat.

"Yes, ma'am?"

"This is my third move in less than a week. What the hell is going on?"

He hesitated, as if judging his words. "We're not sure."

Beth frowned. "So if you're not sure, then you can't assure me it won't happen again, right?"

It was obvious Ames didn't like the question. His expression was condescending, as was the tone of his voice. "We'll make sure, okay? You leave the worrying up to us."

Beth shuddered, remembering Sarah's sightless eyes and the vision of Dewey's body sprawled out on the living room floor.

"That's easier said than done. It's my life on the line, and people are dying because of me."

"We've upped security," Ames said.

She heard him, but she no longer trusted the process. She blinked away tears as she leaned back in the seat. She'd been raised smarter than this. Her people had called the Appalachian Mountains home for over five generations. Life was hard there, but they were not the kind of people who sat back and waited for someone else to solve their problems. Wherever the Feds were taking her was fine, but she needed a backup plan. If something like this happened again and she lived through it, she was gone.

Ike Pappas was having breakfast when his phone rang, informing him of the second failure. He listened without comment and, once the message was delivered, hung up without a goodbye.

He sat for a moment, looking down the table at his son, who was picking at his food without much interest.

As if sensing his father's scrutiny, Adam looked up.

"Is everything okay?"

Ike nodded.

"Mom's service is this afternoon. Don't forget," Adam said.

"I won't forget."

The scent of Ike's favorite coffee and the omelet he was having suddenly turned his stomach. His beloved son was grieving because of something he'd done.

Ike wasn't a man who cringed at the sight of blood or ever second-guessed himself about the choices he'd made. Lorena had given him no choice, but he regretted the need. Unfortunately, Adam would never see it that way.

However, the phone call had left him with larger concerns. He wasn't as disconcerted about the death of Pacheco, one of his most reliable cleaners, as he was about the fact that Beth Venable wasn't dead, too. That was a real problem. The longer she stayed in the wind, the riskier his position with Adam became. He couldn't let his son find out what he'd done and be faced with the impossible situation of what happened next. Either the legal system would execute Ike, or Adam would try to do it for them. There were questions he had yet to ask himself, like: Could he let his own son take him down? Or would he be able to do to Adam what he'd done to Lorena? But Ike hadn't risen to control of the organization by being indecisive. His eyes narrowed as he shoved his plate aside and stood up.

"See you later, son, and don't worry. I'll be back before it's time to go to the church."

"Where are you going?"

"I'm going to check on a couple of things."

"Do you need me to go with you?"

Ike shook his head. "You stay here. Do what you have to do." Then he left the room.

It wasn't a problem sending someone else to finish the job he wanted done, but it might be a problem to find the target. He began running through a mental list of people as he headed out the door to where his car and driver were waiting.

Beth had no idea where she was, or even what the outside of the third safe house looked like, because they'd whisked her inside so fast she'd barely seen the color. As Ames had promised, they'd upped security considerably, but she wasn't sleeping well. When she did go to bed, she slept fully dressed.

Now there were three agents instead of two keeping her company at all times. She didn't remember their names, and they called her Miss Venable. They were as clinically anonymous as they could be and still do their jobs, and unlike the previous location, there were no fast-food deliveries here. Food was cooked on the premises or brought in by agents coming on duty. To keep herself occupied, Beth often did the cooking, even though her appetite was gone. She felt hopeless, even aimless. Until Ike Pappas was brought to trial, she was stuck in limbo. Being proactive, even in these small ways, was what was keeping her sane.

It was a fluke that she had a little over five hundred dollars in her purse from when her own apartment building had been evacuated, not that she had any way to spend it. She didn't know what her employer had been told, but she'd been assured her absence had been explained to the extent that she would not lose her job. Everyone was in charge of her business but her.

A couple of days ago she'd overheard two of them discussing another case and noticed a sack on the cabinet that held some throwaway phones — phones an under cover agent had requested because they couldn't be traced. While they weren't looking, she'd slipped one out and hidden it in the bottom of her purse. She never thought of it as stealing but simply as adding to her own protection — just in case.

During one of the later shift changes an agent had left a map of the city behind. Beth folded it up and put it in her purse, too — another "just in case" addition to her stash.

On the sixth night in the new location Beth made spaghetti with meat sauce and a tossed salad for their dinner. The agents sat down to eat, praising her cooking skills while she picked at the food on her plate and tried not to feel sorry for herself. At least she was still alive. Time to be grateful for small favors.

One of the agents finished up before the others and leaned back in his chair with a groan.

"That was great, Miss Venable. Thanks."

"You're welcome," she said, while trying to remember his name, then deciding it didn't matter.

He would be gone by the next shift and someone else would take his place. As soon as she cleaned up the kitchen she was going to go watch some TV in her room. If she were lucky, she would fall asleep and wake up to a better day.

Gunshots!

Beth woke up with a start, her gaze going straight to the television and the old Western movie playing out on the classics channel.

It took another moment for her to realize the TV had been muted and what she was hearing was coming from inside the house. She flew out of bed just as a bullet came through the wall and smashed into another wall near where she'd been lying. In a panic, she crawled toward the window that overlooked a back alley, praying the attackers had not surrounded the house. She didn't see anyone outside, but it was a moonless night, and there was no way to be sure.

Another spray of bullets came through the wall. She stifled a scream as she slung her purse strap over her shoulder and pushed up the window. Her heart was hammering, her hands shaking, as she crawled out into the alley and slipped away into the night.

Beth ran blindly through the neighborhood without looking back, taking dark alleys instead of well-lit roads, running until her legs were shaking and her lungs were burning, crossing streets only after traffic had passed to make sure she wasn't seen. Once, as she ran past an overflowing Dumpster, an alley cat suddenly darted out from under it with a hiss and a squall, startling her into missing a step. She fell hard in the dirt and debris, catching herself with outstretched arms.

Pain shot through her hands and up to her shoulders as she stifled a scream. Within seconds of hitting the ground, she was back on her feet. The palms of her hands were cut in what looked like a dozen places, and blood was dripping all over the ground and on her clothes. The knee of her jeans was torn and bloody, but she could still move. Ignoring the pain, she glanced over her shoulder and slipped away in the dark.

She had no idea how much time had passed before she came out of an alley near an all-night quick stop. The worst of the bleeding on her hands had stopped, except for the places where the cuts were deeper, but the pain was growing worse the longer her wounds went unattended.

She eyed the flickering fluorescent lights over the pumps, then looked through the windows to the lone clerk inside sitting behind a counter.

Mickey's One-Stop-Shop was open for business.

After a hasty glance up and down the near-deserted street, she waited for a couple of cars to pass, then crossed and slipped inside.

The clerk looked up as the door opened.

Beth hoped she didn't look as desperate as she felt.

61

"Ladies' room?"

He pointed.

She headed toward a hallway with her head down, then locked herself inside, and quickly used the restroom and washed her hands, wincing as the water hit the open wounds. The blood had dried, which made it harder to get off, and some cuts were deeper than others. In the real world, she would most likely have gotten stitches, but not in this one. Eventually everything would heal — if she lived long enough.

If the worst thing that happened to her tonight was the injury to her hands, she would consider herself lucky. Meanwhile, she was far enough away from the safe house to take a few minutes to gather her thoughts. What she needed now was help from someone she trusted. Someone Ike Pappas could not buy off.

She dug the throwaway cell phone from her purse and dialed a number she knew by heart. It rang four times with no answer. On the verge of panic that her call was going to voice mail, she heard a click, then a whiskey-rough voice with a soft, Southern drawl.

"Will Venable."

The familiar voice of her uncle was as welcome as rain on dry ground.

"Uncle Will . . . it's me, Beth. I need help."
She meant to take a breath, but it turned into a sob, and then exhaustion took over and she started to cry uncontrollably.

Will had a soft spot for his brother's only child and had been a stand-in father for Beth ever since her parents' deaths four years earlier. Hearing her distress unnerved him.

"Bethie, honey, what's wrong?"

She began choking back sobs as she tried to explain.

"I witnessed . . . there was a murder . . . and we called . . . and the police came and . . . Oh, Uncle Will, it got my best friend killed."

Will couldn't believe what he was hearing. "What in hell? Sugar? Where are you?"

She took a deep breath and made herself focus. "A quick stop on the south side of L.A. called Mickey's One-Stop-Shop. The FBI hid me in a safe house, because they said the killer would try to get rid of me like he did Sarah, but then they moved me, because they said the location was compromised, and they took me to a second house. I wasn't there long before they found me. One agent was killed and I was shot at. Oh, my God, Uncle Will, there were so many shots being fired, I don't know how he missed me. The killer is some big-time mob guy, but his people keep finding me. They just shot up the third safe house tonight, and I don't know what happened. I don't know who's dead and who's still alive. When I heard the shooting start I went out a window. I don't trust them to keep me safe anymore."

"Sweet Jesus, Bethie . . . I'm so sorry." As a long-haul trucker, it was a hell of a time for him to be on the other side of the country. His mind was in a panic, but he couldn't let on. "Look, honey, here's what we're gonna do. Do you think you can get a cab from there at this time of night?"

"I don't know. Hang on while I ask," Beth said, and hurried out of the bathroom to the night clerk. "I need a cab. Do you know of a driver who'll come here this time of night?"

The clerk's eyes widened, but he didn't hesitate. "Maybe. Depends on where you want to go."

Beth put the phone back to her ear.

"I heard him," Will said. "What's the address there?"

"What's this address?" Beth asked.

The clerk rattled it off.

Will recognized the area and immediately shifted gears. "I heard. Skip the cab. You're

64

not far from a wholesale warehouse. Just stay there, honey. Whatever you do, don't leave. I'll find someone to come pick you up."

"Pick me up? Who do you know who'll pick me up? Where are you, Uncle Will?"

"I know truckers, honey. Lots of 'em. Right now I'm on the other side of the country, but I've got friends. We're gonna get you out of L.A."

"But I don't know where to go that will be safe."

"I do," Will said. "You are going to your granny Lou's."

Beth gasped. Back to Kentucky? Her thoughts immediately went to Ryal.

"But —"

"No buts. I know what I'm talkin' about. There are thousands of places to hide in those hills, and Venables take care of their own. I'll set up the rides. We'll use trucks to relay you cross-country. All you have to do is get in. I'm in North Dakota, but I'm already leaving Minot. I'll meet you on the road and have you home before you know it."

"Okay," she said softly, then walked away so the clerk couldn't hear. "I'm scared, Uncle Will."

"I know, baby. I'm scared *for* you, but you

just stay there until someone comes for you. It will be okay. I promise."

"How will I know who it is I'm supposed to trust?"

"They'll be haulin', honey, so look for a semi. When the driver comes in, he's gonna call you Angel. He'll take you as far as he's going, but I'll make sure there's another trucker to keep you moving east until we meet up. You can trust these men just as if they're family, and I'll be in contact with them — and you — every step of the way. I love you, Bethie. I won't let anything bad happen to you, I promise."

Beth hung up and dropped the phone back in her purse. When she turned around, the clerk was staring.

"So do you still want a cab?"

"No. Someone is coming to get me."

It hadn't taken Will long to find out who was in L.A. A few shout-outs on his CB radio and he had a half-dozen names of men he trusted, *and* the numbers to their personal cell phones. What he had to say didn't need to go out over the air. When he saw Bo Jackson's name on the list, he started to relax. He'd known Bo for more than twelve years. He was a good man, and happily married with a wife and three daughters. If Will was lucky, he would catch Bo before he left L.A.

His expression was grim as he punched in the number, and he didn't relax until he heard Bo's voice.

Bo Jackson hadn't questioned Will Venable's request to pick up his niece. All he had to hear Will say was "she needs help and keep it off the air," and he was on the job. He had just loaded up for a run back to Flagstaff and was still close by. It would be a ten-minute detour, and he knew the area. Finding Mickey's One-Stop-Shop would be a piece of cake.

Beth picked up a small tube of antiseptic cream for her hands, some painkillers, a honey bun and a Coke to eat while she waited, and headed for the checkout counter.

The clerk saw her fumbling with bills and change as she was trying to get money out of her purse.

"What happened to your hands?"

"I fell."

"Do they hurt?"

"Some."

"Want me to open your soda for you?"

Beth was surprised by the kindness of the

offer and almost smiled. "Yes, please."

He took her money, then unscrewed the soda cap and pushed the bottle across the counter.

The condensation burned a little, but the cold felt good on the scratches.

"Thanks, mister. Look, I have a ride on the way. Not sure how long it'll take for them to get here. Okay if I wait up front?"

"Yeah, sure," he said, then watched her walk away.

Beth found a spot where she could see traffic coming and going, and settled down to wait. A couple of minutes later she heard the clerk walking up behind her. He was carrying the stool he'd been sitting on.

"Might as well have a seat while you wait."

Thankful for the kindness of strangers, she nodded. "Thank you."

She eased down onto the stool, grateful to take weight off her sore knee. Once she was settled, she opened the honey bun and took a bite. The slightly crunchy sugar-sweet icing and the soft, sweet bread tasted as good as anything she'd had in days. She finished it off, washing down bites with intermittent sips from the Coke while watching the traffic.

Cars came and went, as well as an occasional pickup or an SUV, but no big rigs.

She made a quick trip to the bathroom again, then washed the sugar off her hands and finally used the antiseptic cream on her cuts before she came back out to resume her wait.

It was coming up on thirty minutes since she'd talked to Uncle Will, and she was getting anxious. She was about to call him again when she saw a semi pull to a stop at the traffic light down the street.

Her heart started pounding as she got to her feet. Was this her ride? Please, God, let it be! She needed to get out of this city.

The truck took a right at the light.

Her heart skipped a beat. It was coming this way! *Oh, God, please let this be my ride.*

Air brakes squeaked and hissed as the semi pulled up at the pumps. Big rigs used diesel, but this one had stopped at the gas pumps, which meant he wasn't here for fuel. Unconsciously, she pulled her purse around in front of her like a shield and watched as the driver swung down from the cab.

He was a stocky man of average height, maybe in his mid-forties, with warm brown skin and long black hair pulled back in a ponytail. He was wearing faded blue jeans, a green John Deere T-shirt and cowboy boots run down at the heels. He walked with an easy stride, and when he saw her standing inside the doorway, a slow smile spread across his face.

If this wasn't her ride, it suddenly hit her that he might think she was a hooker. Alone at this time of night, blatantly visible in the lighted doorway, it could easily appear as if she were soliciting. She took a quick step back and held her breath. Then the door opened, and she saw the expression in his eyes. Empathy. Kindness.

"Angel?"

Beth felt like weeping. God bless Uncle Will. He'd done it.

She nodded.

"I hear you're in need of a ride."

"Yes, please."

He held out his hand. When she reached for it, he saw her palm and stopped.

"You're hurt."

"It's not so bad," she said softly.

Bo glanced at the clerk and frowned, then slid his hand protectively onto Beth's shoulder.

"My name's Bo. Come on, Angel. Let's get you out of here."

Special Agent Ames was not a happy camper. Not only were his superiors ticked, but the state attorney general was also furious. Everyone above him was on his ass for losing their witness. It didn't matter that he hadn't even been on the premises when it happened. He was the lead on the case, and their only witness against Ike Pappas was gone.

He'd already gotten a snide, in-your-face phone call from Detective Burroughs at the LAPD asking if it was true that they'd lost Beth Venable. He hadn't answered, because he didn't have to, but he didn't like the man's attitude. However, it was Burroughs's next question that made his gut knot. That one he'd already asked a dozen times himself.

"How do you know she's running? What if the shots from out front were nothing but a ruse, so someone could drag her out the window?"

Ames didn't answer Burroughs and soon disconnected. His gut was telling him that she was on the run. If Pappas's men had seen her in that bedroom, he was convinced they would have simply shot her. They wanted her dead, not held for ransom. However, what he thought was immaterial. Right now it was just a waiting game to see how long it took for her body to show up. Or maybe they would get lucky. Because if she *was* on the run, she would eventually slip up — use a credit card, make a phone call, do something they could trace — and then they could go get her. He was praying for the latter, but fearing the worst.

FOUR

Adam Pappas was taller than Ike, but he had his father's swarthy complexion and muscular build. His hair was black and wavy, his eyes dark and soulful, and he knew the ladies loved him, both for his looks and his money. He'd known before he was twelve what his father did, even though his mother had tried to hide it. Instead of being horrified, he'd been intrigued. By the time he was sixteen, he'd made it perfectly clear to Ike that he wanted to follow in his footsteps. He knew his father had been surprised, but he'd also seen a measure of pride that only added to his intent. The only rule between them had been that his mother must never know.

And now she wouldn't. For Adam, watching the pallbearers carrying her casket to the grave site felt like an out-of-body experience. He could not believe he would never hear her voice again, or feel her arms around his neck. Knowing how she'd died made him sick with anger. All he wanted now was five minutes alone with the son of a bitch who'd killed her. He didn't want the man caught and arrested. He wanted him dead, and he was doing everything in his power to make that happen. He had connections of his own, and the word was out that he would pay a lot for a name. With that news out on the street, the assortment of mob bosses at the funeral was telling. None of them wanted to be conspicuously absent and unintentionally incriminate themselves by giving the Pappas family the impression that they weren't sorry for what had happened.

The head of the Russian Mafia had sent a huge basket of flowers.

The leader of the Chinese tong had come to the house last night to pay his respects, and the drug lord from the barrio had been the first one to speak to Adam at the church.

T-Boy Lollis, who ran women and numbers in South Central L.A., had been trying to catch his eye ever since the prayer service began at the cemetery. If Adam hadn't been so heartsick about his mother's murder, it would have been comical. Thank God for his father, who'd been a rock through the entire ordeal. He glanced up at Ike, then unconsciously stood a little taller, a little straighter, measuring his worth against his father's power.

Ike was hiding his expression behind dark glasses, hoping it came across as subdued sorrow for his son as well as the death of his ex-wife. He had a plan to make this go away, but he had to get rid of the witness first. After that, he would find a patsy to take the fall for Lorena's murder and the problem would be solved.

When he saw tears rolling down Adam's face, he slid an arm across his son's shoulder, pulling him close, blood of his blood, flesh of his flesh . . . and cold enough to take him out if he ever found out what he had done.

Beth crawled up into the sleeper bunk of the truck cab behind Bo Jackson's seat. She stretched slowly, easing her bruised knee into a comfortable position, and then noticed the photo taped to the low ceiling above the bed. A pretty, dark-eyed woman holding a baby, with two other children standing beside her. She guessed this was Bo Jackson's family. She thought of all the time he had to spend away from them just to give them a good life and wondered how he coped. Then she rolled over onto her side and closed her eyes.

Hours later, when she woke, there was a moment of panic, of trying to remember where she was; then she saw the picture and relaxed. She rolled over and parted the curtains, saw the long black ponytail hanging down the back of Bo's head, then looked over his shoulder to daylight on the horizon.

Bo heard her stirring.

"You okay back there?"

"Yes." She was stiff and sore as she climbed out of the bunk and into the seat beside him. "Where are we?"

"Coming into Flagstaff, Arizona. This is where I leave you. Your next ride will be with a trucker named Rob Louis."

There was something that needed to be said, and Beth had to say it before they parted company.

"I don't know what Uncle Will told you, but I want you to know that you saved my life."

Bo eyed her briefly. "I'm glad I was able to be there for you at the right place and time." He dug a cold bottle of water out of a small ice chest, opened it, then handed it to her before he exited the highway and began winding his way through city streets. Before long they were pulling into the shipping yard of a large warehouse. Several eighteen-wheelers were in the process of being loaded and unloaded.

"Sit tight while I go find Rob," Bo said.

Beth dug the painkillers out of her purse, downed them with a gulp of water, then called her uncle Will. This time he answered before the second ring.

"Bethie?"

"We're in Flagstaff, Uncle Will. Bo said I'm supposed to ride with a man named Rob Louis. Is that right?"

Will heard the uncertainty in her voice and hated it that he wasn't right there.

"Yes, that's right. I know you're uneasy about getting into trucks with total strangers, but I need you to understand. I know these men. I wouldn't pick one I didn't trust you with, okay?"

Beth felt easier. "Okay. Where are you now, Uncle Will?"

"I'm southbound on the I-29, driving through South Dakota. I'll meet up with you in Oklahoma and take you the rest of the way myself."

"When will you sleep? Aren't there rules about driving only a certain number of hours before you have to stop and rest?"

"I picked up a friend who's riding shotgun with me. He'll take over after we cross into Nebraska, and I'll catch a few hours' sleep."

"Does Granny Lou know I'm coming?"

"Yes, honey. Don't you worry. I've talked to her twice since your call. She's organizing stuff on her end. All you need to know is that you're no longer alone in this."

She struggled to keep the tears out of her voice as she said, "I can't wait to see you."

"It won't be long."

"Okay. I love you, Uncle Will."

"I love you, too."

She dropped the phone back in her purse, and then wiped her eyes and blew her nose. Whoever Rob Louis was, she didn't think he would want a bawl-baby hitchhiker in the seat beside him. All of a sudden the door opened. Bo pulled himself up onto the steps and then held out a hand.

"Your ride is here. Do you have all your gear?"

She slid the purse strap over her shoulder and nodded.

Bo steadied her elbow. "Easy does it," he said, as he helped her down.

"Thank you. Thank you so much," she said.

His dark eyes softened. "You're welcome, Angel."

At that point a tall, heavyset man walked up. "Is this Angel?"

Bo grinned. "It sure is. Angel, this is Rob.

He'll take you from here. Safe journey."

Rob seemed aware of her hands and didn't offer to shake them. What he did do was smile, then point toward his truck.

"That's my baby. Her name is Missy. She's the prettiest purple truck on the road. Don't mean to be rude, but I thought you might want to wash up a bit before we head out."

"If that's a polite way of asking if I need to use the bathroom, then I'm saying yes."

Rob grinned. "Then let's get this show on the road. I always wanted an angel riding with me. I finally got my wish."

It had been raining on the mountain since noon. Ryal was in his woodworking shop, hand-sanding a small table he'd just finished and listening to the rain peppering down on the roof. It was times like this that fed his soul — the peace of living on the mountain while working at a job he loved. If he could only shake the feeling of dread, he would be completely satisfied.

A few moments later a large clap of thunder rocked the mountain, rattling the glass in the windows enough that he jumped. At that same moment, his cell phone rang. A little surprised that he was able to get a signal during this kind of weather, he glanced at the caller ID, then frowned.

Lou Venable.

He couldn't imagine why Granny Lou would be calling him. He hadn't seen or talked to her since the Walker/Venable family reunion two months ago. Curious, he answered quickly.

"Hello?"

"Ryal, this is Lou Venable. We got a problem, son, and I'm gonna be needin' your help."

Ryal's gut knotted. This explained the sick, unsettled feeling he'd been having.

"Yes, ma'am. What's wrong?"

"Beth is in bad trouble. She witnessed a murder, and now the killer is after *her.*"

Ryal's heart stopped. Beth in danger? She might not love him anymore, but he couldn't think of a world without her in it.

"A murder?"

"Yes. The killer is some big L.A. crime boss. He's already tried twice to kill her. The last time it happened she went out a window during all the gunfire and ran. She called my boy, Will. He set up a relay with some of his trucker friends to get her away. They're bringing her here to Rebel Ridge, and we need a place to hide her until the Feds can get a handle on this mess."

He didn't care why Lou had called him, or take a second to wonder how he would feel to see Beth again.

"You know I'll help. Just let me think a minute about where to hide her."

"I wouldn't be askin' this of your people except we fear if anyone figures out where she's gone, they'll immediately assume it would be to the Venables — not to her mama's side of the family. I realize this might be a bit uncomfortable between the two of you, considerin' you used to be a bit sweet on each other."

Ryal closed his eyes, remembering how it felt to be inside Beth's body. *Sweet on her* wasn't the term he would have used.

"Kin is kin, Granny Lou, no matter how distant, and you know it. We're happy to help."

"And we thank you."

"How much time do we have before she gets here?" Ryal asked.

"Probably no more than another twenty-four hours. Will was in the Dakotas when she called him, and he's driving hard to get to her. I'll let you know more when I hear from him again."

"Yes, ma'am. Don't you worry. We'll figure out a good place to keep her out of sight."

Beth didn't talk much on her leg of the trip with Rob Louis, because Rob never stopped talking long enough to let her. She heard about his life from his first memory at the age of three right up to last year, when he'd gotten divorced from his third wife. They'd stopped in Albuquerque to get fuel and some food. About the only time Beth had spoken through lunch was when she'd given the waitress her order.

When they got back in the truck, Rob began getting some chatter on his CB radio. Beth took the opportunity to crawl into the sleeper bunk, where she noticed the only pictures taped to his ceiling were of him holding a succession of really big fish.

She fell asleep and dreamed of Ryal standing naked beneath the little waterfall above the creek that ran behind his home, and in her dream she cried when he suddenly disappeared.

When she woke it was late afternoon. She crawled out of the bunk and back into the seat. Right after that, they had to pull over at a weigh station. She took advantage of the stop to take a bathroom break. About a half hour later they were back on the road.

Rob picked up his conversation right where he'd left off, as if she hadn't been absent for several hours, and talked all the way to Amarillo. Finally he changed lanes and angled toward an exit off Interstate 40.

"This is where we part company. I go north to Denver from here. You'll be riding the rest of the way with ol' Hank."

Beth didn't know who ol' Hank was, but she hoped he was the strong, silent type. She was thankful for Rob's participation in her trip, but grateful she wouldn't have to listen to him talk any longer. He was starting to repeat himself.

"Come on inside, Angel. We'll eat us some supper in here, and by the time we're done, Hank oughta be here. He's coming in on the I-27 from Lubbock."

True to his word, they were finishing up their meal when Beth saw Rob's face light up. She turned to look as a giant of a man entered. He was huge, both in height and girth, but there was something about the way he looked at her when they were introduced that relieved whatever anxiety she'd been feeling.

"Is this the angel?"

Rob nodded. "It sure is, and she's a sweetheart. Angel, this is Hank Wilson. He's taking you the rest of the way into Oklahoma City to meet Will."

Hank read the nervousness on her face, saw the condition of her hands and clothes, and wanted to put her at ease.

"It's a real pleasure to meet you, Angel. You put me in mind of my oldest granddaughter, Patty, who happens to be the light of my life."

At the mention of granddaughters, Beth started to relax. "I'm glad to meet you, too."

Beth noticed Rob was getting up to leave. "Thank you for everything, Rob, including the food, the ride and the conversation. I don't know what my uncle told you, but you're all helping save my life."

Rob patted her on the head. "Stay safe, Angel," he said, then thumped Hank on the back. "She's all yours. Take good care of her."

Hank sat down at the table with Beth and waved at a waitress, who headed their way.

"I need a couple of burgers with fries on the side and a large sweet tea to go."

"You got it," she said, and hurried away to place the order.

Hank eyed Beth curiously, wondering what she was running from and at the same time conscious that he had a big responsibility on his hands.

"Say, honey . . . if you want to go freshen

up and buy you some snacks or something to drink to take with you, do it now. If you get tired, you can sack out in my bunk."

"You won't be stopping anywhere along the way?"

Hank shook his head. "No. It's a short hop from here to Oklahoma City. Barring any problems, about a four-hour drive. If we're lucky, we'll be there before midnight."

Ike slammed his office phone down on his desk and then strode to the windows overlooking the Hollywood hills. The news he'd just received wasn't what he'd wanted to hear. According to his man in the P.D., the witness had disappeared. The Feds had lost her, and the cops didn't know where she was, either.

Then he started to breathe a little easier. She was running. She didn't want to testify against him. It would seem that the failed attempts to kill her hadn't been a total bust. They'd scared her enough to change her mind about fulfilling her civic duty.

As he looked down, he recognized Adam's limo pulling up at the curb and frowned. The last thing Adam had told him this morning was that he was flying to Vegas. It would seem his plans had changed.

He watched Adam get out, then slam the

door. From the set of his shoulders, Ike could tell that he was mad. He wondered who'd crossed him, then wondered if the man was still alive.

Ike stepped back from the window and went to the wet bar, poured himself a drink, then sat down and waited for Adam to arrive. He would find out soon enough what had set him off. In the meantime, he felt the need to celebrate Beth Venable's absence.

Adam Pappas was wavering between rage and shock. He'd gotten word from a reliable source that his father might know more than he was saying about his mother's death. He didn't know what to think or how to react, and knew his father well enough to know he wouldn't get jack shit out of him if he went in mad. But he *was* mad, and he didn't know how to hide it. By the time he got to Ike's office, his personal pep talk had gone out the window. He strode past Ike's secretary without speaking, and didn't even bother to knock as he strode into the room with his chin up and his shoulders back.

Ike ignored his son's attitude as he stood up and went over to greet him. "Hey, I thought you were going to Vegas."

Adam didn't stop moving until he was in

Ike's face. When he asked the question, he needed to be close, so he would know if his father was lying.

"What the fuck do you know about Mom's murder that you haven't told me?"

Ike blinked.

Adam swung a fist.

Ike blocked it on reflex, then grabbed Adam's wrist. "What the hell is the matter with you?"

Adam was so mad he was shaking. "I want the truth. You know something you haven't told me about Mom's murder."

Ike channeled shock into indignation as he jabbed a finger into Adam's chest. "Have you lost your mind? If I knew anything solid, the situation would already have been resolved. You should know that."

"That's not what I heard."

Ike sneered, then hammered his fist against his own chest. "So, little big man . . . you think you've got better information than me? You can't be that stupid!"

Adam was off balance. He'd been so sure.

"I don't know what to believe," he muttered.

Ike needed this confrontation to be over *now.* He rarely pulled rank on his own son, but this was one of those times when Adam needed to be reminded who was boss.

He put a finger in Adam's face. "You get your ass to Vegas like you planned, and quit thinking you can push me around. You're not big enough, strong enough or tough enough to take me on. You get that?"

Adam glared. He didn't like being talked down to, but he didn't have anything but suspicion. Pissed at being called out, he jabbed a finger in his father's chest.

"I may not be the big dog . . . yet. But if I find out you're lying to me, you're not going to like what happens."

He left as abruptly as he'd entered, once again slamming the door to punctuate his ire.

FIVE

The Feds were still looking at Ike as their prime suspect. If he'd found out what she'd done, that she'd contacted them, then he had a motive. All they had to do was prove it. Couple that with Beth Venable's eyewitness testimony — if they could just find her before Pappas did — and they could nail him to the proverbial cross.

The forensic team had found traces of Ike's DNA on the dress Lorena had been wearing when she died. The federal prosecutor assigned to the case, a man named Ashton Caine, knew a good lawyer could make mincemeat of that. Especially since Ike was in and out of the apartment all the time. But the more evidence they could stack against Pappas, the stronger their case became. What they needed most, though, was Beth Venable. They'd had her, but they'd lost her. It was a royal fuckup all the way around.

■ ■ ■ ■

Beth's ride with Hank Wilson was uneventful, for which she was truly grateful. After the gabfest with Rob, Hank's lack of conversation was a blessing. She went to sleep listening to the chatter on his CB radio and woke up in the dark, hours later, with a sense of relief at knowing she was that much closer to her uncle Will.

Hank heard her stirring. "Hey there."

Beth stretched, wincing as her sore knee bumped the back of the sleeping compartment, then mumbled a hello as she climbed out of the bunk and scooted into the passenger seat.

It was pitch-black outside, but as far as she could tell they were still on the interstate. She would have given anything for a toothbrush, a shower and change of clothes, but she settled for a breath mint she found in her purse.

"Where are we?"

He pointed to a faint glow of lights against the night sky in the distance. "You're looking at the Oklahoma City skyline. Will is already there and waiting for us at a Love's country store outside of the city."

"Thank God."

Hank glanced at her but didn't comment. Whatever was going on with her was none of his business. Within fifteen minutes he pointed again.

"That's our exit. See that bright yellow quick stop with the big red sign? That's where we're heading."

After all she'd endured during the past week, and then the drama of traveling cross-country with total strangers, just knowing she was about to see a familiar face undid her. Her vision blurred as Hank's big rig swerved off I-40 onto the exit road, then slowed even more as he turned into the parking lot.

"There he is," Hank said, pointing toward a well-lit area where a half-dozen trucks were parked.

Breath caught in the back of Beth's throat as she watched her uncle climbing down from the cab of his semi. He'd gotten grayer since she'd seen him last, but he was still a tall, rangy man with a craggy face. He looked so much like her father that it hurt her heart — but then, all the Venables looked enough alike that it was impossible to mistake their lineage.

She started to shake.

Hank eyed the tension on her face and resisted the urge to hug her.

"I don't know what's going on with you, girl, but you got good people behind you and you're gonna be all right."

Then he hit the air brakes. The familiar squeal was her signal to grab her purse as Will walked toward them. When the truck finally rolled to a stop, he climbed up on the passenger side and opened the door.

She fell out into his arms.

"I got you, honey," Will said, as he held her close. "You're safe now . . . you're safe."

She burst into sobs and buried her face against his chest.

The Feds had no idea what had happened to Beth Venable. Despite all the digging they'd done into her background, there was no action on any of her credit cards. They'd confiscated her cell phone and laptop, and even though she could have accessed the laptop from another location, all activity had ended the night of Sarah Steinman's murder.

Her parents were dead, and since she was a freelance illustrator, she had no boss or working buddies to talk to about her daily habits. Still, despite all their investigations, none of their sources had been able to verify if Pappas had ever gotten his hands on her or not.

The pressure to find her was weighing heavily on Agent Ames, and he was dreading the day ahead of him as he drove in to work. As he stopped for a red light, his cell phone began to ring. He answered absently.

"This is Ames."

"Agent Ames, this is Beth Venable."

He was so startled, his foot nearly slipped off the brake.

"Beth! Thank God you're alive! Where are you?"

Beth leaned against her uncle's chest for moral support. His arms encircled her. Finally she was safe — safe enough to unload her fear and anger.

"Yes, I'm still alive, no thanks to you people. As for where I am, you don't need to know."

"Listen, Miss Venable, you don't understand what —"

Beth was through listening as she angrily interrupted. "Oh, I understand perfectly. You want my testimony, but you nearly got me killed. Twice! Frankly, I don't trust your agency anymore. In fact, I don't trust the LAPD *or* the FBI. Both your agencies obviously employ someone who sold me out to Pappas or none of this would have happened to me."

93

"Now, see here. You —"

"You have no room for indignation on anyone's behalf but mine. The LAPD knew about the call from Sarah's apartment and she wound up dead. Then you 'big boys' take over, swagger into Sarah's apartment and sweep me away to a 'safe house,' where I nearly got killed. So you moved me to a second one, then a third. Out of curiosity, how many died there?"

Ames sighed. "Okay, I'm hearing you. So why the call?"

"To let you know that I will still testify. But I won't show my face in L.A. again until Pappas has been arrested and is in the courtroom on trial. I don't suppose he's been arrested and a date has been set for a hearing or a trial or whatever you people call it?"

"Not yet."

"Then when you give me a date, I'll be there. Until then, you can pretend I'm dead."

"But how can I contact you to let you know?"

"You can't. I'll call you again to check in. In the meantime, make something happen."

Will laid a hand on Beth's shoulder as she dropped the phone back in her purse.

"Feel better, darlin'?"

Her shoulders slumped. "I wish I could forget that all this has happened, but I can't. I didn't want them to think I ran out on them, and I don't want Sarah's killer to get away with murder. I just want to stay alive until they get their act together."

He frowned. "Were you happy in L.A.?"

She shrugged. "I wasn't *un*happy."

"Did you have anyone special?"

Ryal Walker's face slid through her mind; then she cast it out, just like he'd forgotten her ten years earlier.

"If you mean, was I dating, then the answer is no. Never met anyone there I felt like spending that much time with."

"Just asking," Will said, as he eyed her purse. "I'm guessing you don't have a change of clothes in that bag you're carrying."

She shook her head.

"No problem. We can fix that. I've been waiting for you to get here to eat. How about we chow down, and then we find ourselves an all-night Walmart and get you some clothes?"

"And a place to take a shower?"

"I think we can make that happen."

Beth threw her arms around her uncle's neck. "Thank you, Uncle Will. Thank you."

"You don't need to thank me, darlin'. That's what family is for."

Ryal had called a meeting of the Walker clan, and they'd come by the dozens, spilling out of his house and into the front yard, sitting beneath shade trees and on the tailgates of their pickup trucks. Once he filled them in on what was happening to Annie Walker's girl and how the Feds had nearly gotten her killed, whatever lingering feelings they had about how Annie's betrayal had split the two families down the middle, the hard feelings of the past were suddenly gone.

The mere mention of the federal government was all it took to rouse them to indignation on her behalf. There were generations of people in Appalachia who didn't have any use for the Feds, and they didn't have to be told twice how important it was to stick to total secrecy. They all offered to assist in any way, should Ryal send out a call for help.

In the end, it was his mother who suggested the perfect hiding place: the mountain cabin where she and her brothers and sisters had been raised. Her father had passed away a little over a year ago, but everything was still as he'd left it. The family used it now and then if they were hunting that high up, so the basic comforts, though very simple, were still available.

Ryal's brothers, James and Quinn, volunteered to go up early, clean it and stock it with food, and get the power turned back on. Satisfied that he'd done what needed to be done, Ryal settled in to wait.

The next night Lou Venable called as Ryal was getting out of the shower. He ran to answer, dripping water as he went.

"Hello?"

"Ryal, it's me. Will and Beth are due in late tomorrow, probably after dark. He wants to know if you could pick her up at the foot of the mountain where the county road meets the highway and bring her up to me."

Even though Ryal was soaking wet and naked, he feared the shiver that ran through his body had nothing to do with being chilled. How was it going to be, seeing Beth again after all these years? Then he realized Lou was still speaking and made himself focus.

"It may seem selfish, but I haven't seen her in ten years, and I want one night with her before you hide her away."

"That's not selfish at all, ma'am, and you

know I'll do it."

"I thank you. I wouldn't ask, 'cept Will can't drive his big rig up the mountain on this danged narrow road."

"You give me a call and let me know what time. I'll be around all day tomorrow. Sleep well, Granny Lou."

"I'll sleep when I know my girl is out of danger."

"Yes, ma'am," Ryal said, and disconnected, but Lou's vow had gotten under his skin.

Now *he* couldn't sleep, either. Every time he closed his eyes, he found himself reliving their love affair, from the first time he'd kissed her to the first time they'd made love, right up to the day she and her family disappeared.

He finally fell into a fitful sleep, but by the time dawn broke, he was already up and hard at work. He'd always found the best way to make time pass was to stay busy, and if he was going to be gone for an undetermined amount of time, the more work he got done before he left, the better.

He waited all day for that call from Lou — the call that was going to change his world — and it came as he was cleaning up his supper dishes.

■ ■ ■ ■

Ryal's cell phone was on the counter. He was rinsing off a plate when it began to ring. When he saw it was from Lou Venable, he ran to answer.

"Hey, Lou."

"Will just called. He said they should reach the turnoff in about an hour and a half. Can you still go get her?"

Her voice was shaking. He could tell how unnerved she was by the danger her granddaughter was in. She had already buried Beth's parents. He could only imagine the thoughts running through her mind.

"Yes, ma'am. Don't you worry. I'll be there waiting, and as soon as Will drops her off, I'll bring her right up."

Lou started to cry. "I can't thank you enough, Ryal. I remember what the two of you were once, and I'm sorry as I can be if this is difficult. But this isn't about us, or our families, or what once was. This is about Bethie and keeping her alive, and I want this night with her. It's been ten years since I've seen her sweet face."

Ryal sighed. There was nothing to be said that would make a difference to the past. Then he heard her blow her nose, and when she spoke again, that matter-of-fact tone was back in her voice.

"I'll see you soon."

"Yes, ma'am."

He grabbed a jacket and headed for his truck. Better to be too early than have them wait on him. After all the turmoil Beth Venable had been going through, he didn't want to be the one to put another measure of fear in her heart.

Storm clouds had been gathering in the Kentucky sky all afternoon. By the time it got dark, Will and Beth could see intermittent flashes of lightning in the distance.

"We're driving right into that rain," Will said.

Beth looked nervous. After the day and a half they'd been on the road together, she couldn't bear to think of a delay. She was beyond thankful for everything that had been done on her behalf, but she would hold no regrets if she never rode in another big rig as long as she lived.

However, it wasn't just the weather that was making her anxious. When Will finally told her it would be Ryal who was going to take her into hiding, her heart sank. He'd let her go once, and now *he* was the one who was going to help hide her? Why did life always have to be so hard?

"If it starts raining before we get there, will the weather keep Ryal from driving down the mountain?"

"No, honey. Remember, us mountain people don't have fancy cars, and we're used to driving in all kinds of weather. The road up the mountain isn't paved, but it's a good gravel road. If I know Ryal, he'll be waiting when we get there."

Beth frowned. "What's his wi— his family going to think about him going off somewhere to babysit me through this mess?"

Will frowned. "It's not babysitting. This is a matter of keeping you alive, Bethie. Anyway, Ryal never married."

She eyed Will briefly, then looked away. Everyone knew what they'd once been to each other, but no one knew that, in her heart, at least some of the love she'd had for him was still there. He'd broken her heart, but she had never been able to hate him. She knew facing him now, when she was at her most vulnerable, wasn't going to be easy.

"I wish you could stay," Beth said.

"I do, too, but remember what we talked about. If someone starts looking into your family history, it won't take long to find out your folks are dead. As your dad's oldest brother, I'm the obvious choice to look at, and if I've suddenly deviated from my routine in any way, they'll suspect I've taken you into hiding, and then one thing would lead to another, and you know how that would go."

Her gut knotted as she thought about Sarah. "The last thing I want is for someone to think you know where I am. They killed my friend because of me. I couldn't stand it if anything happened to any of my family because of this."

"None of this is your fault, and we're not stupid, girl. We've covered our backs just fine here. I'm scheduled to pick up a load in Richmond at noon tomorrow. If I stay on schedule, there will be nothing to find."

"Okay."

He grinned. "Damn right it's okay. You're with family now. I'm still dealing with the guilt of not bringing you back home when Sam and Annie were killed, but you were no longer a minor, and I didn't feel like it was my place to tell you what to do after six years of silence from all of us. In our defense, I will say it's the way Sam wanted it, but we should have ignored him. We shouldn't have let him call all the shots, 'specially not once he was dead. However, you're here now, and nothing and no one's ever gonna hurt you again. We'll see to that. Now sit back and relax. We're less than thirty minutes from the turnoff."

Ryal had been waiting close to forty-five minutes when he saw the lights of an eighteen-wheeler come up over a hill on the highway. It wasn't the first one he'd seen pass by since he'd gotten here, but this one appeared to be slowing down. When he saw the turn signal come on, his muscles tensed. This was good. At least they were making the transfer before the storm hit.

As soon as the truck came to a complete stop, he got out of his pickup, then stopped by the front fender, watching as the driver climbed out of the big rig's cab. He recognized Will's tall, lanky frame as he walked in front of the headlights to the passenger side.

Ryal shifted from one foot to another, suddenly anxious about what Beth looked like now. Ten years in L.A. could change a lot about a person. He frowned slightly as he waited for their approach.

And then she stepped out from behind Will and started toward him, backlit by the headlights of the truck. All he could see was a dark, womanly silhouette of long legs, slow, lanky steps and a long swath of hair that swung in perfect opposition to her stride.

His gut knotted. The closer she got, the faster his heart began to beat. He didn't know whether to run or stand his ground and take the punishment he felt coming.

Then she stopped before him, and even though the light wasn't the best, he saw only the fear and uncertainty in her eyes. When she extended her hand, his attitude shifted from defensiveness to a great sense of wanting to protect.

"Beth, it's good to see you again." He reached for her hand, then caught a glimpse of the raw, ugly cuts and crude bandages, and stopped short. "What happened to your hands?"

Thinking he'd been disgusted by their condition, she yanked them back against her chest.

"I fell in an alley near a Dumpster when I was running away from gunfire."

Shattered by the matter-of-fact tone in her voice, she undid him.

"Lord have mercy," Ryal said softly, then wrapped his arms around her. There were ten long years and some bad family history between them, but right now that could all go to hell. She looked as if she was about to fall apart.

Breath caught in the back of Beth's throat. She hadn't expected this. What was worse, she didn't want it to stop, but it didn't last long as thunder suddenly rumbled overhead and Ryal turned her loose.

"I better get you to your granny Lou's before she comes looking for the both of us."

Unsettled by his tenderness, Beth struggled for a reason to turn away. Her uncle's need for a hasty exit gave her the excuse she needed as she walked into his arms and hugged him fiercely.

"Thank you for everything, Uncle Will."

Will returned the hug, along with a kiss on the cheek. "You've got my number. All you have to do is call and I'll be here."

"I know."

Will handed her duffel bag to Ryal. "I don't have to say it, do I?"

"No, sir. We'll take real good care of her."

"That's all I ask," Will said, as he brushed a lock of hair from Beth's face. "Trust him, Bethie. Trust all of them. Despite the past, they're family. They know the mountain. They'll keep you safe."

Ryal touched her arm.

She jumped.

"Sorry," he said, and pointed to the sky.

"We need to leave now."

Beth quickly climbed into his pickup. He set the duffel bag on the floor beside her feet, then closed the door, shutting her away from the inclement weather.

The first drops of rain began to fall as Will pulled back onto the highway. Beth watched the taillights of the semi disappearing around the bend, then caught Ryal watching her and shivered.

"It's gonna be okay. I promise," he said.

Beth wanted to scream at him — to tell him that, for her, nothing would ever be okay again, certainly not between them — but it was painfully obvious he'd long ago gotten over her, so she wasn't going to give him the satisfaction of knowing he could still hurt her.

She had yet to see his face clearly. Even now it was barely highlighted by the dashboard light. But his voice was like warm whiskey on a cold night, and she kept remembering what his lips felt like on her skin when they made love.

Ryal started his pickup and turned around. In moments they hit the gravel. The road they were on looked like a dark scar on the mountain, but the farther up they drove, the heavier the woods became and the safer she began to feel. It was as if the mountain itself was sheltering her. She shivered.

"Are you cold?" he asked, and reached toward the dash to turn on the heater.

"No, just exhausted and scared half out of my life."

"I'm really sorry, Beth. This is a hell of a thing to be going through."

"I need to hide. Can you hide me, Ryal?"

"Yes, and I will. In fact, we're all in this together. Every Walker on Rebel Ridge knows what happened to you, and every one of them is ready to help at a moment's notice."

She shuddered, then leaned back against the seat and closed her eyes.

"I didn't know anyone back here even remembered I existed."

Ryal's fingers tightened on the steering wheel as the wind began to blow a little harder. There was anger in her voice, which didn't make any sense. She might not have had a choice about leaving, but she *was* the one who'd chosen not to come back.

"We'll be at Lou's in a few minutes. I hope we beat the storm. It would add insult to injury if I brought you back cold and wet, now, wouldn't it?"

Beth frowned. So he was ignoring her comment. Fine. Two could play that game.

Six

The farther up the mountain Ryal drove, the more anxious Beth became. Her memories of Granny Lou were wrapped up in childish things. The molasses cookies Granny Lou kept in an old brown bean pot. The cool taste of spring water from her well. The scent of clean sheets dried on a line outside as Beth snuggled into bed and closed her eyes.

Lightning flashed on the ridge up ahead. She flinched at the crack of thunder that followed.

"We're okay. Remember, storms are always loud up here," Ryal said, wanting to reassure her.

Beth glanced at his profile as he drove — his hands steady on the steering wheel, his gaze firm and straight ahead. She was curious about the man he'd become. Despite the broken bond of their relationship, he'd answered her grandmother's call without hesitation. The word *dependable* came to mind. And then he sensed her look and momentarily took his eyes off the road to meet her gaze. Startled to have been caught staring, she quickly looked away, hoping he hadn't seen more than curiosity in her expression.

When he began slowing down, she leaned forward, anxious for that first glimpse of her granny Lou's home.

"We're here," he said, as he turned up a narrow one-lane road and into a clearing where a small, two-story log cabin with a big front porch sat nestled among a stand of tall pines.

The porch light was on, and the curtained windows were backlit from within, giving the home a welcome feeling. Then she saw a woman move away from the door and come down the steps. The growing wind had plastered the skirt of her dress to her legs and was pulling wisps of gray hair from the braid wrapped around her head like a crown, but Beth would have known that tall, spare figure anywhere.

"Granny Lou."

Lou Venable had been a widow for nearly thirty years. She'd come to this house built on the side of Rebel Ridge as a newlywed with her husband, Doyle, and raised four children — two boys and two girls. Years later she'd buried Doyle and then, four years ago, buried her son Sam and his wife, Annie. Their deaths had nearly killed her. Just the thought that now someone was stalking her granddaughter made her physically ill, and she wasn't going to feel easy until she saw her again.

Another rumble of thunder sounded outside. She glanced at the clock as she paced the floor. The storm was getting closer and Ryal still wasn't here. Her imagination was in overdrive, fearing everything from Will wrecking his truck to a breakdown on the side of the highway, which, in theory, could give the people who wanted Beth dead time to catch up. She paused to look out the front windows as she had a dozen times before, when all of a sudden lights swept across the trees at the end of the drive.

Someone was turning in. It had to be Ryal!

She flipped the switch on the porch light and stepped outside, then immediately regretted the lack of a sweater as a chill wind engulfed her. She glanced up at the rolling clouds highlighted by intermittent lightning strikes and shivered. The storm was upon them.

As the truck stopped at the edge of the

yard, she came down off the porch, then stopped. When Ryal got out then ran around to the passenger side and opened the door, she frowned. He seemed to be helping Beth out of the truck. Was she hurt in some way? Then she focused on a tall woman with dark hair who turned and looked toward the house, and her vision blurred. It was like looking at a female version of Sam. "Bethie girl, is that you?"

For Beth, everything after that seemed to happen in slow motion. Getting out of Ryal's pickup as the storm bore down upon them . . . the feel of Granny Lou's arms around her . . . the sweetness of her grandmother's kiss before she hurried them both inside.

"Just in time!" Ryal said, following them in as the sound of raindrops began hitting the roof.

He set Beth's bag against the wall, then turned to face her. That was when his thoughts scattered. He'd seen her face by moonlight, then by the dashboard light of his pickup, but seeing her in this light added a whole new layer of intrigue.

There was no mistaking she was a Venable. She had long legs and dark hair, with eyes the color of milk chocolate, and he saw Annie in the curve of her cheek and the stub-

111

born cut of her chin. The young Beth Venable he'd fallen in love with had grown into a beautiful woman.

It was a time of understanding for Lou, as well. When she saw Beth's hands in the full light, she understood why Ryal had helped her down from his pickup truck. The palms looked as if they'd been shredded. Parts of them were beginning to heal, but she could only imagine how painful it was for Beth to clench her fingers.

"Bethie . . . darlin', what happened to your hands?"

Safe now after the terror of the past few days, relief welled up inside her as she started to shake, then spilled out in the hot, blinding tears rolling down her face.

"After the shooting began at the third safe house, I jumped out my bedroom window and began running. I stayed in the alleys where it was dark, running from block to block to get as far away from that place as I could before they realized I was gone. I was running through an alley when I tripped on something and fell on the debris beside a Dumpster."

"Honey, honey, I'm so sorry this is happening to you, but you're no longer alone. You're with family now, and we won't let you down." Lou smoothed the windblown wisps of Beth's hair away from her face. "You need to get some food in your belly and then into bed. The bathroom is the last door on the right down the hall. I'm going to warm up some stew and corn bread. Ryal, I'm expecting you to stay the night. No need driving home in this weather when you'd only have to come back in the morning anyway."

"Yes, ma'am," Ryal said, grateful he wouldn't be driving farther up the mountain in the storm.

Beth swayed on her feet as Lou left the room.

Ryal caught her. Again their gazes met, but this time Beth didn't look away.

Ryal wanted to pull her closer. Instead he let go and shoved his hands in his pockets. "Do you need help?"

Beth shook her head, quelling the urge to just close her eyes and lean on someone else for a change. "I can manage. I'm just a little tired."

"I'll go help Lou."

Beth turned around and headed for the bathroom.

Ryal watched her walk away, but his heart was heavy as he headed for the kitchen.

The food Lou served was simple — rabbit

stew with small potatoes and carrots, and a wedge of hot-buttered corn bread, but to Beth, it could have been filet mignon. She hadn't had food like this in years, but she remembered the taste, and it was good.

Being back in this house, she also began remembering Sunday dinners with her parents and the rest of the family, and wading in the creek below the house with her cousins, while the men played horseshoes and the women sat on the porch in the shade, and cheered and jeered for their hits and misses. After she got older and began noticing boys, it was always Ryal Walker who caught her eye.

Their first kiss had been behind this very house. Beth remembered the warm feel of his lips on hers, and how it had started to snow as they'd quietly pulled apart. There had been a look in his eyes that she'd never forgotten. He'd wanted her in the way that a man wants a woman, but he'd never pushed. Instead, he had let Beth lead the way, giving her all the freedom she needed to feel safe with him. And when they'd finally made love that next spring, it had been magic.

She sat quietly, thinking of the day her family had left Rebel Ridge, and how she'd cried and begged her father to take her back, insisting that she didn't want to leave Ryal. But he'd just kept telling her that she was too young to know what she wanted, and that they were a family and family stuck together.

Lou laughed at something Ryal was saying, and Beth watched the laugh lines deepen at the sides of her grandmother's face. Lou Venable had laughed a lot in her life, and it showed. But there were frown lines dug just as deep into the flesh between her eyes. She was also a woman who'd known great grief, yet somehow life had taught her how to live with both without breaking.

That was something Beth had never really mastered: how to laugh within the pain. She kept thinking about how solitary her life and her parents' lives had become after they moved to L.A. Even when Sam and Annie were still alive, the three of them had lived an insular existence. No large Sunday dinners — no friends over from the neighborhood. It was just the three of them behind the walls of the house Sam rented. They did nothing that would indicate they were putting down roots.

After the wreck, and after she'd finally healed and Uncle Will had helped her get set up in her own apartment, it had never occurred to her to come back here for a visit. Sometime during the past ten years, Beth had reached the conclusion that they were unwelcome here. Now, listening to her granny and Ryal talking about their families in such a fond and loving way, she realized that living in L.A. had felt like being in exile because her mama and daddy had never talked about Kentucky again.

"Granny?"

Lou was still smiling from something Ryal had said when she turned to answer her granddaughter.

"What, honey girl?"

"Why did Mama and Daddy really move away from Rebel Ridge? I thought for years it was because I pushed them too hard to accept Ryal, even though he was older." Beth's face flushed, but she wouldn't look at him.

Lou glanced at Ryal, her face flushing slightly as she lifted her chin. "What did they tell you?"

"That they didn't want me growing up here. Daddy said there weren't any good men on this mountain except his own brothers, and since he didn't want to work the mines and there were no other job opportunities, they moved away and made me go with them."

"That's not entirely the truth," Lou said.

"Then what *is* the truth?"

Lou glanced at Ryal again.

Finally he leaned forward, resting his elbows on the table between them. "What your granny doesn't want to say, because it could be construed as a slur against my side of the family, is that your mama, who was a Walker, had an affair with her sister's husband. Your granny talked Sam out of killing his own brother-in-law, but then Sam surprised everyone, including Annie, by moving all of you to the other side of the country. I guess your daddy no longer trusted your mama. They didn't move because of us. They moved because of Annie's affair."

Beth was stunned, but it explained a lot of the sadness she'd always felt between them. Then something occurred to her.

"Was the affair before I was born?"

"Oh, my Lordy, no," Granny said. "You're Sam's child. You know that. All you have to do is look in a mirror."

Beth sighed, relieved that she still knew who she was, but this also meant that her parents had lied to her. They hadn't been upset to find out that she and Ryal had been making love. Ryal hadn't crossed a line. Her mother had. However, she wasn't about to ask him how he felt now, especially in front of her granny.

Lou frowned. "I'm sorry to give you this kind of news in the middle of all your other troubles."

"They're dead, Granny. There's nothing worse than that."

Lou slapped the table lightly. "Well, that's in the past, so enough history for tonight. We all need rest. Tomorrow will come too soon as it is. Ryal, the last bedroom down the hall is yours tonight. It's the one Will stays in when he stops by. Bethie gets the one across the hall from me."

"Yes, ma'am, and thank you again for the invitation," Ryal said as he got up from the table. "Is there anything else I can do to help?"

"No, but I thank you for asking. We'll be fine."

Ryal glanced briefly at Beth before looking away. "Then I'll see the both of you in the morning."

He walked down the hall with the soft murmur of their voices behind him, then into the bedroom. The colorful hand-braided rug at the side of the bed was a popular choice around here, as was the oil lamp on the bedside table, ready for the times when the power would go out, which

in the mountains was a common occurrence.

Even after he was lying in bed, he could
hear Lou getting Beth settled, fussing over
her comfort and making sure she had
doctored her hands again.

Finally the house got quiet and everyone
had fallen to sleep, lulled by the dying winds
of the passing storm and the sound of
raindrops on the roof.

Beth was dreaming, but in the dream, the
horror was all too real.

She was walking back into Sarah's apartment again, seeing the light flickering
through the open door to Sarah's bedroom,
going in to tell her that she was back and to
thank her again for putting up with all the
trouble she'd caused.

Only this time her heart was pounding,
her steps slow and unsteady as she pushed
the door inward, because she already knew
what she was going to find. But then the
dream morphed into a horror she hadn't
expected. Sarah was still dead, but when
Beth walked into the room, Sarah suddenly
blinked, then slowly focused on Beth's face.

Beth saw her lips moving. Blood began
bubbling at the corner of her mouth, and
then she started to cry.

"It should have been you who died, not me. Not me. *Not me!*"

Beth screamed.

The piercing shriek woke both Lou and Ryal at the same time. He was struggling to get out of bed when he heard the patter of Lou's bare feet as she flew out of her room and across the hall into the room where Beth was sleeping. He could hear Beth sobbing, and the soft murmur of Lou's voice. He wanted to help, but knew he would be intruding, so he sat on the side of the bed instead and listened in, excusing it on a need-to-know basis.

Lou crawled into the bed beside Beth just as she used to do when Beth was small and had suffered a bad dream. She wrapped her granddaughter in her arms and cuddled her close.

"It was just a bad dream, Bethie . . . just a bad dream. Granny Lou's here."

Beth buried her face in her grandmother's bosom as she sobbed.

Lou hurt for what Beth was going through, but she knew from experience that sharing a load made it lighter to bear.

"Talk to me, Bethie. Get rid of the ghosts. Don't let them pester your dreams."

Beth's thoughts went faster than the

words she managed to mutter, but it didn't matter. Lou didn't need to hear the details as much as Beth needed to purge.

"Oh, Granny . . . Sarah was . . . best friend . . . my fault. Shot . . . her blood . . . pillow and bed. First safe house wasn't safe . . . moved me to a new place, but they found me. Thought it was pizza delivery, then . . . shooting everywhere. I fell down behind the sofa . . . bullets over my head. Moved me to a third house . . . all over again . . . scared . . . so scared . . . more bullets and shouting and . . . jumped out a window and ran."

Ryal closed his eyes. The wall between them was a symbol of more than distance, but it was the terror in her voice that united them in a mutual goal. She needed him — she needed all of them to keep her safe — and when it came down to it, no matter how distant and no matter what lay between them, that would always be enough.

Granny Lou was still in bed with Beth when dawn broke. Beth felt the warmth of her granny's arm across her belly and opened her eyes, relaxing as she remembered where she was.

She hadn't looked too closely last night,

but now, in the quiet of first light, she was surprised at how familiar this room actually seemed. She remembered sleeping here as a child, and that this wasn't the first time her grandmother had come to her bed to comfort her after a bad dream.

The plain white walls needed a fresh coat of paint, but it was still neat as a pin and with the same decorations: the picture of Jesus on his knees praying in the garden, an old cuckoo clock that no longer kept time, and a photo of her and her cousins, taken at some family gathering years ago. It took a moment for Beth to realize just how much family she still had here, and that she was only one of Lou Venable's grandchildren. She wondered what had happened to all of them, and where they were now. Like her, they would all be grown, but unlike her, they were probably married with children.

Beth's life had been stunted by her mother's betrayal, but her parents had let *her* bear the burden of thinking they'd left Rebel Ridge because of her. She felt sad for all she'd lost. Had she not witnessed a murder, she might never have come back here.

It was obviously too late for her and Ryal, but she prayed it was never too late to reconnect with family. She sighed, then realized that her grandmother was awake and watching her face.

"How's my sweet girl this morning?" Lou said softly.

Beth smiled as she turned to face her granny. "I'm good, Granny Lou. In fact, I'm better than I have been in weeks."

"That's what I like to hear," Lou said, and then threw back the covers in a matter-of-fact motion and sat up. Her long gray braid dangled over her shoulder as she swung her feet off the side of the bed. "I'd best be up and get us all some breakfast before you leave out."

"Where am I going next?" Beth asked.

"I'm not sure, but that's for your safekeeping, not because I don't care. That way, if someone asks, I can truthfully say I don't know."

Beth's eyes widened as she thought of someone threatening Granny Lou to make her talk. What if Pappas's hired killers found out where she was and followed her here? Would her presence get her own family killed?

"Oh, Lord, Granny, I don't want to put anyone here in danger. Maybe I shouldn't have —"

"You hush now. This is exactly where you should be. God will take care of the rest," Lou said, then eyed Beth's hands. "Just come on into the kitchen as soon as you're dressed. Bring your hairbrush, and I'll brush out your hair just like I used to when you were little."

"Thank you, Granny. I would love that."

Lou smiled and winked. "I haven't had a chance to do anything for you in far too many years. It's for me as much as it is for you."

She left the room on bare feet and closed the door behind her.

Beth got up and went down the hall to the bathroom. When she came out, Ryal's door was open and she could hear the sound of voices in the kitchen. So he was up early, too. She shivered, wondering what this day would bring.

Special Agent Ames was waiting in his boss's outer office to inform him that he'd heard from Beth Venable. He didn't like to admit that Pappas could have a mole in the Bureau, but knew it was likely, considering how many safe houses had been breached. For that reason, he'd told no one that he'd heard from her. The chief was going to be the first to know.

When the phone rang on the secretary's desk, he looked up. When she nodded at him, he let himself into the boss's office.

Ames eyed the Bureau chief, Mac Harrison, who preferred to be addressed as "sir," as he stood up behind his desk. When Ames entered, Harrison nodded and gestured toward a chair.

"Good morning, Ames. Have a seat."

"Good morning, sir. Thank you." Ames sat, resting his elbows on the arms of the chair as Harrison settled into his seat.

"So what is it you have to tell me that couldn't be said over a phone?" Harrison asked.

Ames leaned forward. "How certain are you that this room is safe?"

Harrison frowned. "If you're referring to the possibility that my office could be bugged, I can assure you that it is not, and I'll try not to be insulted by the question."

Ames flushed but held his ground. "There's a leak in the organization somewhere, because I have two dead agents, a third in intensive care and a missing witness to prove it. Sir."

Harrison's cheeks reddened, but he didn't argue. Facts were facts.

"What do you have to tell me that I *don't* know?"

"The missing witness called me."

"Where is she? Have you already picked her up? We need to let the federal prosecu-

tor know. It's Caine, right? I'll give him a
—"

"Sir. Wait. She wouldn't tell me where she
is. She called to tell me that she'll still
testify, but she's not coming back until Pappas is sitting in a courtroom being tried for
his crime."

Harrison's eyebrows knitted angrily.
"That's preposterous. She doesn't get to
call the shots like —"

"She doesn't trust the LAPD and she
doesn't trust us — and with good cause on
both fronts. I don't like it, either, but I
understand where she's coming from."

"Then find her!" Harrison said angrily.

"Or . . . we could proceed with gathering
evidence against Pappas and trust her to
keep her word and come in when she's
needed."

"I don't —"

Ames sighed. Harrison wasn't getting it.
"Sir, may I be honest?"

Harrison's frown deepened, but he reluctantly nodded and leaned back in his chair.

"We both know she's right. There was a
leak in the LAPD that got her friend killed.
And like it or not, we have a leak in our
security, too. It's highly likely that bringing
her back would be signing her death warrant. We already had her in protective

126

custody at three different locations, and they were all breached. We nearly got her killed. I can't blame her for not wanting to come back."

Harrison stood abruptly and strode toward the windows overlooking the city.

Ames waited silently. He'd said all he needed to say.

Finally, Harrison turned around.

"I'll let Caine know. In the meantime, you and your men keep digging. If we have a leak, I'll deal with it. As for Pappas, there's got to be a weak link in *his* organization, as well. Man or woman, find it."

Ames didn't comment, although he could have told Harrison that wasn't going to happen. No one who worked for Ike Pappas would ever roll over on him. The world wasn't big enough for them ever to hide and escape the man's wrath. Still, he left the office with a lighter step. The knowledge of Beth Venable's promise had been passed on to a higher authority. Now if someone found out she'd called in, it wouldn't be from his lips.

SEVEN

Ike was in his office on a long-distance call to Chicago when his secretary knocked quietly, then slipped inside.

He frowned as he covered the mouthpiece. "I told you I wasn't to be disturbed."

"I'm sorry, sir, but they wouldn't wait." She stepped aside as two federal agents walked in flashing their badges.

Ike's frown deepened, but he didn't let his displeasure show in his voice as he took his hand from the mouthpiece.

"Carlo . . . I'm sorry to interrupt, but something just came up. We'll talk again tomorrow . . . same time, okay?"

He hung up the phone and then stood. He was a big man. He didn't like anyone looking down at him when they spoke.

"At the risk of sounding clichéd, to what do I owe the honor?"

One of the agents, a stocky redheaded man with a burn scar on his cheek, spoke up. "I'm Agent Burke. This is Agent Browning. Federal Prosecutor Ashton Caine wishes to speak with you."

Ike recognized the name, but he didn't react.

"I'm sorry, but my schedule is full today. I can move some time around tomorrow and —"

"Technically, this isn't a request," Burke said.

Ike's chin jutted. "Do you have a warrant?"

"Surely you're as interested in finding out who killed your ex-wife as we are?"

They had him, and they knew it. It pissed off Ike. If he raised hell, it would only make him look guilty. But after the way Adam had gone off on him last night, being taken in for questioning wasn't going to be easy to explain away.

"Of course I am. You should have said what it was about in the first place, but why are the Feds investigating that? I thought LAPD had the case."

Neither agent commented.

Ike picked up the phone and buzzed his secretary. "Cancel my appointments and reschedule what's necessary. I'll be down at the federal courthouse if you need me."

"Yes, sir," she said.

Ike disconnected, then began making another call. "I'm calling my driver to pick me up out front."

"You can ride with us," Burke said.

Ike smiled, but there was no friendliness behind it. "Unless I'm under arrest, I don't ride with cops, even if they're federal ones."

Burke didn't blink.

"Well? Am I?"

"Are you what?" Burke asked.

"Under arrest?"

"No, sir," Burke said.

"Then I'll meet you at the fucking courthouse."

"We'll follow you there."

Ike was ticked. They were keeping him on a tight leash, and he didn't know why. Why had the Feds taken over Lorena's case? What did they know that he didn't? Maybe he shouldn't have let up on finding that witness. If she was back in the city, he had a whole other set of problems.

The introductions and seating arrangements inside the federal prosecutor's office were a matter of protocol as Ike Pappas was escorted inside. Ashton Caine was on one side of the desk and Ike was on the other. The two agents stood quietly at the back of the room. It offended Ike to think they would believe him so stupid as to cause trouble in a public building, and a federal one at that. But he kept a calm demeanor and an open expression on his face as he settled into the chair. In no way did he want anyone to think he was defensive.

He watched Caine's face, thinking to himself that the man reminded him of a bulldog — not very tall, but muscular, with a short neck and a nose that had been broken more than once. Caine was supposedly busy sorting papers in a file, but Pappas knew it was nothing more than a ruse to try to make him nervous. It wasn't working.

As for Ashton Caine, he was amped to be working on the Pappas case but had no intention of letting it show. Getting a conviction would make his career. Caine decided he'd given Pappas enough time to get ticked and finally looked up.

"Thank you for coming in."

Caine wasn't the only one with moves. Ike leaned back and crossed his legs, as if settling in for a nice cozy visit.

"I'm happy to do anything that would help you in finding Lorena's killer. My son, Adam, is devastated."

"But you're not?" Caine said.

Ike shrugged. "We've been divorced for

several years . . . amicably, of course. Adam and I dined with her at least twice a month, as I'm sure you know, often in her apartment. Lorena likes . . . liked to cook."

Caine scanned a sheet of paper before him. "You own the apartment building where she was killed?"

"Yes."

"And you set her up in the apartment as part of your divorce agreement?"

"Actually, no. She got the Miami estate in our divorce decree, but she wanted to be close to Adam so I set her up in one of the larger apartments in town."

Caine made a note.

Ike wished he'd brought his glasses. He was pretty good at reading upside down.

"Was your ex-wife seeing anyone?" Caine asked.

Ike shrugged. "I have no idea, but it wouldn't have mattered to me if she was. I date when the urge hits me. I assume she did the same, but she would never tell me something that personal. You might ask Adam. He was more aware of the personal aspect of his mother's life than I."

Caine made another note.

Ike was getting ticked. "What's this all about? I canceled an entire morning's worth of appointments to comply with your request, and yet you haven't asked me one damn thing that hasn't already been asked by your agents and the LAPD."

Caine responded with a question. "Can you explain why the surveillance system wasn't working at the building where your ex-wife lived?"

"That's a dumb question, Caine. We both know you found the security guard dead, so I assume the killer was responsible. Surely you came to the same conclusion. Believe me, if I knew who did this, he'd already be dead. By the way . . . do you have any suspects?"

Caine's gaze never wavered. "Yes."

Ike's voice went up an octave. He hoped it indicated disbelief and not panic.

"Then why the hell haven't you made an arrest?"

"We're still gathering evidence," Caine said. "When we make the arrest, we want to make certain it sticks."

Ike inhaled slowly. That felt like a threat, but he wasn't about to take the bait.

"So what's the real reason you called me down here?"

"We would like a DNA sample."

Ike frowned. "Come on, Caine. You've got my whole life on file, including the women I've fucked, so don't play the innocent game with me. What do you really want?"

"A confession."

Ike flinched. "You're a son of a bitch."

Caine buzzed his secretary. "Send in the lab tech."

Ike silently suffered the indignity of the mouth swab, then waited until the tech was gone before he turned on Caine.

"Are you through harassing me?"

Caine rebutted. "This isn't harassment. This is part of an ongoing investigation."

"Into what? Me? You people don't have anything on me, and you know it, so what's this latest gig about? If you're trying to set me up for Lorena's murder, you'd better think again. I have a rock-solid alibi, remember?"

"From your son."

Ike leaned forward. "Who would personally cut my throat if he thought for a second that I'd hurt his mother."

"Tit for tat?" Caine asked.

Ike flushed. Lorena had died because her throat was slashed. Even if they'd had a witness, that witness was gone. They were fishing, but without a motive, not to mention evidence, they couldn't pin it on him.

"Merely a poor choice of words," Ike snapped. "This is beginning to sound like an interrogation, in which case I need to call my lawyer. So unless you have something else to discuss with me, I think we're done."

Caine hadn't needed to talk to Pappas. He'd done it to let the man know he wasn't off the hook, and for now, his job was done. He nodded to the agents at the back of the room, who promptly escorted Pappas out of the building.

When it came time for Beth and Ryal to leave, Lou wouldn't let Beth say goodbye, only that they would see each other again soon. It took away enough of the impact of why she was there that Beth was able to leave with a smile on her face.

But the moment she was alone in the pickup with Ryal, the tension returned. They'd been cordial in front of Lou, but she didn't feel cordial. The silence between them was awkward. Something needed to be said, but for the life of her she couldn't come up with how to begin.

Ryal knew she was uncomfortable, but so was he. It had taken years to come to terms with how to live without her, and he wasn't always happy about the outcome, but it wasn't his call. Now all of a sudden she was back in his life as abruptly as she'd left, and as prickly as a porcupine every time she looked at him.

He wondered what she was thinking but didn't want to ask. They were going to be spending a lot of time together during the next days, maybe weeks, and they needed to be able to do it without making each other miserable. But even if he wasn't sure what needed to be said, this silence couldn't endure.

"Beth, I know you're uncomfortable with me, but I want you to know it's not necessary. We don't need to talk about the past unless you want to. I don't have any hard feelings, and I hope you don't, either."

Beth resisted the urge to glare. "*Uncomfortable* is hardly the word I'd use, but it's not just you, Ryal. It's the whole ugly mess."

His eyes narrowed as he slowed down for a curve in the road.

"I don't know everything that happened, but I know enough to realize you're lucky to be alive."

"Pretty much, and I have Uncle Will to thank for that."

"That's not what I heard. You were pretty damn brave, Beth, but then, you always were."

The unexpected praise brought tears to her eyes, but she quickly blinked them away.

"Mama used to say that a person never

136

knows what they're capable of until they're faced with adversity."

Ryal cast a quick glance at her.

Beth turned toward him, and for a moment their gazes locked. She was the one who looked away.

Ryal sighed. So much for that hoped-for truce.

Beth had seen a question in his eyes, and by keeping her silence she felt as if she'd somehow let him down, but there was no footing between them. Every time she looked at him she felt hot and achy . . . as if she couldn't quite catch her breath. She needed to change the subject.

"Where are you hiding me?" Beth asked.

"Remember my grandpa Foster?"

"Your mother's daddy?"

Ryal nodded.

"We're staying at his place, because it's the highest house on Rebel Ridge and completely isolated."

"Oh, Ryal, I don't know. What's he going to think about people just moving in on him?"

"He won't mind. He died about a little over a year ago."

"Oh. I'm so sorry. I didn't know."

Ryal shrugged. "How could you?"

Beth frowned. She didn't like his attitude.

"What does that mean?"

Ryal frowned back. "Don't use that tone of voice with me, Lilabeth. It means, how could you know when you no longer lived here? It means how could you know when you broke contact with everyone and everything you left behind without a damned word? Not to me. Not to Lou. Not to anyone. That's what that means."

Beth flinched. The anger in his voice was impossible to miss. But he wasn't the only one who'd felt hurt and betrayed.

"I didn't want to go!" she yelled, and then groaned. She hadn't meant to say that out loud. "I thought you would fight for me. But you didn't. I thought you would come get me. But you didn't. No one wrote back to me no matter how many letters I sent. No one called. After that, I got the message. There wasn't anything to come back for."

Ryal stomped on the brakes and slammed the pickup into Park. The morning sun coming through the windshield highlighted the dust motes in the air between them, but the heat was nothing compared to the heat of the anger between them.

"I didn't know I needed to fight for you until it was too late. I woke up one morning and you were gone. All of you. No one even knew which direction you'd gone until months later, when Lou finally got a letter from your dad. I begged for the address. I wrote a dozen letters to you in one month's time and every one of them came back unopened."

Ryal's face began to blur. Beth swiped at the tears running down her face. If what he was saying was true, then that meant her parents had lied to her a thousand times over, blocking both her letters and his.

"I don't believe you!" she screamed.

He reeled as if she'd just slapped him, then took a deep breath, put the pickup in gear and started driving.

The silence between them was painful, but the longer it stretched, the less likely it became that it was going to end on a good note.

Beth took a slow, shuddering breath and swallowed back tears, refusing to let him see her cry. She made herself focus on the view and started recognizing houses tucked back in the woods, roads cut into the hills that wound upward before they disappeared from sight. She'd been gone ten years, and yet nothing here had really changed. The only industry in this part of Kentucky was the mines. A majority of the population lived below the poverty line, and it showed — in the run-down houses and in the ramshackle cars parked in front, some with wheels, some without.

When she realized they were near his old family home, she began to get nervous. Surely she wasn't going to have to face all of them now. He took the turn she remembered and resisted the urge to argue.

The road was shaded by trees on both sides, but the underbrush was gone. It looked neat and well cared for. When the house she remembered suddenly appeared in front of them, she felt sick. The one-story clapboard house was still there, but it appeared that they'd added on a room, a wraparound porch, narrow gray shutters and a fresh coat of white paint. But all she could remember was the last time she'd been here with him, when they'd made love beneath the waterfall in the woods below the house.

Ryal slammed on the brakes and killed the engine, but he wouldn't look at her.

"I need to pick up my stuff. Would you like to come in and use the bathroom before we head up? It's about an hour's drive to Grandpa's cabin."

Beth wanted to say no, but she knew better. "I guess I should." But when she reached for the door, he stopped her.

"I'll get that. The door sticks, and you'll

hurt your hands."

He bounded out of of the truck and around to the passenger side before she could disagree, opened the door and put a hand under her elbow to steady her as she slid down from the seat.

She started to say thank-you, but he turned his back on her and walked away. She followed him up the stone walk to the front porch.

He unlocked the door, and then stepped aside.

"After you."

The hair rose on the back of Beth's neck as she walked past him and into the house, only to be greeted by silence.

"The bathroom is still down that hall and to the left," he said, and left her standing in the living room.

It took a few moments before she could make herself move. She didn't recognize anything about the place. Not the furniture, not the layout — nothing. Walls had been moved. Everything was more open, and the furniture was all different. That was when she remembered Uncle Will saying Ryal made and sold furniture for a living. She wondered if he'd made any of this. It was simple, but beautiful.

Finally she came to her senses and headed

for the bathroom. When she got back, he was standing in the living room with a suitcase in his hand.

"I've already loaded up the perishables," he said.

"Where's your family?"

"They don't live here anymore. Dad died the year after you left. Mom moved down the mountain to be closer to my oldest sister — you remember Meg, right? James is married, and Quinn lives on his own. I live here alone. Do you want a drink or anything?"

She shook her head.

He thrust a packet into her hands and then walked out the door, leaving her to follow.

Startled, Beth looked down at what he'd handed her. A handful of unopened letters tied up with a ribbon. She recognized the handwriting, and then her name. Her stomach knotted as she saw the dates on the postmarks.

Sweet Lord . . . he had written to her after all.

She looked up. He was standing at the door, waiting for her to exit. She started to say something, but his expression was cold, and enough had already been said between them. She lifted her chin and walked past him.

Ryal watched her walk out of the house with her head up and her shoulders straight. He could tell by her stride she was pissed, but so was he. He'd known this wouldn't be easy, but he hadn't been prepared to feel old anger and pain, and obviously neither had she.

"God help the both of us," he muttered, then locked the door and followed her to the pickup.

Pappas was at his favorite restaurant, sipping ouzo as he waited for his meal to appear. The man sitting across from him neither ate nor drank. Instead, he sat watching Pappas like a rat watching a cobra.

Moe Cavanaugh was middle-aged, skinny and going bald, but his skills had nothing to do with age or looks. His reputation for finding people who didn't want to be found was well-known, and when he'd gotten the call to meet Pappas, he'd relished the opportunity. He didn't like the man, but the money he paid out was worth a lot of angst. Now he sat, patiently waiting for Pappas to speak.

Pappas knew Moe was getting antsy, but he liked to keep people who worked for him a little off guard. To draw out the suspense, he took another slow sip of ouzo, then

143

glanced at Moe and slid an envelope across the table.

Moe quickly picked it up and slipped it in his jacket pocket as Ike began to speak.

"I need you to find someone for me. Her name is Beth Venable. She's an artist of sorts . . . illustrates children's books. I gave you her address, but needless to say, she's not there. The Feds had her in protective custody, then lost her, so mind how and where you do your searching, especially on-line. You don't want to let the Feds know you're looking. When you find her, I'll take it from there."

"I'll get right on it," Moe said.

"Time is an issue," Ike said. "Find her quickly and there's another ten thousand in it for you."

"Yes, sir, I'll do my best," Moe said. "Is there anything else?"

Ike's eyes narrowed thoughtfully as he saw Adam walk through the door. He hadn't expected to see him. They were still at odds, and he couldn't help but wonder if Adam was tailing him.

"That's all. You can go," Ike muttered.

Moe was out of the chair and through the door before Adam was halfway across the room, but Adam recognized him. By the time Adam reached Ike's table, he was curious.

"May I join you, or are you expecting someone else?"

Ike leaned back, eyeing his flesh and blood with a wary air. He wasn't going to make it easy for Adam. The little bastard had insulted him.

"I didn't know we were back on speaking terms."

Adam flushed, but he didn't apologize. "I didn't ask for a hug. I asked if I could sit down."

Ike grinned. "Spoken like a true Pappas. Yes, sit your ass down before you make a scene."

Adam sat. He was still suspicious of his old man, though he had nothing but a gut feeling to go on.

"Have you already ordered?" Adam asked, as he hailed a waiter.

"Yes."

Adam pointed toward Ike. "I'll have what he's having, and bring me a coffee," he told the waiter, who quickly sped away to adjust the table order.

Ike shook his head, as if in disbelief. "A Greek who doesn't like ouzo. Shameful."

"Half Greek, half Italian," Adam said.

Ike bowed his head in acknowledgment. It

was a subtle reminder that Lorena's unanswered murder was still between them.

Adam leaned back and crossed his hands over his belly. Ike grinned. His own father had always done that when pondering the way to broach a subject.

"What's funny?" Adam asked.

Ike pointed. "My father always did that, too — crossing his hands over his belly as you do. Must be the Greek half of you."

Adam smiled, then regretted it. He didn't want his father to think he was off the hook.

"So who did you send Moe Cavanaugh after?"

"Your mother's killer."

Adam blinked, stunned by the answer. "You know who he is?"

Ike shrugged. "I've been thinking . . . maybe it was wrong to assume it was a man."

Adam leaned forward, lowering his voice. "What do you know that I don't?"

"Right now, nothing," Ike said. "But I would have found out by now if it was one of my enemies, and I can truthfully say I don't think it was. What do you know about the people your mother associated with?"

Adam frowned. "I know some names, but I don't know much else."

"And neither do I. Know your friends and

your enemies, I always say, because it is often the friend who will betray you first."

Adam's thoughts were racing as he fiddled with a spoon; then he blurted out an apology before he could rethink it. "I think it is time to say I'm sorry for accusing you of having anything to do with Mother's death."

Ike stifled the urge to grin. Now was not the time to gloat.

"Thank you, son. That means everything to me." Then he saw the waitstaff approaching with their food and quickly changed the subject. "Ah . . . here comes our meal. It's time we eat and forget about the harsh words. There should be no bad blood between father and son, right?"

"Right," Adam said.

Ike smiled. Now he could gloat.

EIGHT

The packet of letters in Beth's hands was a ticking time bomb. If she opened them, the contents were going to destroy the memories she had of her parents. The lies they'd told her to cover up her mother's indiscretions were bad enough, but to accept that they'd purposefully destroyed the relationship she'd had with Ryal proved they'd been selfish and self-serving. They'd sacrificed her happiness to make sure she never learned what her mother had done.

Beth was appalled at their lack of concern for her. Part of her wanted to throw the letters out of the window and pretend they'd never existed, but she couldn't. Even though it was too late for her and Ryal, she needed to know, for her own self-worth, that he hadn't walked away from her after all.

Ryal's silence was worse than when they'd been yelling at each other. The anger and abandonment they both thought they'd gotten over had been resurrected with a vengeance. Beth couldn't imagine what the coming days would be like, isolated together, miles away from everyone and everything. They would be forced to face whatever feelings they had left, whether they liked it or not. She stifled a groan. Right now she didn't know who she was more afraid of, the man who wanted to kill her, or Ryal. Still lost in thought, she was unprepared when Ryal suddenly slammed on the brakes.

From out of nowhere, a deer had suddenly bounded out of the trees onto the road in front of them. As Ryal braked, Beth flew forward toward the windshield. It was instinct that made her jam her hands against the dash to keep from ramming her head into the glass.

Within seconds, she realized what she'd done, but it was too late to take it back. The pain in her hands was so intense that all she could do was double over in the seat, moaning as she cradled her hands against her breasts. The wounds that had just begun to heal had broken open and were bleeding again.

Ryal panicked. When he heard the moan he thought she'd hit her head, but then he saw her protecting her hands, then saw the

149

blood, and felt sick, realizing what had just happened.

"Oh, my God, Beth . . . sweetheart, I'm sorry. I'm so sorry."

He jumped out of the truck, pulled a first-aid kit from behind the seat and then ran around to open her door.

Beth was white-lipped and shaking, and when their gazes met, he saw tears.

"Ah . . . honey . . . Beth . . . I —"

Her teeth chattered from the pain as she tried to reassure him.

"It wasn't your fault. I didn't fasten my seat belt."

The fact that she wasn't letting herself cry made him feel even worse. If it would have taken away her pain, he would have cried for her.

"You didn't fasten it because your hands were too sore. And I didn't help you because I was feeling sorry for myself. I would give anything for this not to have happened."

"It's all right," she said.

Ryal slid a hand beneath the fall of her hair as he cupped the back of her neck.

"No, honey . . . it's not, but like a lot of things that have been said and done today, it's too late to take it back. However, let's see what we can do about the end results, okay? I have some antibiotic spray. I think it will be less painful than cream, because I won't have to touch anything that's re-opened. We'll do one hand at a time. Are you ready?" he asked, as he removed the old bandages.

She nodded, then inhaled sharply as the spray hit the open wounds. He quickly sprayed the other hand, wincing with her as new pain shot up her arm, then put a gauze pad on each palm and taped them down.

"It's pretty sorry first aid, but it'll keep the blood off your clothes. When we get to Grandpa's house, I'll do a better job, okay?"

She nodded.

As soon as he finished, he tossed the first-aid kit on the floor near her feet, then grabbed her seat belt and leaned in to fasten it.

"There, better late than never."

Beth shivered. He was so close she could smell the faint scent of his aftershave. If he turned his head just a little bit and lifted his chin, all she would have to do was lean forward and they would kiss, but the moment she thought it, she wished the urge away. Being this close to him and not touching him was enough to make her crazy.

"There now," Ryal said, then picked up the letters and laid them back in her lap. "You okay?"

"I will be."

A faint smile came and went as his gaze swept her face.

"When did you get so tough?"

She didn't answer, but the question had apparently been rhetorical anyway, since Ryal was already on his way back around the truck. He gave her a quick glance as he got inside, then put it in gear and drove away. The deer that had caused the near-accident was long gone, but he drove with a closer eye on the road.

A few minutes later he glanced over at Beth.

"Doing okay?"

She nodded. She had never been this far up Rebel Ridge and thought what it must have been like for Ryal's mother to have grown up here.

"This is a long way up."

"Yes, and it's why we chose it to hide you. In fact, the road ends at Grandpa's house. Anyone wanting to go farther up Rebel Ridge goes it on foot. It's nearly one o'clock, but we'll be there soon. You're probably getting hungry. James and Quinn stocked the house with some basics, but I brought some precooked stuff from my house, too."

"There's power and running water?"

Ryal nodded. "Different members of the

family have stayed here a few times since Grandpa died, usually during hunting season. No one wants to live this far out of the way, but we're sentimental enough about the old place that we didn't want to see it go to ruin."

Beth shivered. "I don't care how far up it is. I'm ready to get lost."

"I can only imagine," Ryal said.

Minutes later he pointed. "The house is just beyond that dead pine. There's a small clearing in front of it, but it's surrounded in the back by trees, which should make it hard to see from the air."

Beth's eyes narrowed. She hadn't thought about it from that angle but was glad they had.

"How are your hands?" he asked.

She peered beneath the gauze. "They quit bleeding, but they'll be sore again."

He frowned as he drove past the dead pine. What was done was done.

"There it is," he said, wondering how she would view the unpainted wood, the tilting porch roof and the simple furnishings.

Beth leaned forward. "So this is the castle that's going to protect me from the enemy. Nice, but where's the moat?"

Ryal hadn't expected humor. He laughed.

"Would you settle for a rusty knight and a rifle?"

His laugh wound around her heart and made it ache, as did the smile on his face. There had been a time when laughter had been often and easy between them.

She smiled back, then saw Ryal pointing at the house.

"Looks like James and Quinn are still here. When you get inside, make sure they brought everything you're going to need for at least the next couple of weeks, okay? If not, they can bring it next time they come up."

Beth was a little nervous about seeing Ryal's brothers again. "Are they mad at me, too?" she asked.

Ryal flinched. "No, Bethie . . . no. God. I'm not mad at you, either. I'm not throwing out blame to hurt your feelings, but the truth is, you and I became collateral damage in your mother's affair."

"I know. I'm sorry."

"You have nothing to apologize for, okay?"

"Okay."

Within moments Ryal pulled up and parked. Both his brothers came off the porch. James was smiling as he opened the passenger-side door.

"Hey, Beth. Welcome back." Then he saw

the gauze pads on her hands. "Ryal didn't tell us you were hurt."

"I'm healing," she said. "Help me out, okay?"

"I'll do better than that," James said, and scooped her up in his arms and lifted her down from the cab of the pickup, then set her on her feet. "How's that?"

Despite the fact that James was happily married and just being his usual self, a little jealousy hit Ryal and reared its ugly head. "Stop showing off," he muttered. "You guys grab the bags and the box of food, okay?"

"Beth, good to see you," Quinn said quietly, then grabbed an armload of bags and walked away without commenting on James's gallantry.

Beth watched him walk away, then turned toward the old weather-beaten house.

"What do you think?" Ryal asked, as he walked up behind her.

Beth shrugged. "That I'm glad to be here and don't care if it's a month before I have to get back in a vehicle again."

James walked past her, carrying the box of groceries from Ryal's house.

"Hey, Ryal, do I smell ham?" he asked.

Beth remembered how James had always been hungry. "I see some things haven't changed."

Ryal slid a hand under her elbow. "That's for sure. Let's get you inside before he eats it all."

The front step creaked as they walked up onto the porch. "That needs fixing," Ryal said. "I know the place isn't much, but —"

Beth paused on the threshold. "Stop saying that, okay? I'm still the same person I was before I left, only older and a whole lot wiser. I don't need fancy. I need safe."

Ryal cupped her elbow. "Then I guess all I need to say is, your castle awaits."

"That's better," Beth said, and walked inside.

She was caught off guard by the faint scent of lemon oil, then touched by the gesture. They'd even dusted the place. It was, as Ryal had stated — not much, but it was enough. The front room was oblong, with an old rock fireplace at the far end. The furnishings were old, and the cushions in the sofa were sagging. The curtains at the windows were faded and a little tattered. There were stairs off to the right, leading up to a sleeping loft, and a short hallway to the left that branched in one direction toward bedrooms and the bath, and in another toward the kitchen. Despite its rather forlorn appearance, the place felt welcoming.

"Come this way," Ryal said. "You're getting the bedroom where the grandkids used to sleep. The mattress is the newest one, which isn't saying much, but everything's clean."

"Stop apologizing for everything. You're making me feel like a —"

Ryal tugged a lock of her hair. "Like a princess?"

She sighed. "Whatever."

Ryal eyed the tension in her expression and guessed she was close to a meltdown.

"Follow me." He dropped her bag off in her bedroom. "Bathroom is across the hall. I'm going to rescue our dinner from James before he eats it all. Come to the kitchen when you're ready."

She nodded, then couldn't help but watch as he walked away. His shoulders were bigger, his body more muscular, but he still had the same long, lanky stride. It was surreal to know she was with him again — that she could touch him and talk to him anytime she wanted. But it wasn't the reunion she'd always dreamed of. The anger and tension between them simmered just below the surface, ready to explode at a careless word or a judgmental look.

When she went to use the bathroom, she calmly ignored the cracked linoleum and the rust line in the toilet bowl, thankful there was an indoor bathroom rather than an old outhouse. After she finished, she took the gauze pads off her hands and carefully washed, then winced when she tried to dry. Until her hands began healing again, she was definitely limited as to what she could do. After a glance at her windblown hair, she smoothed it down and then started toward the kitchen.

She was still coming down the hall when she heard Ryal laugh out loud at something James had just said, and she stopped, letting the sound wash over her. She had always loved his laugh. It felt good to hear it again.

When she got to the kitchen, she paused in the doorway. Ryal was filling glasses with ice and then refilling the old ice trays so they could refreeze. There were no ice makers in this kitchen, although the refrigerator wasn't as old as she might have imagined. The stove was gas, which explained the propane tank she'd seen at the side of the house when they'd driven up.

Quinn was at the counter making sandwiches. She noticed Ryal kept watching him, and wondered why.

"Hey, there you are!" James said when he saw Beth standing in the doorway. "Come sit, girl, and tell me what you've been doing with yourself the past ten years . . . besides getting prettier."

Beth smiled. "You first. What have you been doing?"

"Your cousin Julie and I got married. We've got two kids, a four-year-old girl named Meggie, and James Junior, who's a little over a year old. I got me a small patch of tobacco and a couple of milk cows, and I'm the substitute mail carrier for Rebel Ridge. Maybe one day, when old man Hennings retires, I'll get the job full-time."

Quinn picked up a handful of potato chips and started eating, then stopped and handed her one.

"Watch the salt. It'll sting your hands."

Touched by his thoughtfulness, Beth smiled.

"Thank you, Quinn."

Again Ryal felt a surge of jealousy, but he shoved it aside. Whatever had been between them was gone, which meant jealousy had no place here, either.

"You still like mustard with your sandwiches?" Ryal asked.

Beth's eyes widened — she was startled that he'd remembered such a small thing.

"Yes, please."

Ryal finished making the sandwich that

Quinn had started, then cut it in quarters to make it easier for her to hold. When he slid the plate in front of her, he saw her face flush.

"Is something wrong?"

She looked up, surprised by his concern.

"No, I'm just so appreciative of how thoughtful all of you are being."

"Mama raised us right," James said and winked.

"I put your drink in a mug, so you wouldn't have to grip a whole glass. Is that okay?" Ryal asked.

Beth's gaze locked onto his, and for a moment the silence between them was palpable. "So far you're batting a thousand."

Ryal smiled. Things had to be getting better. She'd almost bragged on him. He put his food on a plate and sat down at the table beside the others. Within a few minutes the tension was gone and they were talking among themselves as easily as if the past ten years had never happened.

Oddly enough, it was Quinn — and not Ryal — who brought the subject of the past up again.

"So what have you been doing with yourself since you moved away?" he asked.

Beth shrugged. "I graduated high school in L.A., which was a nightmare compared to Rebel Ridge. I went to a local community college and then began working before I graduated."

"Where do you work?" Ryal asked.

"Where *did* I work is the better way of asking that," Beth said. "I have no idea what any of the people I work with think about my sudden absence, although I was assured by the FBI that they had everything covered."

"So where *did* you work?"

"I freelance, but on a regular basis, at a couple of publishing houses. I'm an illustrator, mostly of children's books. I use Lila Bethany as my professional name."

"That's amazing," Ryal said, and leaned back, eyeing Beth with newfound respect.

"You're kidding!" James said. "Like, what are some of the books you've done?"

"I've done a lot of different things, but I've been working on a series for nearly six years that's pretty popular. It's called The Hitchhiker series, about a little ladybug —"

Ryal suddenly smiled. "Named Bitsy, who hitchhikes on the backs of different animals and birds, and learns something new with every trip she takes."

Beth's smile lit her expression from the inside out. "Yes! You've seen it?"

Ryal was stunned by the fact that all these

years he'd been seeing the name Lila Bethany on the cover of his niece's books and never once thought of Beth.

"Those are Meggie's favorite stories. I have to read at least one every time she visits."

James beamed. "Meggie is smart as a whip, and my boy is already ahead of his age developmentally."

"Says the proud papa," Quinn drawled.

"Well, it's true," James insisted, then eyed the clock over the stove. "And speaking of family, I need to be getting back to mine. I have a milk cow that freshened up, so I'm milking every evening now."

"I'm ready when you are," Quinn said, then eyed Beth's hands. "Next time I come up, I'll stop by Aunt Tildy's and bring something for your hands. They'll be well in no time."

Beth instantly recognized the name of the old herb woman who lived on the mountain. When money was short, which was often on Rebel Ridge, locals went to Aunt Tildy rather than down to a doctor in the town. "I can't believe she's still alive. I thought she was ancient when I was a kid."

"She isn't as spry as she was, but she's still mobile," Quinn said.

"Is there anything else you want them to

bring?" Ryal asked.

Beth shook her head. "I wouldn't ask for more. I'm just grateful for what you've all done." Then her voice broke, and it took her a moment to collect her emotions. She wouldn't look at Ryal and couldn't look at the others without crying, so she fixed her gaze on a spot near the toe of her shoe. "I was so scared. Every time they found me, I thought for sure I would be dead before it was over, but somehow I managed to live through it. I couldn't imagine anything ever being all right in my life again . . . until now. I know what an imposition this is. I know how much you're all sacrificing to do this, but thank you, all of you, so much."

"Group hug," James said, and they all embraced her, making her laugh.

Ryal followed his brothers out, then moved his pickup to the back of the house, beneath the trees, as they drove away. When he started up the back steps, he paused. Something didn't sound right. He stood for a moment, listening, then quietly walked across the porch and peered in the screen door.

Beth was leaning across the table sobbing, her head buried in her arms.

"Well hell," Ryal said softly, then took a deep breath and walked inside.

Caught by surprise, Beth straightened

abruptly, but it was too late to hide the tears.

"I . . . uh —"

"Hush, girl," he said, then pulled her up out of the chair and wrapped her in his arms. "No explanations needed. You've been blindsided in more ways than one. If it was me, I would be crying, too."

Beth went limp in his arms and buried her face against his chest. His heartbeat was rock-solid against her cheek. His arms were strong, and his grip was sure. It was the final confirmation. She'd done the right thing by coming home.

NINE

Moe Cavanaugh had been digging into Beth Venable's background for six hours and had yet to uncover anything that might tell him where she'd gone. At this point it was his opinion that the woman had no life beyond work and the occasional workout at a gym. But this was only the beginning. By the time he was finished, he would know more about her than she did. It was why he got paid the big bucks.

So far he knew her parents were dead. She had no siblings. Her best friend was also dead, recently murdered. She was a freelance illustrator, mostly for children's books, and had an apartment in a medium-income part of the city. She was solvent, but not rolling in dough, and she didn't use credit cards. He wouldn't mind finding a woman with that particular quality, but he was guessing they weren't that plentiful.

She didn't attend church. She didn't do

volunteer work, and as far as he could tell she didn't have any hobbies. He'd pulled her phone records and accessed the names of every person she'd called for the past year, and not one of them had turned out to be a boyfriend. He was beginning to wonder if Beth Venable was a lesbian. Maybe she and this Sarah Steinman who'd been murdered had been a couple? It could explain the reason why she'd been at Steinman's apartment the night Steinman had been killed.

It took him another hour to find a small news item about a gas leak at Venable's apartment that had warranted an evacuation. When he noted that the evacuation and the murder of Sarah Steinman had happened within the same twenty-four hours, he realized his theory about her sexual orientation was no longer as solid as it had been. Venable had gone to a friend's house rather than a hotel after being forced to leave her own apartment. Not an uncommon occurrence.

Now that he'd run into a small wall on Beth Venable, it was time to expand the search, which meant running backgrounds on her parents. Even though they'd been deceased for several years, he might pop up some extended family in the area.

He started with Samuel Venable. The man hadn't shown up in the California DMV records until ten years ago, and after a quick search of property tax records, it was obvious he had never owned property in the state, either.

Moe leaned back in his chair and reached for a handful of pretzels. He liked the crunch and the salt, and the chewing it took to get them down helped him think. What he needed was a birth certificate and a social-security number. Not a problem.

He stopped long enough to get up and get himself a cold longneck, then took a big swig on his way back to his office. Beer and pretzels were food for the gods — at least the gods that Moe worshipped.

He popped a couple of tiny twists into his mouth, and then centered his fingers on the computer keyboard and let them fly, running through firewalls and password-protected sites as easily as a kid going from the swings to the slide to the merry-go-round. Within an hour Moe had a fresh trail to follow that led him right out of California and across the country to Kentucky and more Venables than he could count. If she wasn't still in California, he would bet money she'd gone home. However, betting wasn't an option when it came to Ike Pappas. Pappas was paying him for a sure thing, which meant Moe needed to book himself a flight. He checked the screen again, making notes to himself before he got back online. He didn't know where the hell Rebel Ridge, Kentucky, was located, but he was about to find out. He hit MapQuest and typed in the address, then stared in disbelief. According to the computer, Rebel Ridge did not exist. Great. Every good plan always had a hitch.

Night had finally come to the old Foster home. Beth was taking a bath, and the supper dishes had been done. Ryal wanted to talk to Quinn, to see if everything was set up as they'd planned. He couldn't help but worry about his younger brother. At this point, getting him mixed up in what amounted to a tense, warlike situation was about the worst thing they could do to him, but Quinn wouldn't be dissuaded. He was a Walker. Beth was his kin, too, distant though the blood link might be. And of all the Walkers, he had argued successfully, he was the most suited for the job.

Ryal picked up his phone to call but couldn't get a signal in the house, so he walked outside into the yard, moving and turning until he got a clear signal, then made the call. Quinn answered almost immediately.

"Yeah?"

"It's me," Ryal said. "Are you settled in?"

"Yep. Tent's up. Gun's loaded. Cold camp. Plenty of water."

"Come eat with us in the morning."

"I'll swing by and pick something up, but I won't be dawdling."

"Good enough," Ryal said, and then felt obligated to ask, "Are you still okay with this?"

"Stop worrying, damn it. I would feel the same if we were hunting turkey or deer. I'm just better at hunting men than the rest of you are."

"I am well aware of that. I am also aware that the U.S. Army wouldn't let you re-up for a third tour, and we all know why."

There was a moment of silence, then a low chuckle. "Yeah. At the moment, I'm a shade on the crazy side."

"Shut the fuck up," Ryal drawled.

Quinn laughed softly. "Stop worrying. Make me some biscuits in the morning."

"Consider it done. Sleep well, brother."

"It's all good," Quinn said.

The enigmatic comment didn't fit what Ryal had said, which meant Quinn probably wouldn't sleep at all. But Ryal knew there was nothing he could do to change the situation. He disconnected and headed back to the house.

Beth had crawled into the old claw-foot tub, ignoring the chips and rust stains as she sank wearily into the deep, warm water. There were two things she was grateful for tonight. One had to do with the fact that she was no longer going cross-country via eighteen-wheeler, and the other was that there were no FBI agents around. She was home. Surprisingly, it felt good to be here. But she didn't linger. Instead, she washed her hair, then herself, as best she could and got out.

When she came out of the bathroom in her pajamas, her hair clipped up at the back of her head, the house was quiet — too quiet. Even though she knew Ryal was somewhere close by, she felt vulnerable.

"Ryal?"

He didn't answer.

Droplets of water from her still-wet hair ran down the middle of her back as she walked through the house to the front room, then looked out. He was standing out in the yard, a short distance away from the house, and talking on the phone. He was probably trying to get the best signal, since cell-phone reception was spotty, at best, in the mountains. She wondered who he was talking to. Just because he wasn't married, that didn't mean he didn't have someone special.

As soon as she had that thought, her stomach knotted. She didn't want to think about Ryal making love to anyone, but thanks to her parents, he no longer owed his heart or allegiance to her. Not anymore.

Saddened at the loss of what might have been, she turned away. With no television, there wasn't anything to do but talk, and they'd said enough to each other for one day. Even though they had called something of a truce, there were many things still unsaid between them. But that conversation wasn't happening until she read the letters. Granted, she was reading them ten years too late, but she wanted to know what his state of mind had been. She'd lived with the anger of thinking he'd abandoned her, although she knew that was no longer the case. At least that part of their history could be resolved.

Once back in her room, she turned on the lights, then crawled up onto the bed with the packet of unopened letters in her lap. She didn't have to read them to know they were going to be hurtful, but she'd learned a long time ago that to get over pain, she first had to go through it.

Her fingers shook slightly as she picked up the packet, then untied the ribbons holding them together. Every one of them had been marked Return to Sender.

She shuffled through the postmarks until she found the earliest, but as she was about to open it, she heard footsteps in the hall. Ryal must be back. She stilled, waiting to see if he passed by her door. When he did, she breathed a quick sigh of relief. This was something she needed to do in private.

There was a knot in her stomach as she slid a finger beneath the flap. The glue was old — the envelope opened easily. She pulled out the page, but when she unfolded it, something fell out into her lap. She started to brush it off her leg, then realized it was a flower that had been tucked within the letter — a tiny mountain violet. The colors were still as vivid as they'd been the day he'd slipped it inside.

Beth felt like crying. The first time they'd made love had been under a tree near the spring at her parents' house, next to a bed of mountain violets. She slid the flower into the envelope for safekeeping, then began to read.

Beth,
What's happening? I've been going

crazy, trying to find out where you went and why. If it hadn't been for your granny Lou, I don't know that I would have ever had a way to contact you. All the Venables shut down. They won't talk to the Walkers, and I don't know why.

Lou finally took pity on me and drove up to our house just to give me this address. It's only a post-office box, which still doesn't tell me where you are, or I would have already been on your doorstep asking these questions in person. I love you. I thought we were forever. Why did you leave me without a word? Are you coming back? If you say the word, I'll come get you. Write to me, darlin'. Tell me what to do.

All my love,
Ryal

Beth didn't even know she was crying until she realized the spots on the paper were her tears. She put the tiny flower back into the letter and slipped it into the envelope. The pain in her heart matched the pain she'd felt in Ryal's words. What must he have thought?

Her first instinct was to go find him, but then she stopped. That was just the first letter. She needed to read them all before they talked. Her parents' betrayal, which was shocking, to say the least, couldn't be denied. Somehow she was going to have to find a way to forgive them, too, but tonight was not a night for dwelling on the past. She had too much on her plate with her present situation.

She heard footsteps again, and then a knock on her door.

"Hey, Beth, can I come in?"

"Yes, sure," she said, and shoved the letters beneath the pillow.

He came in carrying her hairbrush from the bathroom.

"Did you get your hands doctored okay?"

She turned them palms up, showing the Band-Aids she'd put on the larger cuts that had reopened.

He waved the hairbrush in the air. "Uh . . . I saw the shampoo and guessed you might have washed your hair. I brought your brush in case you need help combing it out."

"Thank you," Beth said, and took the clip out of the back of her hair and let it fall. "I'm warning you, it's a tangled mess."

Ryal's smile was genuine as he moved toward her. "Tell me if I brush too hard or if it's pulling."

"I will," Beth said, and turned around so that her back was to him.

Ryal took a deep breath. The thick fall of dark hair was still damp, which always made it curl. He thought about running his fingers through it on the pretext of combing out the worst of the tangles first but knew better than to start something he couldn't finish. It was tempting enough to be in a bedroom with her and know she didn't have a thing on under those flimsy pajamas.

Instead of focusing on his lust, he started at the ends of her hair, working out the tangles. As he worked his way up to the crown, he felt her begin to relax. He could only imagine how horrifying the past few days had been for her, and the thought of someone trying to hunt her down enraged him.

A few minutes later he paused.

"You doing okay?"

"Yes, thank you."

"Hey, it's no big deal. Besides, I'm nearly finished."

He worked his way through the last couple of sections until her hair was smooth and shiny. In the process, most of it had dried, as well.

"There you go, soft as a baby's cheek and shiny as a new penny."

Beth grinned. That was an expression

she'd only heard in the South, and she loved
it.

"Thank you so much."

Ryal wanted to lay her down on that bed
and make love until daylight, but that wasn't
going to happen, so he just smiled back.

"You're welcome, and when you need help
with anything, all you have to do is ask."

The awkward silence that came afterward
didn't last long. Ryal left, quietly closing the
door behind him before Beth could call him
back.

"Just as well," she muttered, then dug the
letters out from under the pillow, found the
next one and carefully opened it, wondering
if there would be another violet pressed
between the pages.

And there was. "Oh, Ryal." She bit her
lip, then began to read.

Beth,
It's been four days since I sent the first
letter, so I know it's too soon for you to
send one back. At least that's what I
keep telling myself. I don't know how
you're doing, but I'm not doing so well.
I can't sleep, because every time I close
my eyes I see your face. Sometimes
you're laughing. Sometimes you're crying. I don't know if it's just my imagina-

tion making this mess worse, or if that's really what's happening. I can't eat. The food tastes like dust in my mouth, and what I manage to get down keeps wanting to come back up. This is making me crazy. Write back. Soon.

Love you,
Ryal

Beth's lips quivered as she replaced everything, including the pressed flower, back in the envelope, and pulled out the next letter and the third violet.

Bethie,
It's been eleven days since I first wrote. I don't know what to think. Every horrible thing you can imagine has gone through my mind. I keep replaying our last day together over and over, trying to remember if there was a clue I missed — if there was something you were trying to tell me that I misunderstood. If there was, I'm sorry. More than you can know. Was something wrong? Please, honey . . . write to me.

All my love,
Ryal

Beth's anger was growing. She wondered

what her parents had been thinking as these had arrived, and how they'd justified it to themselves when they'd had them sent back unopened. She picked up the fourth one and opened it. The mountain violet fell out into her lap, and the words on the page broke her heart.

Beth,
Are you pregnant? It's the only thing I can think of that might make your parents react in such a crazy way. But if you are, why take you away? They know I love you. They know I would marry you in a heartbeat, and that I was only waiting for you to get out of school to even broach the subject. I was going to give you an engagement ring for Christmas. You would be eighteen by then to my twenty-five. I'm not that much older. Tell me that's not what's wrong.

Love,
Ryal

Beth was sick to her stomach. She'd thought he'd let her go without a thought, and he'd thought she'd dumped him. What a mess. What an awful, awful mess not of their making. The fifth letter was a repeat of the fourth, but the tone of the sixth letter had changed. His hurt was turning to anger, just as hers had done, and the omission of the mountain violet was just as telling as his words.

Beth,
I'm not real sure why I keep writing these letters, but you know how I am. I don't like unfinished business, and there's a hell of a lot of that between us. So what do you want me to do? Forget I ever knew you? Not as easily done for me as it seems to be for you. Oh. There's something you should know. I just found out about it last night. Not sure what it has to do with us, but at least now I know why your parents left. If you don't already know, I'm not going to be the one to tell you. You're going to have to ask your mother about that. The gentlemanly thing to do would be to wish you well, but I'm not there yet, so the only thing I have left to say is goodbye.

Ryal

Beth slid the letter back into the envelope, retied the pile with the ribbon he'd used and put them in her bag. After reading these, she was heartbroken that he'd never received any of the letters she'd sent to him.

179

There was no thought of going to talk to him now. Whatever they said next would be said in the bright light of day with plenty of space between them. Not now, while emotions were high.

She turned out the light and then crawled into bed.

Moonlight came through the part in the curtain and onto the quilt across her feet. Earlier she'd raised the window beside her bed to let in some fresh air and had forgotten to close it. But now she could hear the night sounds on the mountain and realized she could identify everything she was hearing. From the occasional hoot of an owl to what sounded like the howl of a panther, they were far removed from the sounds of city life she'd become accustomed to, and worlds away from being awakened by the sound of gunfire, which had become Ike Pappas's calling card. She thought about shutting the window, then took a deep breath and closed her eyes.

Ryal sat down on the side of the bed. The house was quiet. He thought about the talk he'd had with Quinn, who was standing guard in a camp about a mile down the road from the house. If anyone came up the mountain, he would know it and warn them.

Ryal thought about the ceiling fan over his bed back home and wished for a little moving air to cool the situation. The rifle he'd brought from home was loaded and in the corner beside his bed. He didn't think anyone would find them here, but this was Beth's life they were talking about, and it paid to be overcautious.

Something was making a scratching sound in the closet. Probably a mouse. When his grandpa Foster had been alive, he'd had a dog and a couple of cats. Afterward, one of Ryal's uncles had taken them home with him, and now the place was suffering the consequences. He would dig around the kitchen tomorrow and see if he could find some traps to set out.

When it dawned on him that he had yet to shave, he jumped up and headed for the bathroom. Anything was preferable to sitting and thinking about being under the same roof with Beth again. He moved quietly, aware she would be nervous in a strange place and he didn't want to disturb her rest.

He didn't even turn on the light until he'd closed the bathroom door, and then he went about the business of shaving. By the time he'd finished, he could hear the pine boughs brushing against the roof. The wind must be up.

He hung the towel on the rack, and then walked, shirtless, out into the hall and paused. There was a draft, which was odd. The only explanation was an open window, but he hadn't opened any, because the screens were all gone. It had to be in Beth's room.

He moved to her door and started to knock, then changed his mind and opened it just enough to peek in. She was curled up on her side, eyes closed and breathing steady. He looked past her to the window beside her bed. Curtains were flapping in the brisk wind coming through the open window. Taking care not to wake her, he tiptoed over and pushed the window down, then hurried out before she woke.

He thought about going to bed, too, but it was far too early for him to be sleepy. If he'd been home, he would most likely still have been in the wood shop working on a piece of furniture, but there was nothing to do here. He wandered into the kitchen, got a couple of cookies and a can of Coke, and went out on the back porch.

He had such fond memories of being in this place. It felt odd, almost wrong, to be using it as a hideout. *Hiding* wasn't in his vocabulary, at least not since he'd outgrown playing hide-and-seek with his brothers. He didn't walk away from confrontation, but then, he'd never had the head of an organized-crime family trying to kill him, either.

After he'd learned what had happened to Beth, he'd been mad at Sam and Annie all over again. If they had just stayed here and made Annie face what she'd done instead of running away, Beth would never have been put in this situation. He broke a cookie in half and stuffed it in his mouth, chewing thoughtfully as he watched clouds moving swiftly across the night sky. It wouldn't rain tonight, but he would lay bets it would be raining by this time tomorrow.

As he sat, he heard rustling in the brush. Within a few minutes a possum came waddling out of the shadows with its nose to the ground. Ryal was downwind, so it kept moving, unaware it was no longer alone.

When Ryal broke off a piece of cookie and tossed it out into the grass, the possum heard the sound and scooted backward. But it didn't take long for the scent of the cookie to change the little critter's mind. It waddled forward, found the bit of sweet and began to nibble, while Ryal sat motionless, watching.

Because no one lived here anymore, the

animals had lost their fear of human habitation. Grandpa Foster hadn't been dead much more than a year, but already they were beginning to reclaim the woods as their own.

When the possum finished eating the cookie, he snuffled the ground a little more, then waddled away. Ryal ate the other cookie, washed it down with the Coke and went back into the house. He was just passing Beth's bedroom when the door suddenly opened.

"Ryal, is everything okay?"

He jumped, then hastened to reassure her. "Yes, everything's fine. I'm sorry, did I wake you?"

"No. I woke up on my own, but the window was shut. I remembered it had been open when I lay down and —"

"I'm sorry that frightened you. I closed it earlier. There aren't any screens on the windows, and we're a long way up the mountain. I didn't want a critter crawling into bed with you."

She shivered. "I knew the screen was missing, but it was stuffy earlier. I didn't mean to fall asleep with it open. Thank you for taking care of me."

The tremor in her voice was evident.

"That's why we're here, remember? We're

all taking care of you, honey."

Beth shivered. "I'm afraid my life will never be okay again."

He thought a moment about what he was going to say, then decided it fit the situation.

"That's how Quinn feels, too."

"Quinn? Why?"

"He's done two tours in Iraq. He's only been home about eighteen months."

Beth was horrified. "Oh, no! Is all this stuff about me affecting him? Does he suffer from PTSD? I'm so sorry. He shouldn't involve himself in this. Why did you let him?"

Ryal wanted to hold her, but he knew if he touched her it wouldn't be enough, so he shoved his hands in his pockets instead.

"Quinn does what Quinn wants. The only reason I even mentioned it was because he never thought he'd make it back alive, even though he kept going back, but he did. He's getting better, and you will, too."

"You're right. I'm sorry I freaked out on you earlier."

"You have the right," Ryal said. "Sleep well, Bethie."

She backed into the bedroom and closed the door without taking her gaze from his face.

He went into his room, shed his jeans and pulled back the covers. He didn't know what that look on her face had meant, but he was too tired to figure it out. Within a few minutes he was belly down on the bed with his feet hanging off the end of the mattress. He slept without dreaming, and when he woke, it was morning.

TEN

The hooker was high-class. Adam Pappas wouldn't have it any other way. He was naked — sprawled out on the hotel bed with a couple of pillows behind his head, watching her dance for him. She'd already pleasured herself a dozen times while he watched. It was something he didn't talk about, but for Adam, being a voyeur was as good as being a participant. He already had a hard-on with a mind of its own, but his purpose with her was twofold. Yes, she was good at blow jobs, and since he hated condoms, that was his method of choice for getting off. But it was her other clients who interested Adam most, and he paid top dollar for the pillow talk she picked up.

"Talk to me, Maria."

The lithe beauty reached up and removed the clip from her hair, then tossed her head, spilling platinum-blond waves across her shoulders and down her back. She cupped

187

her own breasts and pinched the nipples, moaning beneath her breath as she sashayed toward him.

"You like this, too, baby? Do I make you hard?" She watched his eyes narrow and his nostrils flare.

"What do you think?" he growled.

She crawled up on the bed and then straddled his legs as she grabbed his penis and gave it a quick stroke.

Adam frowned. "Not yet, damn it."

She rocked back on her heels, smiling to herself as his gaze went straight to her pendulous breasts. They were all hers. No implants. It was only part of why she was in high demand.

"Let me do you first, Adam. Afterward, you'll see why."

"But I —"

"Trust me. Let me make you fly. Then we'll talk."

All the while she was talking, she was stroking his penis. But then she quit talking and took him into her mouth, and he forgot about everything but the rush of blood and the mind-blowing feeling of what she was doing with her tongue.

He rode the buildup with every ounce of control he could muster, wanting it to last as long as possible. But Maria was too damn good, and he was too damn horny.

Less than two minutes later, the orgasm swept through him hard and fast. He grunted. Grabbing the back of her head with both hands, he pushed her down onto his dick as far as she could take him and shot his juice all the way down her throat.

Maria knew her business. She'd learned to breathe and swallow without choking years ago — yet another skill that netted her the big bucks. When there was nothing left of Adam Pappas but a quivering mass of male flesh, she rose up and licked her lips, smiling at him as she did.

Adam grinned. "Damn, baby, you sure know how to fuck."

"That was just a little blow job, Adam. Someday, if you want to really fuck me, I'll show you a real good time."

Adam shivered just thinking about it. "Clean me up, then we'll talk," he ordered.

She walked naked into the bathroom and came back moments later with a warm, wet washcloth. When she finished, she poured them each a glass of champagne. It was the ritual he wanted, and she always met her clients' demands.

It wasn't until Adam held up his glass for a refill that he pushed her for info.

"We did this your way tonight, but why all

the secrets?"

Maria sat down at the foot of the bed facing him, then crossed her legs, well aware that he now had a bird's-eye view of her bare-naked crotch as she took a small sip of champagne.

"Please know that what I'm going to tell you is not meant to spoil your evening, but I am certain it's something you would want to know, okay?"

Adam frowned. "How could you spoil my evening?"

Maria shrugged apologetically. "It's about your mother's murder."

Adam's frown deepened as he leaned forward. "What about it?"

"There was a witness."

Adam gasped. "How do you know that?"

"A certain federal agent is a regular of mine. During one of my visits, he got a call. Usually he lets the phone ring, but this time, when he saw the caller ID, he made me get up and leave the room. I overheard him talking, though."

"Exactly what did you hear him say? Do you know the witness's name?"

"All I heard was his side of the conversation, but that was enough to know that the witness they'd had in protective custody had gone missing."

190

Adam set his champagne glass aside and scooted closer to her. "The Feds had a witness to my mother's murder in protective custody? What the hell? Why didn't they just arrest the killer instead of hiding the guy who saw it?"

"Hiding *her.* The witness was a woman. I know that much because I heard him say, 'What the hell do you mean, she's gone?' "

"This makes no sense," Adam muttered.

"I heard something else that might mean something to you."

"What was it?"

"He also said, and I'm quoting, 'That's just great. Our key snitch, the only one who could have helped us take him down, is murdered, and now the woman who saw her die is missing.' After that, I figured I'd better flush the toilet and make him think I was doing my business instead of listening in, you know?"

Adam felt sick. He couldn't think — *wouldn't* think — of what all that meant. Not now. He needed to be alone and in total control of his senses, not buck naked with a limp dick.

He rolled out of bed and strode to the dresser, opened the drawer and pulled out a wad of cash. He counted out twenty one-hundred-dollar bills and tossed them in her lap.

"I'll be in touch," he said briefly. "Get dressed. We're done here tonight."

"Yeah, sure, honey," Maria said, then dressed quickly and was soon out the door.

Adam was in shock. *Key snitch.* The one who could help take *him* down? That meant his mother had been a snitch, but who had she been helping the Feds to take down? The moment the question ran through his head, the answer hit him like a fist to the gut.

"My father. It has to be my father. Son of a bitch! Why would Mom do something so —"

One more time, reality dawned. The only thing that would enrage her enough to betray Ike Pappas was if she found out that Ike had taken Adam into the business. He'd grown up hearing them argue about it, and he knew for a fact that his father had promised his mother on the Holy Bible that he would keep their son away from organized crime. That would be reason enough.

But his thoughts were still spinning. So there was a witness to the murder. Great. But why would the witness have to be hidden?

"Oh, shit." Adam grabbed his pants and

started dressing.

You hide a witness when they're in danger. And they're in danger when the killer already knows he's been made. Now he knew what the meeting between his father and Moe had been about. Moe Cavanaugh was the best investigator in the business. He had no qualms about what he did or who he did it for. It was all about the money for Moe.

Maria said the Feds had lost the witness, and that she was on the run. Ike said he'd hired Moe to find his mother's killer. But what if Ike had lied to him? What if he already knew who'd killed Lorena? What if Ike wasn't looking for a killer but for the witness who'd seen *him* do it?

"Holy God," Adam murmured, then felt his stomach heave.

He staggered into the bathroom and threw up his guts until there was nothing left but dry heaves. Finally the spasms passed, and as he was washing his face, he caught a glimpse of himself in the mirror.

The horror of what he was thinking nearly overwhelmed him. He'd vowed to kill the murderer himself if he got the chance, but could he do it? He closed his eyes.

Her throat had been slit from ear to ear.

When he looked up, the answer was there

on his face. Not only yes, but hell yes, he could do it and he *would* do it. Out with the old, in with the new — which meant *he* would step into his father's shoes and deal with dissenters afterward. The only questions were when and how he could take care of things without giving himself away.

Ike was on the putting green of his country club with two business colleagues when his cell phone began to vibrate. When he took it out to look at the caller ID, one of the men chided him.

"Come on, Ike, let it go to voice mail."

"Sorry, I need to take this," he said. "Play through. I'll catch up with you later."

"We've heard that before," the man said, then left Ike on his own.

Ike couldn't remember ever receiving a direct phone call from this man before, but he knew better than to let it go to voice mail. If Giovanni Valenti called, it was never good news. He answered briefly as he moved out of earshot.

"Hello."

"Pack a bag and bring your passport."

"Uh, can —"

"Shut up and do what I say."

"Yeah, sure, Gi—"

"Don't say my name. Don't fucking say

my name, you asshole. Just do what I said, and make sure you're here before midnight."

The line went dead in Ike's ear. There weren't many people who could put the fear of God in Ike Pappas, but the boss of the New York crime syndicate was one of them. The only thing he could think of was that they'd gotten wind of the Feds breathing down his neck. But what the hell? The Feds were always breathing down their necks. How was this any different?

Still, there was no denying the man. Ike's golfing partners were already on their way to the next hole. He sighed, dropped his club into his golf bag, got into the cart and headed for the clubhouse. On the way, he called his driver, the pilot of his company jet and his housekeeper, Beatrice. By the time he got home and changed, his bags would be packed and his driver waiting to take him to the airport. But the uneasiness in his gut continued to grow. It was the tone of Valenti's voice and the order to bring his passport that made him think his days were numbered. However, this was his life. He would hear Valenti out, then make his own decisions.

He thought about telling Adam, then realized he couldn't. Adam would ask questions for which Ike had no answers. Better to just leave a message with Beatrice to tell Adam he had to make a quick trip to New York City and leave it at that.

Less than two hours later, Ike was in the air and, except for the pilot and copilot, alone in the plane. Plenty of time to think. Plenty of time to worry.

Adam drove home in a rage. The closer he got to the Pappas estate, the angrier he became. He'd asked his father once if he knew anything about Lorena's murder, but he'd never come out and asked him if he'd done it. Now he wanted to put his hands around his father's neck and ask. He would know by the look in his eyes if he'd done it.

He took the turn onto the estate on two wheels, slammed the brakes long enough to open the gates by remote control, then peeled out again on his way to the house without acknowledging the startled guard. When he braked again in front of the mansion, the car slid sideways. A gardener on the other side of the lawn looked up, then quickly looked away. The staff knew enough to be invisible when the need arose, and this appeared to be one of those times.

Adam jumped out of the car and stormed into the house. The door flew back against the wall with a bang, bringing Beatrice running. She saw him striding angrily through the foyer and stopped.

"Oh. It's you, Mr. Adam. I didn't know —"

"Where's my father?"

"I packed a bag for him earlier today. He said to tell you he had a meeting in New York City."

"Did he say when he was coming back?"

"No, sir."

When Adam hit his fist against the side of his leg, Beatrice flinched. "Will you be home for dinner tonight?" she asked.

"No. In fact, I won't be living here anymore," he said, and ran upstairs into his father's room.

He knew Ike was too smart to leave anything lying around that could incriminate him, but he intended to piss off his father. He also knew the confrontation they would have afterward, when the truth came out. He stopped in the middle of the room and then started looking around. The three pieces of art that hung on the walls of his father's bedroom had cost nearly three-quarters of a million dollars. The rug beneath his feet was the finest Turkish carpet money could buy, woven in rich colors of crimson, royal blue and deep yellow. The bedroom furniture was handmade; the bed, which was once and a half the size of a king-size and three feet longer, had handmade white satin sheets and a white silk comforter. The chandelier was a stunning construction of cut-crystal diadems.

He kept picturing his mother with her throat cut and the blood spilling out of her body, and in that moment, he knew what he was going to do.

He opened his pocketknife and pushed up his shirt sleeve. Without hesitation, he jammed the blade into the fleshy part of his arm, then swung his arm over the bed from top to bottom and all around the edges while his blood flowed, until the bed looked like something out of a horror film. Red blood on white satin.

He walked into the bathroom, dripping blood onto the Turkish carpet and the white tile flooring, grabbed a hand towel and wrapped it around his arm, and then strode out of the room without looking back.

He threw several days' worth of clothing into a bag, along with his toiletry items, then stormed back out of the house and drove himself to the emergency room to be stitched up. After that, he bought a bottle of Scotch and headed out of town for the family lodge up in the hills. It remained to be seen how the future would play out, but he'd spent the last day of his life under a roof with his father.

Ryal could smell coffee and bacon. Either Beth was already up or Quinn had let himself in. He rolled out of bed, put on his jeans and made a trip to the bathroom before he followed his nose to the kitchen.

Quinn was standing at the stove taking crispy strips of bacon from a cast-iron skillet. He turned around as Ryal walked in.

"Mornin', brother."

"Mornin'. How did it go last night?"

"Had visitors. A raccoon, two young bucks and a porcupine. They left me alone, and I returned the favor."

Ryal grinned. "Who's there now?"

"Vance. He'll stay until I get back this evening."

Vance Walker was another member of the clan and a young enough man not to have a family to tend to.

"Did he take off work from the mine to do this? 'Cause if he did, the boss man will frown on that."

Quinn shook his head. "No. It's his day off."

"Okay, then. Hey, Quinn, I'd be happy to spell you tonight. You could sleep here, and I'll take the watch."

"No, thanks. I like the solitude, and I'm pretty sure you and Beth still have things to discuss."

Ryal quickly turned away, unwilling for Quinn to see what he was feeling. "I don't know that Beth and I have anything to talk about beyond keeping her alive."

Quinn snorted lightly as he removed the last of the bacon.

"It's your story. Spin it however you want."

"Are we having eggs with that, or are you planning on bacon sandwiches?"

So Ryal wanted to change the subject. Quinn could live with that, too. "I figured you'd want eggs. Is Beth up?"

"I don't think —"

"Yes, she's up," Beth said, as she walked into the kitchen. "And something sure smells good." She handed the hairbrush she was carrying to Ryal, along with a hair band.

Ryal eyed her sleepy look and tousled hair, and wished he'd been the one to mess it up with a session of morning lovemaking, but since that was nothing but a fantasy, he ignored the sexual pull and focused on the task at hand.

"Turn around."

Beth promptly obeyed, wincing slightly as he immediately got the hairbrush tangled in her hair.

"Quinn's already made bacon and coffee. Want some eggs with that?" he asked, as he slid the hair band over the long ponytail he'd just brushed up, then gave it a couple of twists to keep it tight.

"Thank you, Ryal. As for the eggs, I'll have one over easy."

"You got it," Quinn said, and began cracking eggs into the hot grease. "Oh, Beth, I almost forgot. I stopped by Aunt Tildy's yesterday evening and picked up some ointment for your hands. It's in that little blue jar by the sink."

She eyed the small jar and picked it up. "Thank you."

"Don't thank me until you smell it," Quinn drawled.

Ryal saw the look on Beth's face and hid a grin. The old woman had a tendency toward vile concoctions, even though they were usually effective.

Beth opened the lid and sniffed cautiously. The aroma of mint was strong and refreshing.

"You guys were teasing, right?"

Quinn shrugged. Ryal was still smiling.

"It smells good, anyway," Beth muttered. "However, I'll wait until breakfast is over before I use it, or all we'll smell and taste is mint."

Ryal began taking plates out of the cabinet. "Yeah . . . there's all kinds of ways to use mint. Like mint eggs, mint bacon, mint toast, mint salt, mint —"

Beth threw a pot holder at the back of his head. "Enough, funny man."

Quinn laughed out loud, then stopped abruptly and turned back to the eggs, but Ryal caught it.

He hadn't heard Quinn laugh very many times since he'd come home from his last tour of duty, and it was a good feeling to know it could still happen.

A couple of hours later, with the dishes done and Quinn asleep in Ryal's bedroom, Beth's hands had been doctored with Aunt Tildy's remedy and she was rocking in the porch swing just outside the kitchen door, trying to figure out how to bring up the subject of the letters with Ryal, who was still out beneath the trees where he'd parked his pickup. The hood was up, and he was checking the oil and fiddling with the radiator hose with so much intensity you would have thought he was searching for car bombs. She'd been out there for almost an hour, and not once had he turned around to acknowledge her presence or say hello.

Beth frowned. She suspected he was as much at a loss as to what to do with her as she was with him. She knew how they'd gotten this way, but it was pitiful how it had come to pass. He was nursing a ten-year grudge at her, as she was at him, and though none of it was of their making, somehow that didn't seem to matter. She'd called him a liar, and he'd given her the letters to prove her wrong. The next step was up to her.

Ryal cursed beneath his breath as he checked the oil and transmission fluid for the fifth time. There were only so many things that could be checked in a car engine without crawling underneath the vehicle, but if he stopped and turned around he would have to face Beth, and he didn't know what to say.

All of a sudden he heard the squeak of the old screen door, and then a bang.

Thank God. She'd finally gone inside.

He slammed the hood down on the truck and was wiping the grease off his hands as he turned toward the house. Then he stopped short.

Shit.

Beth was leaning against the porch post, her arms folded across her chest and her chin up. She looked as if she was ready to fight.

And she'd tricked him.

"I thought you went inside."

"Obviously, or you'd still be hanging upside down inside that pickup."

He didn't answer.

She didn't move.

An entire minute went by without a word passing between them. Finally Ryal broke the silence.

"How long are you going to stand there?"

"Not as long as you dug around underneath that hood."

His eyes narrowed. Her tongue and her wits had sharpened perceptibly over the past ten years. Bethie Venable was all grown up.

Beth stepped off the porch and started toward him. "We need to talk."

He straightened his shoulders. "I know."

"My schedule's free. How about yours?"

He grinned.

She frowned. "What?"

"You've changed," he said.

"Ten years will do that to a person." But her frown deepened. "Changed how?"

"It's all good. Don't get defensive on me."

"Ryal, don't start —" Beth stopped, closed her eyes and took a deep breath, and then started over. "About that talk . . ."

"Let me wash up," he said.

She stepped aside as he walked past her into the kitchen. She heard the water running at the sink. Such an ordinary act, but she couldn't get past the fact that she was back in Kentucky with the only man she'd ever loved, and all because someone wanted her dead.

It was nothing short of a dream come true turned into a nightmare.

The sun was hot on the back of her neck. The scent of Aunt Tildy's mint ointment wasn't as potent as it had been, and her hands weren't as tender. Thanks to Quinn, at least one good thing was coming out of this day.

The screen door slammed. She took a deep breath, and then turned around and walked back up on the porch where Ryal was standing.

"I popped the top for you," he said, handing her a cold can of Pepsi.

"Thanks," Beth said, as she sat back down in the porch swing and took a sip.

He slid into the seat beside her and took a big drink from his own can. "Good and cold."

"I read your letters."

Ryal felt naked. Every ounce of love he'd ever had for her had been put on those pages and he'd been rejected, or so he'd thought.

Beth took a deep breath, willing herself to a calm she didn't feel. "I am ashamed and appalled at what my parents did to us. I'm sorry."

"You have nothing to apologize for any more than I do," Ryal said.

"I wrote to you, too. Now I know why you didn't answer. Dad was meddling with both our letters. I should have suspected something when I didn't hear from you. My heart told me you wouldn't just forget me so abruptly, but I was a naive seventeen-year-old girl who'd never been farther than fifty miles from where I was born, and I'd just been uprooted and taken to what felt like the other side of the world. Daddy kept saying the Walkers couldn't be trusted, and after weeks of your silence, I began to believe him. For that I am very sorry."

Ryal shrugged. "I'm sorry, too, Beth. I was older. When I finally found out about the affair between your mother and her sister's husband, I should have known there was more to my not hearing from you than I thought."

Beth felt like crying, but the tears wouldn't come. "It's ironic that we would be thrown together again like this."

"How so?" he asked.

"You know . . . before we were separated by something bad my mother did. Now we've been brought together again, this time by something bad I witnessed. I think the universe has a sick sense of humor."

Ryal chuckled. "I never thought of it that way."

When he laughed, Beth managed a slight smile. "I'm thankful for one thing," she added.

"What's that?"

"That ten-year-old knot in the pit of my stomach is gone."

"Same here," he said, and slid his arm across the back of the porch swing and gave her a quick hug. "This feels like church."

"I don't get the connection."

"Well, we've just confessed our sins, and now we're thankful for the mercies being shown to us. The only thing missing is someone passing the collection plate."

Beth laughed out loud.

Ryal grinned. That single sound had just made his day.

Without thinking, Beth laid a hand on his knee.

"Oh, Lord, that felt good."

"What felt good?"

"Laughing. I haven't laughed like that in

such a long time."

Ryal laid his hand over hers. "I always knew how to make you feel good."

A blood rush shot straight to Beth's belly so fast that she felt faint.

"Yes, you did," she said.

"So . . . are we good now?" he asked.

She nodded. "We're good."

The weight of ten years of guilt was gone — just like that. Still clasping her hand, he set the porch swing moving with the toe of his boot. The gentle movement matched the peaceful quiet between them.

For the moment, this was enough.

ELEVEN

Ike Pappas's private jet landed in New York City just after 7:00 p.m. He was pissed about being summoned on such short notice but knew enough to keep his emotions to himself. As the pilot was lowering the steps, he saw a car waiting for him on the tarmac. So Valenti had sent a ride. Damn considerate, considering it was his fault Ike was even there.

"Fuel up and be ready for my call," Ike told the pilot as he left the plane.

"Yes, sir," the pilot said.

During the hour-long ride to Valenti's estate, the sky turned dark and began threatening rain. He hoped it held off until he at least got inside. There was something about rain-splattered clothing that put a man off his game. At least it did for Ike, and he couldn't afford to be off his game with Valenti.

Even though Ike and Valenti were on equal

footing within their respective organizations, Valenti made him nervous. The man had come up through the ranks as a cleanup guy and still had the instincts of a stone-cold killer. If someone pissed him off, he took them out point-blank and dealt with the consequences afterward.

Finally the car began to slow down. When it took a turn into a tree-lined drive, Ike's pulse kicked up. Whatever Valenti had to say, he would know soon enough.

When they pulled up beneath the three-story portico, the driver looked up into the rearview mirror at his passenger.

"I'm to take you back to the airport when your meeting is finished, Mr. Pappas. I'll be right here when you come out."

Ike nodded, relieved to know an exit for him was already in place. It saved the worry that Valenti had planned to do him in. Moments later he was inside and being escorted to the library.

Valenti was standing at the window with his back to the door. Ike paused as the escort left him on his own. There was no way Valenti had missed hearing their footsteps on the marble flooring, but he didn't turn around.

Now Ike was pissed. He hadn't come all this way to be dissed. The longer he stood there, the more indignant he became.

"You got five seconds to turn your ass around and tell me why I'm here or this meeting is over."

Valenti turned slowly and pointed to a chair. "Close the door and sit down."

The hair bristled on the back of Ike's neck. "This better be good."

Valenti waited until Ike was seated, then sat down on the corner of his desk.

"You fucked up."

Ike stood abruptly, his fists doubled. "You don't talk to me like that."

Valenti moved so fast Ike staggered backward. Before he knew it, one of Valenti's hands was under his chin, the other at the back of his head.

"I'll talk to you any way I want to," Valenti whispered. "You're in the crosshairs of the FBI, which means we're all at risk. I don't like you. I've never liked you. But you did your job. I did mine. It's all for the common good, right? Then you piss off your wife —"

Ike glared. "I'm not married."

Valenti's fingers tightened. Not enough to stop Ike's breathing, but enough for Ike to know Valenti could snap his neck with one simple twist.

"You think you're in the clear, don't you?"

Valenti asked.

Ike frowned. "In the clear about what?"

Valenti cursed softly, then smiled.

That's when Ike's panic really hit.

"The Feds are onto you. They know you killed Lorena. They have your DNA on her clothes and all over the apartment. She was mad at you for bringing her baby boy into the business. Everyone knows you'd promised to keep him out. But you broke your promise, didn't you? You broke it, and she found out. Did she tell you she was going to go to the Feds?"

Ike felt like throwing up. "You don't know what you're talking about," he blustered. "Besides, what happens in my personal life is none of your business."

"The hell it's not!" Valenti shouted. "The five bosses had a meeting. If you're indicted, we're all implicated, and we don't like that."

"I'm not going to be indicted!" Ike shouted back. "I had nothing to do with Lorena's murder. Hell yes, my DNA was probably on her clothes and all over the apartment. I'm in and out of there all the time."

"You can't sell me your crock of shit, Pappas. I already *know* you did it. What *you* don't know is that she'd already gone to the Feds. They have enough circumstantial evidence already for an indictment. If they hadn't lost their witness to the murder, you'd already be behind bars."

Ike sat down. "How do you know she'd already gone to the Feds?"

"You ask me such a question? I know things the same way you know things. My snitches happen to be better than yours, that's all."

"Shit."

Valenti finally sat back down on his desk.

"Yes, and it's about to hit the fan," he said. "Did you bring your passport?"

Ike looked up. "I'm not running. I have things under control."

Valenti's eyes darkened. "You better know what you're talking about, Pappas. You get taken into custody, you won't leave the jailhouse alive."

Ike wanted to puke, but he held his ground. "I won't be taken into custody. The witness isn't going to live long enough to testify. There isn't going to be an arrest or an indictment or a trial. If you're done, I've got a plane to catch."

Valenti shrugged, then stood up. "I'm done. Consider yourself warned."

It was nearly midnight when Moe Cavanaugh landed in Lexington, Kentucky.

213

Things had gone wrong from the first leg of the trip all the way to his destination. Weather delays coupled with grounded planes and missing pilots had turned what was to be a simple flight into an all-day marathon of fuck-ups.

By the time he got his suitcase from baggage claim and headed toward the kiosk to pick up his rental car it was after midnight. At least he'd had the foresight to book a room at a Lexington hotel during one of the layovers. Armed with directions and the GPS in the rental car, he soon found his hotel. A half hour later he was in his room, checking messages and maps on his laptop while he waited on room service.

He had a basic idea of where he would be going tomorrow from info he'd gathered from the funeral home that had buried Sam and Annie Venable; he needed to get on Interstate 64 and head east.

When his food finally came he was almost too tired to eat it. He set the tray with the leftovers out in the hall, then crawled between the sheets. He was asleep within moments of his head hitting the pillow.

Beth's first full day at the cabin with Ryal had gone much better than expected. After their mutual agreement to let go of the past, the day had moved smoothly. They made sandwiches at noon, and for lack of anything better to do afterward, Ryal took her for a walk through the woods where he and his siblings had played when they were young.

"See that stand of young pines?" Ryal said.

"Yes."

"There's a cave behind it. James, Quinn and I used to hide in there, and then jump out and scare the girls when they came looking for us."

"I imagine the three of you were little terrors," Beth said.

"We had our moments, for sure. Wanna see inside?"

"Do you have a flashlight with you?"

"No."

Beth arched an eyebrow. "Then, no, thank you. There could be anything from a bear to a panther to a nest of snakes in there, and I've had all the excitement I can take this month."

Although he stood his ground, he had the strongest urge to pull her into his arms and kiss that smirk right off her face.

He grinned. "It was worth a try."

Beth snorted lightly. "You didn't seriously think I would fall for that, did you? I know you, remember?"

Ryal stilled. "I know *you,* too." It was the

tone of his voice that made Beth glance up. The look on his face stopped the sarcastic remark on the tip of her tongue. All of a sudden the mood had gone from light to dark. She panicked, then wondered why was she afraid to see where this led. This was Ryal — her first love. They'd been naked in each other's arms so many times during the year they'd had together that there shouldn't have been a doubt in her mind about what he was thinking.

But there were those damned ten years that had come and gone with nothing but hard feelings and regret between them. She didn't want pity sex. She didn't want hit-and-run sex, either. Truth was, she didn't know what she wanted from Ryal Walker, and until she did, she wasn't falling for that look again.

"Ryal?"

"What?"

"We're not going there, are we?"

The heat in Ryal's belly was already cooling. He'd seen the uncertainty on her face, and until he knew if there was going to be a future for them, pushing boundaries was the last thing he wanted. "I don't think we should. Do you?"

"No. Not yet. Not until —"

He put a finger over the curve of her lips,

sealing whatever she'd been going to say inside.

"Don't put a date and time stamp on this, Beth. Either it'll happen or it won't, okay?"

Her shoulders slumped. This was what she wanted. So why did she feel as if she'd just been kicked to the curb?

"Okay."

He tugged on the end of the ponytail he'd put in her hair this morning. "How about we head back to the house? If Quinn wakes up and finds us gone, he's liable to worry."

"Right," Beth said.

On the way back they talked about her work and his furniture business, the truckers who'd driven her cross-country to meet her uncle Will, how guilty she still felt about Sarah's death — everything and anything they could think of except the obvious . . .

Where did they go from here?

Were there any emotional ties left between them, and if there were, did they ignore them? Or start over? It was like holding a lit match to an open gas jet and waiting to see how long it took for the thing to ignite.

By dark, supper was over, and Quinn was out of the house and back on guard duty. The storm that Ryal had predicted arrived just before midnight. He and Beth had both been asleep when the front hit, announcing itself with a clap of thunder so loud it rattled the windows. Within seconds the power went out, plunging the house into sudden darkness. No night-lights, no glowing face on the alarm clock — nothing but the intermittent flashes of light from the lightning coming through the curtains.

Beth had been dreaming about the safe houses and hiding from the gunshots when the first clap of thunder sounded. She sat straight up in bed just as all the power went off. Still locked into what she'd been dreaming and disoriented by her surroundings, she screamed, thinking they'd been found.

Ryal was already awake when he heard her scream and was out of bed in seconds. He flew out of his room and into the hall just as the door to Beth's bedroom swung open. She ran out into the hallway, straight into his arms, and then screamed in earnest and began fighting him, thinking she'd been caught.

He grabbed her by the shoulders, then held her close within his arms to keep from being hit.

"Beth, Beth, it's me, baby, it's me. You're okay. It's just a storm."

The relief of hearing Ryal's voice was her undoing.

"Oh, my God." She pressed herself against

his chest and wrapped her arms so tightly around his waist that he couldn't have dislodged her if he'd tried. "I was dreaming. I thought the thunder was gunfire, and then everything went dark."

Ryal had one hand against the back of her head and the other around her waist.

"You're okay. You're okay. Remember where you are and what the old-timers say. Storms are louder up here because we're closer to heaven."

Beth couldn't stop shaking. "Yes, I remember," she muttered, and buried her face against his chest.

The warmth of his bare skin and the safety she felt within his embrace were reassuring. Another clap of thunder rolled overhead, followed by a shaft of lightning so close that the momentary illumination outside was brighter than day.

In that brief second Beth looked up. Ryal's gaze was fixed on her face.

The house went dark again, but now she was aware of the rising wind and the steady thump of Ryal's heartbeat against her breasts.

Another shaft of lightning pierced the darkness just long enough for her to see his long, bare legs and a glimpse of white briefs; then the house was in shadows again.

The repetition of dark then light, thunder then lightning, was like being caught beneath the mirror ball in a disco.

Ryal tilted her chin, then paused, giving her time to pull away. When she didn't move, he took it as approval for what came next.

The kiss had been ten long years in coming, but that only made things better. The feel of Beth's lips beneath his, the softness of her body and the way she melted into his arms, were everything he'd dreamed of. Ryal scooped her off her feet and into his arms as another flash of lightning momentarily lit up the hall.

She had only an instant to see his expression, but it was enough for her to get caught in the rising fever between them.

Ryal carried her into his bedroom. Thunder rumbled as he stripped down to his skin, then pulled her pajama top over her head. Lightning flashed as he yanked the bottoms down around her ankles, then put his hand between her breasts. She fell backward onto the bed, and within seconds Ryal was on her, then in her.

There was no time for foreplay, no time for kisses and whispers — just the blood heat of need pulsing through their bodies and the desire to be one.

The moment Ryal entered her body, Beth was whole again. The loneliness of the past, the empty years and broken promises were gone. When he began to move, she locked her legs around his back and rode the rhythm with him.

Outside, the wind and thunder, followed by lightning, continued until the rain finally arrived. The sudden gush of wind-driven rain against the windows mirrored the instant rush of Beth's climax, hitting her with such force that she screamed. Ryal answered with a primal groan that became lost in the roar of the storm that was upon them. And when they had been emptied of the lust and there was nothing left between them but waning passion, they fell asleep in each other's arms.

When they woke again it was morning, and the scent of coffee and frying bacon was once again permeating the air. More of life had happened beneath the roof of Grandpa Foster's old house in the past twenty-four hours than there had been in years.

Beth opened her eyes to find Ryal watching her. She wanted to frown at the intrusion, but being plastered against his body and the erection pulsing against her leg were too interesting to get past.

"I want to make love to you again," he said. "But Quinn's already in the kitchen."

Beth slid her arms around his neck. "As long as he stays there, I don't see the problem."

Ryal arched an eyebrow. "Do you really want to let him hear you scream?"

"I'll restrain myself.

"That'll work," Ryal said, and proceeded to show her.

By the time they got to the kitchen, Quinn was eating the last bite of his eggs.

"Hey," Ryal said. "You must have been hungry this morning."

Quinn eyed the pair standing arm in arm in the doorway.

"From all appearances, not as hungry as the two of you. Grease is still in the skillet. Eggs are in the bowl. I'm gonna take a shower and get some sleep."

Beth blushed as Ryal ignored the sexual inference.

"Did you see or hear anything suspicious last night?" he asked.

Quinn shook his head. "No, and the tent leaks."

Ryal thought of the downpour and how comfortable they'd been, and immediately felt bad.

"Listen, Quinn, I don't care what you say,

I'm taking the watch tonight."

"I do better in the dark on my own. Just let it go, Ryal. For now, it is what it is, okay?"

Ryal wouldn't argue, but when Quinn passed by, Beth stopped him with a touch.

"Thank you."

Quinn eyed her slightly swollen lips and the just-loved expression on her face, then took her hands and turned them over, giving them a quick examination before he gave her a nod.

"Looks like Aunt Tildy's remedy is working."

He walked out without saying more.

Beth turned to Ryal. "Is he okay?"

Ryal shrugged. "Like he said, right now it is what it is. I have to believe that in time he'll be better. Probably never back to the old Quinn, but better. I'd settle for that. Now, how about breakfast? One egg over easy?"

"Make that two," Beth said. "I worked hard last night."

Again Ryal's laugh rocked the silence in the little house.

Down the hall, Quinn smiled slowly to himself, then rolled over in the bed Beth had abandoned for the one Ryal was in and closed his eyes.

Moe drove into Mount Sterling just before two-thirty in the afternoon and stopped at a quick stop to get gas. He filled up, then went inside to pick up some snacks, and fish around for some information, as well. The man behind the counter looked to be in his early thirties, sporting a red birthmark on his right cheek and missing the little finger of his left hand.

Moe grabbed a couple of bags of cashews from a shelf and a cold bottle of water from the cooler. He wanted a beer but had a rule of no drinking on the job. He laid the snacks on the counter.

"I got gas on pump four, too," he said.

The clerk nodded and rang up his purchases. "That'll be $47.12."

Moe laid three twenties on the counter.

"Did you ever hear of a place called Rebel Ridge? I can't find it on the map and was wondering if you could give me some driving directions."

"There are lots of places around here that ain't on no map," the clerk said and handed Moe his change. "You might head on toward Boone's Gap and ask around."

Moe remembered seeing a town called

Boone's Gap on the map.

"Thanks."

He got in the car, set the GPS and then followed its directions out of town. It took nearly an hour of negotiating winding mountain roads before he began to see signs of habitation in the form of rusting trailer houses and old, run-down homes as gray as a December sky. The exteriors didn't appear ever to have seen a lick of paint. The weather was hot, so the windows were open, but few had screens to keep out flies. Some houses had several old rusting car bodies up on blocks sitting off to the side. Others had kids of assorted ages running about, with the occasional dog thrown in for good measure. A few had all three. He seemed to remember discovering during his research that the chief source of income in the area was coal mining. From the looks of the properties, coal mining didn't appear to be a profitable occupation for anyone but the mine owners.

A short while later he came upon a weather-beaten sign that read Boone's Gap, 2 Miles.

When he finally drove into town, he was hit by even more culture shock. Although they'd strung it out into a semblance of four blocks, the entire town would have fit into two blocks of downtown L.A. with room to spare. There were a gas station/deli, a small grocery store, a tiny building that was a branch of a savings and loan company, a post office and a video rental place. He looked farther and saw a couple more businesses and a café called Frankie's Eats. The rest of the buildings were empty. Seven cars were parked in random spaces along the curbing, which told Moe he probably wouldn't have to wait for a table at Frankie's Eats.

It had been hours since he'd had breakfast, and the snacks he'd bought in Mount Sterling hadn't satisfied his hunger. He made a quick decision and parked in front of the café. As he got out, he stretched wearily before heading inside.

The scent of something fried went up his nose as he opened the door. A tall, skinny waitress with a blond ponytail and a grease stain on the front of her apron waved him toward a booth.

"I'll be right with you," she said, and disappeared into the back with a tray of dirty dishes.

He sat down, picked up the menu standing between the napkin holder and the salt and pepper shakers, and scanned the options.

Unsurprisingly, there was nothing vegan on offer. Ah well, he could always do a cleanse when he got home.

"Hey there, how ya'll doin'?" the waitress said, as she slid a glass of ice water in front of him. "Do you know what you want, or would you like a couple of minutes to read the menu?"

Moe shook his head. "No, I'm good. Give me a cheeseburger and fries, and hold the onions."

"You got it," she said. "Anything to drink?"

"I'll have iced tea."

"One sweet tea comin' up," she said.

Moe frowned. "Not sweet tea. I'll have plain."

"Sorry, hon. Only sweet tea here."

"Then I'll stick to water."

She shrugged. "Yeah, sure. Food comin' right up!"

She left to turn in his order, then came back with that big tray and began bussing another table. He watched her for a few minutes and then decided to see if she had any info he could use.

"Hey . . . uh, miss . . . ?"

She looked up and smiled. "I'm SueEllen. Whatcha' need?"

"A little information."

She walked over to the booth.

"Have you lived here long?" Moe asked.

"All my life."

"Great. Maybe you can help me. I'm looking for someone who lives in a town called Rebel Ridge. Do you know where it is?"

SueEllen's smile didn't disappear, but it didn't get bigger, either.

"It sounds familiar. Who you looking for? If I know the name, I can probably tell you where they live."

Moe hesitated. He hadn't planned on divulging the name of the family he was searching for, but he needed to satisfy Pappas within a reasonable period of time.

"I'm looking for a family by the name of Venable. Have you heard of them?"

"Hey, SueEllen! Pickup!"

The waitress held up a finger. "Hold that thought. Your order's ready."

SueEllen's mind was racing as she went to the pass-through to pick up the order. Her mother was one of Sam Venable's sisters. Beth was her first cousin. The whole family knew about what had happened to her. They also knew she was in hiding somewhere up on the mountain. The way SueEllen looked at it, the only strangers who would be trying to find her family were up to no good.

She took a deep breath and picked up the

order, then sashayed back with a big smile on her face.

"Here you go! Nice and hot. You gonna want ketchup with those fries?"

"Yeah, sure, why not?" Moe said.

She scooped up a ketchup bottle from a nearby table and set it in front of him.

"Now, then . . . you said you're looking for the Venables, right?"

Moe nodded as he took a big bite of the burger, then groaned in ecstasy, trying to remember why he'd gone vegan in the first place.

SueEllen pulled out her order pad and a pen, and began writing.

"When you leave here, you need to keep going east on Interstate 64. When you connect to Highway 32 outside of Morehead, head north."

Moe stuffed a forkful of fries in his mouth, talking as he chewed. "You sure about that?"

"Yep, I'm sure. I'm real sure. Here, I wrote it down for you."

"Thanks a lot," he said.

"No problem. If you need anything else, just holler."

"Yeah, okay," he said, already sidetracked by the food.

He wolfed the burger and fries down without thought as to what it would do to his digestive system later, washed it down with water, then chased it with the refill SueEllen poured for him. She left the bill on his table as she walked away.

Moe looked at the ticket. $7.13. Holy crap. This would be fifteen bucks at least back in L.A., or more, depending on where you ate it. He laid a twenty on the table.

SueEllen called out, "Ya'll drive safe now."

Moe didn't respond as he headed back to his car. The sun was already sending heat waves up off the pavement like mini desert mirages. He couldn't wait to get inside and turn on the air-conditioning. As soon as he had the car going and the AC jacked up to high, he entered the directional info into his GPS. The fact that it didn't register as he'd expected concerned him, but this was a blind hunt in more ways than one.

SueEllen watched until the car had disappeared, then grabbed her cell phone.

"Hey, Justin! I'm going outside to make a call. Be right back."

With no other customers in the café, the cook nodded an okay. She made a beeline for the back door and the nearest shade tree to make the call, then nervously counted the rings before she got an answer.

"Hello?"

"Granny Lou, this is SueEllen."

"Hi, sugar, how's your mama feeling since that kidney stone passed?"

"Better, thank you. I called to tell you something. A stranger stopped in here asking about Rebel Ridge and the Venable family."

Lou gasped. "Oh, no! What did he look like? What was he driving?"

"He was a skinny, middle-aged white guy driving a rental. Don't worry. I sent him on a wild-goose chase. He's gonna wind up real lost."

SueEllen could hear Lou's smile as she answered, "Way to go, sugar. I've got to let the others know. I'll talk to you later."

"Yes, ma'am."

Satisfied that she'd done her part to keep a cousin safe, SueEllen couldn't help but wonder how long it would take that man to figure out he was going in the wrong direction, and then she hoped he didn't come back all pissed and looking for her for what she'd done.

It took less than two hours for Moe's belly to start cramping and about a half hour more before he began to break out in a cold sweat. All he could taste was the grease on his tongue from that burger and fries. He knew he was going to throw up. It was only a matter of time. When the urge finally hit, he was still on the interstate. He pulled off the highway onto the shoulder of the road and jumped out just as the first wave of nausea hit. He bent over with a groan and hurled up the burger from Frankie's Eats, along with a good portion of the fries. One wave after another came and went, until there were nothing but dry heaves, before he collapsed against the car. His legs were shaking, and his belly was still cramping.

He didn't know if it was food poisoning or the fact that red meat and grease had not passed his lips in such quantity in years.

Just when he thought the worst was over, he got cramps of another kind and knew his troubles were about to get worse. He tore through the car looking for something to use for toilet paper and then bolted for the woods lining the road.

It was dark by the time he reached another town of any size. He rented a room at the first motel he came to, locked the door behind him as he entered and then collapsed on the bed in exhaustion, only to be revisited again throughout the night by a repeat of his afflictions. On his fourth trip, he staggered toward the bathroom with a vow on his lips.

"Just let me live through this and I swear to God I'll never touch red meat again."

TWELVE

The swing on the back porch had become Beth's go-to place when she wanted to think. There was something inherently calming about the back-and-forth motion. Not that the old Foster house was all that noisy, but being in Ryal's presence made thinking impossible. All she thought about when she was with him was the years that they'd missed.

She longed for a drawing pad to sketch him, even though she knew she would never be able to capture the true essence of the man. The strongest part of his allure wasn't in his physical appearance, although that was exceedingly fine. It was his soul that drew her closest.

He made love to her with all the ferocity of the storm that had broken down the last walls of their resistance. His tenderness was evident in his caress, in his gaze, in the slow, sensual strokes of the hairbrush he ran through her hair. Everything about him was perfection in her eyes, just as it had been when the love between them was new and fresh. They could never get back the ten years they'd lost, but she would happily settle for sharing the rest of his life.

What she didn't know was how Ryal felt about her. She knew he liked to make love *to* her, but she didn't know if he was still in love *with* her. And with the danger hanging over her head, now was not the time to ask.

The swing was slowly coming to a stop, so she pushed off again with the toe of her shoe, giving it new momentum. The sudden squeak of the chains holding it to the ceiling of the porch sent a squirrel in a nearby tree into a frenzy. It scampered farther up the tree before it began scolding her in a high-pitched tone that made her smile.

Again she wished for a drawing pad and some pencils. In her mind, she could already see the little creature coming to life on the page, right down to the indignant twitch of its tail. Aunt Tildy's ointment was healing her wounds nicely, but her hands were still too tender to hold a pencil, so there was no use asking for someone to bring them up on the next grocery run.

Suddenly something banged inside the house. Beth heard footsteps and then the sounds of voices. Quinn must have been up, which was strange, because he usually slept through most of the day. Worried that something had happened, she got up and went back inside.

Ryal was in the front of the house, sanding down the bottom step that he'd replaced. After this was over, he was thinking about coming back up here and giving the old place a new coat of paint. He couldn't remember the last time that had happened.

He could hear the occasional squeak of the chain holding up the porch swing out back and guessed Beth was in it. She'd taken to spending a lot of her time out there. He knew she was still dealing with a lot of guilt about her friend Sarah's murder and had purposefully left her alone. The old Beth would have come running to him with all her problems, but this Beth was a woman grown and had a mind of her own. He was surprised by how much he liked that.

Just as he was sanding off the last rough corner, his cell phone rang. He glanced at the caller ID. It was Beth's grandmother.

"Hello."

"Hey, Ryal, it's me."

He smiled. Lou and cell phones had not made an acquaintance, and he doubted they ever would. She still used the old landline and a phone that had seen better days — definitely not one with caller ID.

"What's up?"

"I called to warn you."

Ryal's heart skipped. "About what?"

"SueEllen called me. You remember she works down in Boone's Gap, at Frankie's Eats?"

"Yes, ma'am, I remember."

"So she had a customer today, a stranger, asking how to get to Rebel Ridge. She said he was a skinny, middle-aged white man driving a rental. 'Course you know the whole family is aware of what happened to Bethie, so she led him into talking until he admitted he was looking for the Venable family."

"Well damn," Ryal muttered. "Excuse my language."

"No need on my account," she said. "A similar thought went through my mind."

"What did she tell this guy?" Ryal asked.

"She sent him on some wild-goose chase that'll take him a long way from here. Eventually he'll figure out he's going the wrong way, but now we can assume those people who are looking for Bethie have figured out she might have come home."

"I was hoping this wouldn't happen," Ryal said.

"So was I, but I'm not surprised. Anyone who dug into her background would eventually learn where she grew up."

"Right. Okay, thank you for the warning, Lou, but now I'm a little uneasy about you. I don't like to think about someone knocking on your doorstep asking questions. Maybe you should go stay with one of your daughters and her family until this is over."

"Certainly not! I won't be run out of my own house. I'll be fine. You just take good care of my girl. That's all I ask."

"I'll do that for sure. We'll be in touch."

He dropped the phone in his pocket and ran into the house. A gust of wind caught the door as it swung shut behind him, slamming it shut. He winced, hoping the sudden noise hadn't awakened Quinn. Even though he wanted him up, he didn't want to scare him awake. But when Quinn came out into the hall with his rifle in his hand, Ryal realized that was exactly what he'd done.

"Sorry, brother. The wind caught the door as I was coming inside. I was going to wake you, but not like that."

Quinn's heart was still pounding from the sudden instinct for survival that had kicked in. He'd grabbed his rifle without thought.

Now he leaned it against the wall.

"What's up?"

"Lou Venable just called. SueEllen said a stranger came into Frankie's Eats asking for directions to Rebel Ridge, then said he was looking for the Venable family."

Quinn's eyes narrowed. "How much time do we have?"

"I'd say quite a bit," Ryal said. "SueEllen sent him on a wild-goose chase, but he'll eventually figure out he's going the wrong way and backtrack."

"I'm getting dressed," Quinn said. "Remember what we talked about?"

"You mean about setting traps along the way up?"

"Yes. There are traps, and then there are traps. I think it's time to set some of mine."

Ryal knew some of the stuff Quinn had learned in the military, but not nearly all of it. He had a feeling they were all in for a firsthand demonstration of what the United States Army had taught one of their own.

Beth walked into the hallway just as he turned around. She saw Quinn and Ryal standing head to head and the rifle leaning against the wall.

"What's happening?"

Quinn picked up the gun and disappeared into the bedroom to dress.

When Ryal started toward her, she wanted to run away, fearing the answer he would give.

"There was a stranger down in Boone's Gap looking for Rebel Ridge and the Venable family."

"Oh, my God! They found me." She felt the breath leave her body as everything went black.

Ryal jumped, then caught her just before she hit the floor and carried her across the hall into his bedroom. She was already coming to when he returned with a wet cloth, and when he put it on her forehead, she grabbed his wrist and pulled herself upright.

"I need to leave! I have to get out of here while there's still time!"

Fear swept through him — fear that she would run in the mistaken belief it would keep both her and them safe. He pulled her into his lap.

"No, Beth. No, baby, your running is over. We're all with you here. You're not alone anymore."

Beth felt sick. "But what happens when they find us? And they *will* find us," she said, and then started to cry.

"Then we'll be waiting," Ryal said. "No one knows Rebel Ridge better than the people who live on it. Trust us, darlin'. Trust us to keep you safe. Promise me you won't run again."

She couldn't stop shaking. "Lord, forgive me for being weak, but I promise," she said, and hid her face against his shoulder.

"Don't cry, Beth."

"I can't help it," she sobbed. "I'm so tired of being scared. I want my life back. I want all this to be over. I need to give Agent Ames another call. He needs to make something happen, and fast, or I won't be alive to testify."

The thought was horrifying. "Don't say that, woman. Don't even talk about dying. I just got you back. I'm not going to lose you, not ever again."

THIRTEEN

By the time night came to the mountain, Beth had gone through something of a transformation. The first shot of fear had passed, leaving her feeling fatalistic. She was beginning to understand that whatever was coming, she would eventually have to face.

Quinn had disappeared right after the phone call, and she was worried about the effect on his fragile state of mind if this came to actual gunfire. She was also debating with herself about whether to call Agent Ames or not. There were still some minutes left on her throwaway phone, so it wouldn't be traceable if she kept her calls short, but it was the thought of being tracked down by Ike Pappas's killers that settled the decision.

They'd already had their supper and Ryal was taking a bath when Beth got the phone and went outside on the back porch, hoping for a good signal. The sky was clear and the moon was full. Her daddy would have said it was a good night for running the dogs. As she settled down on the porch swing to make the call, she heard an owl hoot from a nearby tree, and a few moments later she heard another one call from farther away. She wondered what owls said to each other on a nightly basis, then knew if she was wondering about what owls discussed, she was definitely delaying the inevitable.

She made the call.

It rang four times before he answered.

"This is Ames."

"It's me. Beth Venable."

"How are you?"

"Still alive. Is there any news?"

"Not yet."

"No arrest? No talk of indictment?"

"No arrest, but there's talk. So far that's all it is, though."

"My time might be running out," Beth said.

"What do you mean? Where are you? Are you in danger again?"

"I'm fine so far, but I won't be forever. Make something happen soon."

"It's not my call," Ames said. "Please come back. Let us help you."

"No. I'll call again."

Beth hung up, dejected and disappointed,

then heard the hinges squeak on the screen door and looked up. Ryal was wearing a pair of jeans and nothing else.

"You heard?" she asked.

"Yes. I take it nothing has changed."

Even though it was dark, he saw her shoulders slump.

"Don't be discouraged. It hasn't been long."

She nodded but wouldn't look up for fear she'd start crying. She didn't want to cry. She didn't want pity. She wanted to be happy. She made herself focus on something else.

"Have you talked to Quinn?"

"Yeah. He's okay."

"Is he coming back tonight?"

"No."

"Is there something else I should know?"

"Does the fact that I want to make love to you count?"

She heard passion as well as uncertainty in his voice, and knew the latter was something only time could erase. She smiled.

"I already knew that, and yes, it counts."

Ryal pulled her up from the swing and into his arms. "They're playing our song," he said, and began slow-dancing her up and down the length of the old porch.

The only things Beth could hear were

bullfrogs and crickets. The absurdity of it made her smile, but the tenderness with which he was holding her stole her heart. For the first time in years she was happy, and she kept wondering why it had taken a tragedy for her to come back to the place where she was born.

She leaned back against Ryal's arm and looked up to meet his gaze.

"It's a little dark out here."

"It's never dark when I'm with you. You are my sunshine, Bethie. I will be forever disappointed in myself that I let other people control what happened in our lives."

"I was just as complicit," she said.

Ryal stopped moving, wrapped his arms around her and pulled her hard against him. His breath was warm against her face, his lips demanding. When they finally paused to take a breath, he swung her up off her feet and into his arms.

Beth gasped, then laughed. "Where are we going?"

"The music is over. It's time for bed."

Beth laid her head against his shoulder as he carried her back into the house and into their bedroom, then put her down.

"I'll lock up," he said.

Beth put her hand in the middle of his chest, where his heartbeat was the loudest,

245

and felt the rock-steady thud beneath her palm.

"I won't be long in the bathroom," she said.

"It doesn't matter how long it takes, I'll be waiting when you come out."

As she headed for the bathroom, she could hear the sound of Ryal's footsteps moving through the house, checking windows and doors.

She took a quick bath, then slipped across the hall in the dark. The door to Ryal's room was ajar. She walked inside, closing it quietly behind her.

His jeans were hanging over the back of a chair, and he was standing at the window looking out at the surrounding forest, completely nude. When he heard the creak of the old door as it swung inward, he turned around.

She saw his erection, and then he came toward her as she crawled up on the bed and rocked back on her knees.

Ryal paused to look his fill. Her skin glowed like alabaster in the ambient moonlight. For him, she was woman personified, from her slender body and long legs to the lushness of her breasts. He heard a catch in her breathing and knew she was anticipating this as much as he was.

"What do you want, Lilabeth?"

"To know if this means as much to you as it does to me."

"If you're looking for forever, you've come to the right place. Does that answer your question?"

"Yes. Make love to me, Ryal."

His answer was a sigh as he climbed into bed beside her and pulled her down into his arms.

Once he'd been the beginning and end of her world. She wanted that back and more.

Ryal slid a hand beneath her hair and pulled her close. Her mouth opened beneath the pressure of his lips as she wrapped her arms around his neck. Her skin was like silk to the touch as he cupped her breast, rolling her nipple between his thumb and forefinger until she moaned from the pleasure.

He tore his mouth from her lips, then moved to the hollow at the base of her throat, pressing kisses all the way down the front of her body until he reached the juncture of her thighs.

At that point he parted the velvety folds and leaned closer.

The rush of blood that shot through Beth was like being struck by lightning. Breath caught in the back of her throat as her body reacted. She had a moment's impression that she was about to take flight and grabbed onto Ryal's shoulders for an anchor. Rational thought was gone. All she wanted was for that mind-bending heat building in her belly to never end. And for a while, she got her wish. One minute rolled into another and then another, while sweat beaded on their skin and the old bed thumped against the wall in rhythm to their lovemaking. She rode the pulse-pounding throb as if it was a rocket to heaven, until it blew up, taking her with it.

The moan that came up her throat was what Ryal had been waiting for. He parted her legs and slid inside her before the orgasm was over, then began to ride it with her. The tiny quivers pulsing around him were like aphrodisiacs. He'd been hard and hurting too long to bother maintaining control. He thrust hard and fast while she met and matched him. Within moments a second orgasm exploded inside her.

Ryal buried his face in the curve of her neck and let go, spilling his seed in one spasm after another, until he was spent and shaking. He rolled over onto his back, taking her with him until she was sprawled on top of his body. He kept thinking, *How have I lived all these years without her?*

Beth was stunned by the flood of emotions. There was too much on the line to wait for the perfect moment. She'd learned the hard way that some people never have a tomorrow. She rose up and looked down into his face.

"I love you, Ryal. I'm saying it because I want you to know, in case this doesn't turn out the way we want it to."

Ryal chuckled as his arms tightened around her. "Ah, God, Bethie . . . you would say all this when I'm so damn weak I can barely breathe. I love you, too. More than I thought possible. I touch you, and it feels like the years we lost never happened. And just for the record, nothing is going to happen to you. Your daddy's people are looking out for you. Your mother's people are looking out for you. That's close to half the population of Rebel Ridge. No stranger will set foot here without one of us knowing it first. Understood?"

"Understood," Beth said, and kissed him.

Ryal groaned beneath his breath as the need for her rose within him again, but this time they took it slow and easy all the way.

The Pappas lodge near the San Gabriel Mountains wasn't really a lodge as lodges go. There were no hunting trophies hanging on the walls, no pelts decorating the floor as rugs. Just the fireplace and the massive mantel. The rest of the two-story structure was a little too elegant to qualify. The walls in the kitchen were a soft butter-yellow. The rest of the walls through the house were the color of old ivory. The furniture was soft leather in varying shades of brown with gold accents. The same colors were picked up throughout the house by throw pillows, curtains and shades. It was beautiful, but a little too classy for Adam's taste. He remembered when his mother had been with them; back then, the place had been a fun, lively place to be. Now it felt hollow — almost sterile.

His arm was throbbing where he'd stabbed himself with the knife, but he refused to take the pain pills the doctor had provided. Guilt over what he'd caused was eating him alive. He'd known his mother wanted him to go straight, yet he'd ignored the one thing he could have given her — and it had cost her life. After all he'd learned, he was certain his father had murdered her to keep her from making good on her threat.

There was a part of him that felt like a child. His mommy was dead, and his daddy was a bad man. But he couldn't go there, because he'd known most of his life what his father was capable of. He'd just never thought he would ever be on the receiving end of that grief.

He glanced at the clock, and then palmed a couple of the antibiotic pills and chased them with a big drink of cola. He eyed the pain pills, but again wouldn't allow himself the relief. He needed to be sharp, not drugged out of his mind. He had no idea what time his father would return from New York City, but he knew when he did, the shit would hit the fan.

Beatrice would tell his father he'd been there. Ike would be shocked, then incensed, and even more importantly, he would recognize the anger behind what his son had done. Adam hadn't decided if he would answer the call when it came. He might make his father sweat. The bastard deserved to be worried.

Adam continued to pace, trying to block the pain throbbing in his arm all the way up the side of his neck. What he'd done had been impulsive and born of fury, but what came next? The urge to shoot his father and watch him die was strong. But that was almost too easy. He wanted him to pay big-time. He wanted him broken, humiliated and spending the rest of his life in prison.

And the minute he thought it, he knew what he was going to do. It was so simple, he was a little disgusted with himself for not thinking of it earlier.

All he had to do was finish what his mother had started.

It was after four in the morning by the time Ike got home. He was pissed at having been called down like a neophyte by a no-neck killer with a complete lack of finesse. All he wanted to do was take a shower and crawl into bed. The thought of lying naked on cool satin sheets was a drug, and he needed a fix. If it hadn't been so late, he would have called his favorite escort service. However, he could always jack off in the shower and call it a day, which was the plan on his mind as he started up the stairs.

The upper part of the house seemed empty, which was strange. Out of curiosity, he bypassed his door and walked farther down the hall to Adam's room and looked in, then frowned. The bed was still made, although there was an indentation in the coverlet, as if something large and heavy had been laid on it. Like a suitcase.

That was when he noticed a couple of dresser drawers were open and the closet door was ajar. Ike frowned. Adam hadn't said anything about any upcoming trips — although, to be fair, he hadn't always announced his whereabouts lately, either.

Adam was an adult, so Ike shrugged off the urge to be irked and went back toward his own room. He was surprised that the lights were on as he walked in. He moved past the small foyer into the suite, unbuttoning his shirt and loosening his belt as he went.

Then his gaze fell on the bed and the carpet, and he froze. What the hell? Blood was everywhere — on the bed, on the floor, all the way across the room into his bathroom.

It took only a moment for shock to turn to rage. The explanation for his son's absence was suddenly very plain.

"Son of a holy bitch!"

His angry roar echoed through the upper level of the mansion, but there was no one awake to hear. That didn't last long. Within minutes, Ike had roused every staff member on the premises and dragged them upstairs.

There was no way Beatrice could have faked the shock and fear on her face as she faced Ike's wrath.

"I don't understand! I swear to God, Mr. Pappas, I don't know how this happened!" She dropped to her knees and began wringing her hands as she rocked back and forth. "Please don't hurt me! Please don't hurt me!"

Ike swore. "What kind of a man do you think I am? Just get off your knees and answer my questions, woman!"

She scrambled to her feet, tripping over the hem of her robe as she did. "Yes, sir. Anything, sir."

"Who was in this house tonight besides the staff?"

"Just Mr. Adam."

Ike's gut knotted at knowing his guess had been right. He had a sick feeling things were coming undone.

"Did anything happen while he was here? Anything that seemed to upset him?"

Beatrice was still wringing her hands. It was obvious to Ike that she didn't want to tell him.

"Damn it! Don't make me repeat the question!"

Beatrice shuddered. "I believe he was already upset when he arrived."

Ike turned on the guard who worked days at the gate. "Did you see him?"

"Yes, sir. He seemed agitated when he drove in."

"Agitated how?"

"He was driving really fast. When he

reached the house, he was driving so fast that one of the gardeners said he thought he would hit the steps."

Ike took a deep breath and then turned back to Beatrice. "Did you talk to him?"

"Yes, sir. He asked where you were. I said I'd packed a suitcase for you earlier and that you said you were flying to New York, but I didn't know when you would return."

A muscle jerked in Ike's jaw as his voice grew quieter. "Then what?"

"I asked him if he would be wanting dinner. And then he said no, and that he wouldn't be living here anymore." She covered her face and began to weep.

The knot in Ike's gut got tighter. "Did he say where he was going?"

"No, sir. I don't know how long he was upstairs. I didn't hear him leave."

"In the morning, get this mess cleaned up. Call in professional cleaners for the rug, and throw away the bedding. It's ruined."

Beatrice nodded.

"Go back to bed. All of you. And say nothing about this to anyone! Do you understand?"

"Yes, sir!" they echoed, and made a quick exit.

Ike thought about calling Adam's number, then changed his mind. He needed to plan what he was going to say, not attack in rage. He didn't know what had precipitated this act. No need jumping the gun unnecessarily. Maybe there was still a way to salvage their relationship, although when he stared at the mess in his room, he seriously doubted it.

He turned around and left the wreckage behind as he moved down the hall to one of the guest rooms. As soon as he got inside, he began to strip. His shower was brief. No hand-job. No standing under the hot-water jets to relax. He crawled into bed and then turned out the lights, but he couldn't sleep. No matter how hard he tried, all he could see was that bloody bed and the rage behind the act.

Moe woke up the next morning with a foul taste in his mouth and the lingering remains of yesterday's sickness. His gut rumbled as he went to the bathroom, but other than a little gas, he felt as if he'd survived the worst.

After a shower and a change of clothes, he tried to get online to check messages but soon realized the motel he'd chosen didn't have an internet hookup or Wi-Fi. Muttering to himself about the lack of civilized conveniences in this godforsaken part of the country, he loaded his stuff in the car and went in search of some coffee. But no food. The way he felt right now, he might never eat again.

When he got in the car, he reset the GPS to the same coordinates he'd gotten yesterday and began the final leg of the journey in hopes of reaching Rebel Ridge today. The sooner he got Ike Pappas off his back, the better he would feel. He stopped at a local gas station to fuel up and get some coffee to go. When he went inside he headed straight for the coffee, filled a large cup and went up to the register to pay.

The clerk was a fiftysomething, heavyset woman with copper-red hair and a tattoo of Elvis on her arm that was sagging from the combined weight of fat and time.

Moe set the coffee on the counter and pulled out his wallet. "I got gas on pump two."

"That'll be $47.30," she said without looking up.

Moe eyed his cash, noted it was running low and handed her his credit card. While she was running the card through, he took a quick sip of the coffee and winced. Not Starbucks quality, for sure, but it was black and hot, and he needed the kick of caffeine. He eyed the tattoo curiously and caught her staring. A little taken aback that he'd been caught, he blurted out the question on his mind.

"I don't suppose you've ever heard of a place around here called Rebel Ridge?"

"That's not a town. That's a mountain," she drawled.

Moe's pulse kicked. "Is it somewhere close by?"

She shook her head. "Naw . . . it's a far piece south of here."

Moe frowned. "South? But I just came from there and was told —"

He sighed. Shit. It was his own damn fault for thinking that just because the people looked like hillbillies it meant they were stupid. If he'd been close to his target location and Beth Venable was actually there somewhere, then it stood to reason some of her people would be hiding her. And he'd given out her name. He groaned. Now she'd been warned. Pappas would be furious if he screwed this up.

"By any chance is Rebel Ridge close to a town called Boone's Gap?" Moe asked.

She nodded. "Yeah. You know where that is?"

"Yes, I know where that is," Moe said, then pocketed his credit card, grabbed his coffee and got back in the car.

He reset his GPS again, and this time there would be no mistakes.

FOURTEEN

Beth woke up in Ryal's arms and then caught him watching her sleep.

"How long have you been awake?" she asked, as she slowly stretched.

Ryal kissed a spot near her earlobe, then nipped it lightly just to hear her groan.

"Long enough to know you don't snore."

Beth grinned. "So what if I did? Would you kick me out of bed?"

A slow, lazy smile spread across his face. "No, but it *would* mean that I'd have to keep waking you up in the night, which wouldn't be all that bad. I like waking you up in the night. I like what we do when we wake up."

Beth laughed out loud.

Before either of them could respond, they heard a door slam in another part of the house.

Ryal frowned. "Quinn must be back."

Beth threw back the covers. "I'm going to the bathroom before he wants it."

"I'll get dressed and start breakfast," Ryal said, and then grabbed one of her hands and turned it palm up to check out her healing wounds. "They're looking good. Don't forget to doctor them again this morning."

"After we eat," Beth said, then grabbed a nightgown and pulled it over her head before darting out of the room and into the bathroom across the hall.

Ryal watched her go, admiring her long legs and curves, then reluctantly got up and got dressed. When he walked into the kitchen, Quinn was making coffee. Ryal eyed the scratches on Quinn's arms and the two-day growth of whiskers, but he didn't ask for an explanation.

"Hey, brother. I'll bet you're ready for a bath and a bed. I'll make breakfast while you finish the coffee."

Quinn poured the water into the pot, scooped coffee into the filter and turned the switch to "on" before he turned around.

"We have two lookout posts in place and four traps. Uncle John's boys are as good as any sharpshooters with their hunting rifles. They'll be in the roosts if the time comes. Uncle Fagan's boys are the best in the county with bows and arrows. You know they always bring down the first deer in bow season. I personally set two of the traps in the woods, in case the bad guys abandon the road for the trees. One's a staked pit. One's not. I won't go into details. Suffice it to say you do not want to be caught in either of them. James is standing watch for me this morning. I'm going to catch five hours sleep, and then I'll send him home. I can have ten men here in less than fifteen minutes, should the need arise. I think we're covered."

It was the emotionless tone of Quinn's voice that bothered Ryal most.

"Quinn, I —"

Quinn held up his hand. "Don't say it, damn it. I'm not going to turn into some raving lunatic and start killing people or shoot myself, okay? I'm no worse than I was before this started, and that's the truth. If anything, this has given me something to focus on besides myself."

"Do you want your eggs scrambled or fried?" Ryal asked.

It took a few moments, but Quinn finally smiled. "Since my brains are already scrambled, I believe I'll have three fried, over easy, and some toast and bacon."

Ryal grinned.

Quinn eyed his older brother as Ryal began pulling food out of the old refrigerator.

"So, how's our cousin?"

Ryal flashed him a disgusted look. "Our very distant cousin is healing nicely, thanks to Aunt Tildy's ointment. As for her state of mind, it's a little bit like yours. Somewhat rattled at the moment, but it will pass."

The coffee machine was burping and gurgling as the coffee streamed into the carafe below. The aroma of fresh brewing coffee permeated the kitchen, along with the scent of the bacon Ryal had begun to fry.

When they heard footsteps coming down the hall, Ryal turned toward the doorway so fast he accidentally slung grease onto the back of the stove.

Quinn chuckled beneath his breath.

Ryal heard the sound and looked over his shoulder. "What's so funny?"

"You. You got it bad, brother. I hope this time you take measures to make it stick."

"Already done," Ryal said beneath his breath.

Quinn nodded. "At least one good thing has come out of this mess."

Beth entered on cue, took one look at Quinn and his scratches, the dirt on his clothes and the gaunt look on his face, then caught Ryal's expression, got rattled by the silent warning and stuttered, "Um . . . uh . . ."

"Most of it will wash off," Quinn drawled. "And like you, the rest will heal. I'm gonna wash up so I'm at least fit to sit at the table with you two. Don't eat all the bacon while I'm gone."

He gave Beth a wink as he passed by and headed down the hall to bathroom.

As soon as he was gone, Beth grabbed Ryal's arm. "Is he okay? He looks . . . he looks like . . ."

"He looks like he did the day he came home from Iraq," Ryal said. "He's back on the hunt, and there's nothing that's going to change that until you're out of danger."

"I'm sorry," she whispered, afraid she might be overheard.

"No need. It is what it is, Beth. Let him be. He'll know better than any of us if he's had enough, and I know my brother. He'll handle whatever he has to handle and deal with the consequences later."

Her chin trembled as she moved past Ryal to begin putting slices of bread in the toaster. The guilt of getting Sarah murdered was now coupled with the guilt of what this was doing to Quinn and his PTSD. Her heart was heavy. Could this nightmare ever come to a good end?

They finished cooking the food and were putting loaded plates on the table when Quinn returned. He'd bathed and washed his hair, but he hadn't bothered shaving. The two-day growth of black whiskers gave him a mercenary look that almost made Beth shiver, and when he looked up and caught her staring, she jumped.

"Boo," he said, then winked. "Pass the jelly."

"You don't scare me," she muttered, as she shoved the jelly across the table.

Ryal frowned. "Leave her alone, Quinn."

Beth pointed at him with a piece of toast. "Don't baby me, Ryal, and Quinn's not the enemy. He doesn't scare me." She pushed the last piece of bacon across the table toward him as a peace offering. "However, I am grateful he's on our side."

Both men burst into laughter that turned her cheeks pink and then made her smile.

Moe reached Boone's Gap a couple of hours after noon, but this time when he stopped to get gas, he had a whole new set of plans. For the past thirty miles he'd seen little to convince him that more than a few of the people in the area lived above the poverty level, which told him he'd gone about everything all wrong before.

This time he had a pocketful of cash from a recent withdrawal at an ATM back in Mount Sterling. All he needed was a break and he would be back on the right track. In the meantime, he gassed up, and bought himself a cold drink and a package of saltines. He was still afraid to put anything solid into his belly and nibbled on the salty crackers as he booted up his laptop inside the car.

He'd done a thorough background check on Beth Venable's father, Sam, but having found the link to Rebel Ridge, he hadn't bothered with her mother until now. He knew from the obituary that her name was Annie, but now he wanted to know what her maiden name had been, and where she'd been born.

His fingers flew across the keyboard, though every now and then he paused to eat another cracker or take a drink of the cold soda. Within a few minutes he found a record of her wedding license. Annie Walker. Sam Venable. When everything fell into place, he did love this job. Now to find out where this Annie Walker had been born and where she'd grown up.

This time he had the answer in minutes. Like Sam, her birthplace was listed as Rebel Ridge. Both had earned diplomas from the same high school. And, after a quick search through the last five census records, he knew they'd grown up in — or *on* — Rebel Ridge, been educated there, lived there as man and wife, and had a child who was close to legal age before they moved away.

That meant Beth Venable's roots here were deep. It was possible, even likely, that either or both sets of relatives could be working to hide her. The question was, how to find out.

He turned off the laptop to keep from draining the battery, then leaned back to watch who came and went. He was hoping for a junkie or a drunk, but in this place, the pickings were slim, due to the small population. Moe was optimistic, but careful. He'd been parked here long enough. He needed to move, but where to?

Boone's Gap's four blocks were nothing to brag about. After that, you were past the city limits. He started the engine and then drove away from the gas station, scanning the small collection of stores. It wasn't until he drove past the post office, next door to city hall, that he realized he'd overlooked the most obvious solution. It was near the end of the month, and people who received monthly checks — whether from retirement funds, the social-security system or county welfare — would most likely be low on funds. Utility bills, traffic fines and bail bonds were usually paid to different offices, but since Boone's Gap was so small, he was betting they were all paid in one location here.

He parked in front of the post office, went inside and bought himself some prepaid postcards, then went back out to the car and pretended to write, all the while keeping an eye out for possibilities.

Cars came and went intermittently. If anyone happened to look his way, he would write more diligently. Nearly thirty minutes came and went, and he was getting antsy. He couldn't sit there much longer without raising suspicion in a town so small.

Just as he was about to give up this idea as only one in a series of dumb ones he'd recently had, an old truck pulled up to the curb near where he was parked. He glanced at the driver, a pale, skinny man wearing jeans and a Coors Lite T-shirt. Moe could tell by the way the man was walking that he was pissed about something. He watched the man enter city hall and waited curiously for him to emerge. When he came out, he was no longer alone.

Moe blinked. Either he was seeing double, or the skinny man had a twin. Although they were wearing different clothing, they definitely had the same face, and it was obvious they were having a deep dispute about something. The Coors Lite man seemed to be cursing at the other one all the way to the truck.

Moe casually rolled down the window just enough to be able to hear and realized one had just bailed the other out of jail.

"I hope you're fuckin' happy! Now we're both broke!" Coors Lite yelled.

The twin's face was as red as his brother's, but he obviously knew enough to keep quiet. They got in the old truck and drove away.

Moe started the car and followed a short distance behind. When they pulled off the highway into the parking lot of what appeared to be a local bar, Moe decided they couldn't be completely broke. Obviously they had enough left to drown their troubles.

They pulled up to the side of the building and were still inside the truck arguing when Moe parked next to them. He made a big production of getting out and unfolding a map of Kentucky onto the hood of his car, and then pretending to pore over it, as if he was lost.

He heard both of the old truck's doors

open and close, but he didn't look up. A gust of wind lifted the corner of the map. He let it catch just enough that the map almost took flight right in front of Coors Lite, who grabbed it out of midair.

"Son of a gun," Moe said. "Good catch."

Coors Lite eyed him curiously. "You ain't from around here," he said.

Twin sidled up on the other side of Moe. All of a sudden it occurred to Moe that he could also be viewed as a prime target to rob. It was time to be proactive, not wait and see what happened next.

"No, I'm not, but I'm damned tired of looking for places that aren't on this map."

"Whatcha' lookin' for?" Twin asked.

"Rebel Ridge." Moe sensed the men looking at each other, but he kept his gaze on the map. "I'm on a deadline. No time to waste. I've got a hundred dollars for anyone who can tell me how to get there, and another hundred for directions to find any family related to Sam Venable."

"Sam's dead," Coors Lite said.

"I know that," Moe said.

He folded up the map and took a step back until he was looking at both men face-to-face. Their indecision was obvious. Their greed, coupled with their need for cash, was overriding whatever inhibitions they might have had about informing on one of their own to a stranger. He knew the moment they looked around to see who was watching that he had them.

Coors Lite swiped his nose with the back of his hand, then casually wiped his hand on the leg of his jeans. "Make it three hundred and I'll lead you straight up the mountain they call Rebel Ridge. I ain't gonna introduce you to none of the Venables, but I'll give you a wave as we pass where one of them lives."

"Who?" Moe asked.

"James Walker. But his wife's a Venable. That's the best I'll do."

Walker. The other family name! Moe felt as if he'd hit the jackpot. "That'll do. You show me the place, and I'll take it from there." He pulled out four one-hundred-dollar bills and handed them over. "Gave you a little something extra to keep this between us," he added.

Coors Lite grabbed the money, then headed for his truck, with Twin right behind them. Their need to drown their troubles had just been overridden by the sudden windfall. It was time to make tracks before someone saw them talking to the stranger and put two and two together later, when they started flashing money. Even though they didn't know why the man was looking for Venables, if it turned out bad, they didn't want to be named as the ones who'd ratted the family out.

Moe got back in the car and followed the twins nearly five miles out of town before the men took a sudden turn off the highway and up a tree-lined blacktop that was barely wide enough for two cars to meet and pass.

He kept an eye on the miles, hoping they weren't driving him into some out-of-the-way place so they could jump him for the money he had left. But to his relief, just after they'd passed the sixth mile, Coors Lite stuck his arm out the window and waved and pointed, then sped off in a cloud of dust.

It was only after Moe braked that he noticed another road leading off into the woods, even narrower than the one he was on. He could just see the peak of a rooftop through the trees. He drove a little farther on until he found a spot to turn around, then headed back down the mountain. Earlier he'd noticed a cut in the under-growth that might be wide enough to hide a car in and had marked the mileage in his mind. All he had to do was come back after dark, get to the Walker house on foot, plant tracking devices in the family cars and see where they went. It wasn't much, but short of taking someone hostage and beating the information out of them, which wasn't his style, there wasn't anything more he could do.

James had finished his mail route before noon and had been working his tobacco patch all afternoon. He was bone-tired and dirty as he headed toward the house. He still had the cow to milk and the hogs to feed, and he'd promised Julie he would put the kids to bed so she could go to a baby shower at their church, which was only a couple of miles up the road from the house.

Less than a mile from home, his cell phone rang. When he saw it was Ryal, he pulled over onto the side of the road to answer.

"Hey, Ryal, how's it going?"

"We're okay. I was wondering if you had time to make a grocery run for us tomorrow. If you're busy, I can leave Beth here with Quinn and do it myself."

"No. I can do that," James said, scrambling for a pen and some paper. "Tell me what you need."

Ryal went down the list, then paused. "Are you going to shop in Boone's Gap or Mount Sterling? You can't always find everything in

Boone's Gap."

"Probably Mount Sterling. Julie needs some stuff for the baby that we can't get here."

"Do you have enough money left from what I gave you? If you don't, just say so and I'll cull the list."

"No, we're good. I'll bring it up tomorrow afternoon. Okay?"

"Yes, it's definitely okay, and thank you."

"Come on, Ryal. We've been through this already. No thanks necessary. Family is family." Then he heard Ryal clear his throat. "What? What's happening that I don't know?"

"About that family thing, Beth and I are —"

James chuckled. "Well hell, brother. I already saw that coming. Besides, I married a Venable, too, you know. Even if she's from Mount Sterling, she's still kin to the rest of them. So tell me something I don't know."

"Quinn. All this preparation for a possible attack has put him right back into soldier mode. He isn't sleeping on a regular basis. Some mornings I don't see him at all. He's pushing himself past the limit of his endurance and argues when I suggest he cut himself some slack."

James's smile died. He loved and worried

about Quinn as much as the rest of the family, but because he was the closest in age to Quinn, he knew him better than most.

"There's one thing we've always had to accept about Quinn that I think you're forgetting. He doesn't share his feelings. He doesn't show weakness. He doesn't quit. It's part of why he was a good soldier. It's also part of why he's struggling with the trauma of what he's seen. He'll be all right in the long run, because he's a strong man, and because he's not alone. We won't let him be."

Part of Ryal's worry lifted. "You're right. I guess I'm feeling guilty because I'm the one who told Lou Venable we'd help, and I did that without thinking about Quinn first."

"Shoot, Ryal. This is Beth, your Beth, we're talking about. You were thinking with your heart, and that's how a good man walks through life."

Another weight lifted off Ryal's shoulders. "Thank you, James. Sometimes I forget that you *are* more than the family clown."

James grinned. "Anything else you need? Otherwise I'll see you tomorrow."

"No, that will do. See you soon."

They hung up.

James put the car in gear and went home,

while Ryal dropped his phone back in his pocket and headed into the house.

By the time it was dark, Moe was back up the mountain, his car concealed in the place he'd found earlier in the day, and on foot heading upward toward James Walker's home. He was wearing a backpack and carrying a flashlight, although he was careful not to use it too often for fear someone would see the light in the darkness.

He was carrying a sack with five pounds of uncooked ground beef and a large branch he would use as a club, just in case he ran into one of the four-footed denizens who dwelled up here. He'd used Google to find the number of animals he could possibly encounter in this part of the state and was not all that thrilled with the options. He couldn't decide which would be worse: cougars, wild hogs or skunks.

He'd heard dogs soon after he'd gotten out of the car and hoped he had enough meat to shift their attention from him to the food. He paused to listen and heard the sound of a car engine coming nearer. Someone was driving by out on the road. Even though he was several yards away in the deep woods, he stopped and crouched down, not wanting to get caught in the headlights. He waited until the car passed before he stood. Just as he started to take a step, he heard rustling in the leaves beneath his feet, flashed the light down and then stifled a scream as a snake slithered past.

"Son of a bitch," he gasped, and then hastened his steps. The sooner he got this job done, the sooner he could get down off this godforsaken mountain.

A short time later he saw a light through the trees and knew he was near the house. He stopped to listen but heard nothing to tell him one way or another if the family owned dogs, but he was guessing they did. Kids and dogs seemed to be everywhere here.

He kept moving until he found himself standing in the tree line of the clearing surrounding the house. He could see lights on in the back of the house and only one vehicle — a dark, older-model truck parked near the porch. By accident he was upwind, but he didn't see any dogs, though he knew that didn't mean a thing. Readying the meat just in case, he slipped through the darkness.

As he got closer to the house, he could see movement back and forth behind the curtained windows in the rear, although the front of the property was dark and quiet.

When he was within a few yards of the truck, he ran, then ducked down behind it and slipped off the backpack.

He'd packed what he needed in an exterior pocket for easy access and quickly pulled it out. In less than a minute he'd put a tracking device up underneath the back fender, and then a second one right beside it, just in case one became dislodged due to the rough roads.

Just as he was finishing up, he heard a dog begin baying from inside the house, so he grabbed up his backpack and ran for the trees. As soon as he hit the tree line, he dumped the meat and kept running. If they let the dog out, he was hoping it would follow his scent to the meat and then stop. That would give him enough time to get back to his car and get away.

When Julie was gone, James always let Big Red, the family dog, into the house to keep one of the kids occupied while he bathed the other, but also because they adored the old hound and were happiest if he was at their feet as they played.

He was helping his daughter out of the bathtub and drying her off when Big Red suddenly bounded up from the threshold where he'd been lying and let out a sharp bark. James frowned. He'd just put the baby down and hoped the noise wouldn't get him to crying.

"Daddy, why is Big Red a'barkin'?"

"I don't know, sugar. Probably some varmint prowling around outside. Hang on a minute while I let him out."

He set her down on her feet and followed the dog through the house to the front door.

"What's out there, Red? What do you hear?" he asked, as he reached for the knob.

The dog woofed softly, and when James opened the door, Red bounded outside as if he'd been catapulted.

James looked out into the darkness but didn't see anything obvious. He shut the door and hurried back to the bathroom, where he'd left his daughter. Without giving the incident another thought, he put her to bed and then sat down on the side of the mattress and began reading her favorite story. This time he paid close attention to Beth's illustrations, marveling that someone he knew was responsible for the charm of the hitchhiker ladybug and all her adventures.

The dog had immediately picked up Moe's scent and shot off across the clearing, barking as he went.

Moe was running full tilt through the trees with the flashlight shining to keep from running into any branches. He knew the moment the dog had been let out of the house and how close he was getting because of how the sound carried.

All of a sudden there was silence. Moe grinned. He would bet a fiver the dog had found the meat, but that wasn't cause to slow down. The sooner he left the area, the better.

Before the barking resumed, Moe was safely inside his car and driving away.

FIFTEEN

Ike woke, momentarily confused as to where he was. Then he recognized a painting on the wall and remembered he was in a guest bedroom in the south wing. Then he remembered why, which made him angry all over again. His worst fear was about to come true, and he didn't know what he was going to do about it. Either Adam suspected Ike had killed Lorena, or he already knew it was true. But before Ike could make any decisions, he needed to know what was in his son's heart. Was this going to cause an irrevocable breach in their relationship, or was there a way to get past it?

He rolled over in the bed and glanced out the window. It was already morning — time to see where he stood. He picked up the phone, took a deep breath and made the call.

The sun was just over the mountain peak

and streaming into the bedroom window near the bed where Adam was sleeping when his cell phone began to ring. He woke abruptly to check caller ID. Just as he suspected — his father was finally checking in.

It rang five more times before it went to voice mail. He laid it aside and got up to use the bathroom. Afterward, as he was washing up, he glanced up in the mirror and paused, eyeing his features with a judgmental eye.

The Greek heritage he shared with his father was evident in his black wavy hair and even features, but he had his mother's mouth. His gaze slid to his eyes. They were a soft brown like hers, too, not the dark, almost black, color of his father's.

Before, he'd been a proud man, even vain. But now it was disconcerting to look at himself. All he saw was a son whose greed and need for power had crossed a line and broken his mother's heart. Even though his father had been holding the knife, Adam knew it was his decision to "go to the dark side" that had caused her death. In the true sense of the word, he was just as guilty as Ike for her murder.

But this was his turning point. Either he redeemed his soul, or he ignored what he knew and continued in the footsteps of the devil who was his sire. In the bright light of day, the decision he'd made last night was still the most viable choice.

As he was drying off, his cell phone rang again. Ignoring it, he began to shave. If he was going to do this, he was going in shining like the diamond in his father's pinkie ring.

Adam was back in Los Angeles before 10:00 a.m. He'd already had a phone conversation with an agent in the Federal Bureau of Investigation and made an appointment with the special agent in charge of Lorena Pappas's murder to discuss the progress of the investigation.

He had to admit that, when he'd entered the building and gone through the body scanners, he'd felt as if he'd just walked into enemy territory. Both Adam and the Feds had an agenda, but he was the only one who knew the extent of where it was going to lead.

Within moments of passing through the scanner he was approached by a woman who identified herself as Special Agent Curran. She proceeded to escort him to his destination.

He eyed her curiously, wondering what

would lead an attractive woman like Curran to want to go into law enforcement, when she could use her looks and her smarts to get so much more for much less. Then he remembered that that was how his mother and father had met, and Lorena's walk on the wild side had not turned out for the best.

When they got on the elevator, Adam put his hands in his pockets in what he hoped was a sexy, casual stance and flashed his best smile.

"So, Special Agent Curran, how did you get into this business?"

She eyed him coolly as the elevator rose. "Just like you got into *your* business. I followed in my father's footsteps."

Adam's smile slipped. "Touché."

The elevator stopped. "I wasn't trying to make points. Follow me, please," she said, and got out.

Adam followed at her heels.

She stopped four doors down and went inside the small office where a rather large man was sitting at a desk, diligently working on a computer.

"Agent Ames, this is Adam Pappas."

Ames stood up as Curran left and pointed to a chair on the other side of his desk.

"Have a seat," he said.

Adam sat. His heart was pounding, and

there was a slight sick feeling in the pit of his belly. He wondered if this was how his mother had felt when she'd come to offer testimony that would send her son to prison.

I'll make this right, Mother. I swear on your sweet soul, I will make him pay.

Ames eyed the younger Pappas curiously. "So, I understand you're here to discuss the progress on your mother's case. You know I can't reveal any —"

Adam held up a hand. "On the contrary, that's not actually why I'm here," he said.

Ames frowned. "Then . . . ?"

"I'm here to offer you a deal."

Ames frowned. "What kind of deal?"

"I know you believe my father killed my mother."

Ames said nothing.

"For the record, I do, too, although I can't prove it."

Ames suddenly leaned forward, his mind racing with possibilities as to where this was going.

"So what are you saying here?" Ames asked.

"You arrest and convict my father of my mother's murder, and I will finish what she started. I will testify against Ike Pappas and the organization to which he belongs. I'll tell you everything I know and help you get

285

proof of all of it. I don't know how many others you can take down with what I know, but my father won't be the only one."

Ames stood abruptly. "Sit tight and let me get someone in here to take your statement."

Adam held up his hand. "No, no, you aren't hearing me. I tell you nothing until my father is convicted of murdering my mother."

Ames frowned. "But if you testify against him, he'll still spend the rest of his days behind bars."

"That's not good enough," Adam said. "My mother deserves her justice separate from what else he's done. I want it known what he did to her, and I want him sentenced for the crime. Once that's a done deal, then I talk. If you can't do that, there is no deal. I say nothing to you and take care of him myself."

Ames flinched. "You do know you're admitting to intent to commit murder."

Adam looked around. "I'm sorry. Are we taping this conversation? Is something happening here that I don't know about?"

"No, of course not," Ames said.

Adam's eyes narrowed angrily, and for the first time Ames saw the resemblance between father and son.

Adam pointed at Ames in an accusing manner. "I can assure you that I will vehemently deny any accusation that I want my father dead. Everyone knows he has enemies. Now, where are you on Mother's murder case?"

Ames's frown deepened. "You know I'm not allowed to tell you that."

"Then let me tell you what *I* know," Adam said. "I know there is a witness named Beth Venable — and my father knows it, too. I know you lost her and that he's sent one of his bloodhounds on her trail. You better find her before he does, or your case against him won't stick. If that happens, my deal is off the table."

Ames's head was reeling. No wonder they couldn't take these people down. The Mob had more intel than the Feds did.

"Who's the bloodhound?" Ames asked.

Adam shook his head. "I tell you, and you blow it by picking him up, alerting my father that you're onto him, and then he disappears. I didn't come in here to do your damned job for you. So what do you say? Do we have a deal or not?"

Ames sighed. He didn't have the power to do what he was about to do, but Adam Pappas was too antsy to wait around for the real word.

"Yes, we have a deal," Ames said.

Adam nodded. "As soon as you get Ike Pappas in court, we talk again."

"We could get him there sooner if you'd tell us what you know about the missing witness."

"I know she's smarter than all of us," Adam said, then stood up and handed Ames a card.

"What's this?" Ames asked.

Adam smiled. "You know what it is. You have all our phones tapped. But just to keep this seemingly kosher, here's where I explain that it's my cell number. I often suffer from insomnia, so feel free to call anytime, night or day."

Ames felt as if he'd just been given the winning lottery ticket as he slipped the card into his pocket.

"I'll walk you down," he said, and escorted Pappas to the elevator, then rode down to the ground floor and stood in the lobby as Adam exited the building. After that, Ames made a beeline for his boss's office. Mac Harrison wasn't going to believe this.

The tracking program Moe had on his laptop had a range of fifty miles, so wherever James Walker went the next morning, Moe wouldn't be more than a couple of miles behind. He drove the twenty miles back to Mount Sterling, got a room at a motel on the edge of the city, and then went to the restaurant next door and scanned the menu. This time when he gave the waitress an order it was all vegetarian.

"I'll have a bowl of tomato soup and some crackers," he said.

"What to drink?" she asked.

"Iced tea."

He forgot until after she'd already walked away that the tea would most likely be sweet, but he didn't mind. In fact, he was learning to appreciate it with sugar, rather than the plain Earl Grey he normally ordered hot.

After he got back to his room, he plugged in the computer, logged on to the tracking system and smiled when he got a clear signal on Walker's truck. The extra money he'd spent on those CIA knockoffs was worth it. He turned up the volume so that if the target vehicle began moving before he woke up, the pinging would alert him, then rolled over on the bed and closed his eyes. Within minutes he was asleep and snoring.

The weatherman had predicted the possibility of thunderstorms later in the day, and it was already getting cloudy. James was rushing around, trying to get Julie to finish her grocery list so he could leave for Mount Sterling and get everything done, then get back with their groceries and deliver what Ryal had ordered, as well, before the storms hit. He hurried back to the porch and opened the front door long enough to shout, "Hey, honey! Are you finished with that list yet?"

Julie came hurrying into the room with the baby on her hip and Meggie only a few steps behind.

"Here it is," Julie said, and tilted her head up for the kiss she knew was coming, because James never left the house without kissing her goodbye.

Their kiss was sweet but brief.

"Mmm, good sugar," James said, kissed the baby's cheek, as well, then picked up his daughter and gave her a big hug and a kiss. "You be good for Daddy and help Mama with your brother, okay?"

"Are you gonna bwing me a supwise?"

James grinned. "Yes, Daddy will bring you a surprise." Then he winked at Julie. "I'll bring you one, too."

Julie hefted the baby on her hip and rolled her eyes. "That's okay. I don't need any more surprises, honey. This little guy was surprise enough for me."

They grinned at each other, and then moments later James was gone.

It was the ping of the tracking system that woke Moe up. He rolled over, then grabbed his reading glasses and eyed the laptop. The program was active. James Walker was on the move.

Moe jumped out of bed and raced around getting shaved and dressed, all the while keeping an eye on the truck's progress. When he realized the truck was actually heading toward Mount Sterling, he grinned. His target was coming to him. How considerate.

He'd only taken the room for one night, so he packed and reloaded his belongings into the rental car, and headed for a McDonald's drive-through to get breakfast. After that, wherever that truck went, Moe would follow. Even the things that Walker might be buying or the places he visited could be clues. Moe left nothing to chance.

Nearly thirty minutes later, the truck was in the city. Moe pulled up a city map, transposed the program onto the screen and then followed the truck turn by turn until he finally caught sight of both it and the driver.

"So that's what you look like," Moe muttered, as he caught a glimpse of James's profile.

After he followed Walker into the parking lot of a supermarket and the other man got out, Moe took a couple of photos of him, then set the camera under the seat and followed Walker inside.

He grabbed a shopping cart and began following James around the store, taking note of what he was buying. For cover, he began tossing items in his cart without paying much attention to what they were. He was at one end of the cereal aisle and James was at the other end when James's cell phone suddenly rang. Moe moved closer until he could hear clearly, while making sure to keep his gaze on the shelves.

James was debating about getting one box of cereal or two when his cell phone began to ring. He answered absently as he reached for the shelf.

"Hello?"

"James, it's me."

He smiled when he heard his wife's voice. "What did you forget?"

She sighed. "Toilet paper. That should just be a given every time we go to the store."

"Toilet paper coming up," he said. "Anything else?"

"I found the list you made for Ryal on the floor."

"Dang, are you sure?" he asked, and began checking his pockets. Sure enough, the list was missing. "You're right. I don't have it. Good catch, my love. Hang on. Let me get a pen and I'll write it on the back of our list." He pulled a pen out of his pocket and then grabbed a cereal box off the shelf to use for a table. "Okay . . . go ahead."

Julie began naming the items slowly, giving James time to write.

About halfway through, James stopped her.

"Wait. What was that last one?"

"Band-Aids. I wonder who's hurt?" she added.

James scribbled as he talked. "Beth is, but I thought I told you. Her hands . . . remember?"

"Oh . . . yes. Quinn stopped by Aunt Tildy's and got some of her ointment. Now I remember. I guess she's getting better if the sores can be covered with Band-Aids now. Good news."

"Right. Thanks again, honey. I'm almost through with our list. As soon as I pick up the stuff for Ryal, I'll be heading home. What's the weather look like there?"

"Still clouding up. Hurry home. I don't

want you that high up on the mountain when the storm hits."

"I will. I don't want to be up that high, either. Not with lightning all over the place. I'm hurrying. Love you — bye."

"Love you, too," Julie said, and disconnected.

James tossed the cereal box he'd been writing on into the basket, then finished filling their grocery list before parking the cart up front and bringing back an empty for Ryal's list.

By that time Moe was already out the door. He wanted to verify some more information before he assumed he'd hit the jackpot, so he began to boot up the laptop while keeping an eye on the supermarket exit.

He typed in the name Ryal Venable. When he didn't get a hit on that, he tried Ryal Walker. Within moments he had an entire list of links, including one for Walker's Handcrafted Furniture.

So a man named Ryal Walker had sent for some groceries via a man named James Walker, and on that list were Band-Aids for a woman named Beth. No way in hell were these names a coincidence.

While he waited for James Walker to return to his truck, Moe ran a search on property owned by people with the last name Walker. To his surprise, he got dozens of options.

Then he searched the local newspapers' online archives for Beth Venable's name, and to his surprise there were several old articles in which her name popped up. Most of the articles had to do with school functions, though one was about an annual family reunion and listed all the attendees. But the article that caught his attention included a photo of several attendees at a local turkey shoot right before Thanksgiving eleven years ago. The picture showed the winners of the contest, including a young man named Ryal Walker. The young girl standing by his side and smiling up at him was identified as Beth Venable.

Moe smiled back.

She'd run home to an old flame.

Now all he had to do was figure out where Ryal Walker was hiding his childhood sweetheart, and then he would be on a plane and back in good old L.A. before sunset tomorrow.

Beth was sick of being housebound and had talked Ryal into another walk through the forest, this time to a waterfall he'd promised to show her. It occurred to her that he had a thing for waterfalls — maybe because she'd seen him naked under one — but she kept it to herself.

She'd been trying to make sandwiches to take with them when Ryal had come into the kitchen and taken over.

"I love you to distraction, Bethie, and I mean no offense, but I can't stomach Aunt Tildy's ointment on my bread."

Beth had relinquished the knife she was using to spread mustard with a smile.

"None taken," she said. "Do we have a sack small enough to pack the food in?"

"Look in that bottom drawer," he said, pointing to the set of cabinet drawers nearest the back door.

"I found one," Beth said, and brought it back to the counter.

Ryal had the sandwiches made and wrapped in wax paper. He dropped them in the sack, along with a small bag of cookies, and then rolled down the top to seal it.

"We're good to go. Wanna use the bathroom before we head out?"

She nodded and hurried back through the house. A few minutes later she joined Ryal on the back porch.

"Should we lock the house?" she asked.

"No. Quinn might need to come in. Besides, there aren't any other people living up this high anymore."

He slid his arm around Beth's shoulders. When she looked up, he kissed her hard and long.

"You sure you wouldn't rather spend the morning in bed?" he asked.

She shook her head. "As good as you are in bed, I need to get out of the house. The walls are closing in on me."

He grinned. "I'll take that compliment and raise you one. You're the queen of my heart, and I have a waterfall to show you, located in the great outdoors. Might even get in a little skinny-dipping while we're at it."

Beth arched an eyebrow. "I knew that was where this was going. Leave it to you to get me naked, no matter where we're going."

He grinned. "Hey, I have ten long years of missed quickies to make up for."

Beth laughed as she wrapped her arms around his neck. This time, she was the one who kissed him hard and fast.

"There's your quickie," she said. "Now show me that waterfall."

They headed off into the woods, talking and laughing as if her absence of the past ten years had never happened and they were safe as houses there on the mountain.

■ ■ ■ ■

When James got home, he unloaded the family groceries and then, at Julie's urging, sat down to the noon meal she had waiting. By the time they finished eating, it was a little after 1:00 p.m. Julie put the baby down for a nap and had settled in the big rocking chair with their daughter to read a book as James headed for the front door.

"I'd better get those groceries up to Ryal. I won't stay, honey, so don't worry. I should be back in a couple of hours, okay?"

"Okay," she said. "Let Big Red in the house when you leave, will you?"

James frowned. Normally, Julie was the one who didn't want him inside.

"Why?"

She shrugged. "I don't know. I'm just a little unsettled, maybe because of all this hiding out and hush-hush drama. Just my motherly instincts on alert, I guess."

James went back and dropped down on his knees beside her chair.

"I'm sorry, sugar. If this is making you upset, I can get one of the cousins to —"

Julie grabbed his wrist. "No. I don't want you to abandon Ryal and Quinn. It's important that we help Beth. I'm just being a

298

worrywart, okay?"

James kissed her, then kissed her again. "I won't be long."

"Love you," she said, as he opened the door.

"Love you, too," James echoed as he let in the dog, and then he was gone.

Moe stayed a good five miles behind James Walker's pickup truck. He didn't need to see him to know where he was going. When he realized James had stopped at his home, he pulled his car off the road into the same tree cover that he'd used last night and settled in to wait.

A little over an hour later, the truck was once again on the move. Moe assumed James was delivering the other set of groceries he'd purchased, and while he would have liked to follow to see for himself, the area was so deserted that he feared there was no way he could do that and not be seen by someone.

It was too big a risk to take.

He would just keep on using the area map to track Walker, then take coordinates when he stopped again and get the hell off the mountain while the getting was good.

Sixteen

The woods were dense, the underbrush thick and often hard to walk through, but they followed the sound of the waterfall all the way to the banks of the stream that it fed. They walked out of the trees, startling a doe that had been drinking at the bank. She bounded across the water and into the trees on the opposite side in one leap.

"Oh, no, we scared her," Beth said.

"She'll come back when we're gone," Ryal said, as he set the sack with their picnic on a nearby rock and pointed to the falls coming over a ledge about ten feet above their heads. It was just large enough to send a spray of water back up into the air, forming its own rainbow.

"There it is. When we were kids we named it Foster Falls, because it was close to Grandma and Grandpa Foster's house, but I don't think it ever had an official name."

"Oh, look!" Beth said. "Look at that

rainbow! Isn't it beautiful?"

"Yes, very beautiful," Ryal said, but he wasn't looking at the waterfall — he was looking at Beth. He put his arms around her and kissed her gently at first, and then harder, hungrier.

Beth leaned into his embrace as he parted her lips with his tongue. A shock wave ricocheted through her as she felt his erection through the fabric of his jeans. That was what she wanted — all that power — inside her. She pulled back and reached for his belt with shaking fingers.

"Ryal . . ."

He heard the question in her voice, but he was already on the same page. His answer was to shed his clothes as fast as he could get out of them, then strip her bare. Before she had time to worry about the temperature of the water, he scooped her up in his arms and stepped off the bank into the swiftly moving stream.

It wasn't deep, no more than knee-high, as he kept walking toward the falls. The closer they got, the louder the water became. One moment the spray from the falls was on their faces, and then, the next thing Beth knew, he'd carried her through the cascade of water to the rock wall behind it and set her on her feet. Their hair was wet and plastered against their heads, and the mist continued to blanket their skin, while the thunder of the water matched the blood rush inside their bodies.

Their gazes locked.

He cupped her breasts.

She encircled his erection with her hands.

His nostrils flared, and for a moment she saw his eyes close in quiet ecstasy.

She moved her hands, and his body followed. The silken feel of his foreskin was in direct contrast to how hard he had become. She thought he groaned, but the sound was swallowed up by the water's roar.

Ryal put her arms around his neck, then picked her up and lowered her slowly onto his shaft. She locked her legs around his waist, breathing deeply in quiet satisfaction as he filled her.

He braced himself against the rock wall with one hand while holding on to her with the other, then began to thrust.

Beth tightened her hands around his neck and held on, her face buried in his shoulder, her breasts flattened against his chest, and rode him hard. There behind the falls, the water thundered against the rocks until they were deaf to everything else — even the beating of their own hearts.

It was the most sensual experience of

Beth's life. She couldn't hear a thing over the sound of the falls. There was nothing but the sensations of their bodies locked together in one pounding thrust after another, the feeling of the blood rushing through her veins and building in the valley between her legs in a ever-tightening spiral of lust and need, until she thought she would die from the pleasure.

Ryal was lost in what they were creating. He had no control. No thought of Beth. No thought of tenderness or care. Just a mind-bending need to keep pounding himself against the wet heat of the woman in his arms.

When the climax hit Beth, she felt as if she were flying into a million little pieces.

When she peaked, the muscles inside her core clamped around Ryal like a warm, wet fist, pushing him over the edge. He came with such force that it nearly sent him to his knees. Still deep inside his woman, he spilled his seed.

When it was over, they both sank into the water, their foreheads touching, their hands still locked in a death grip around each other.

Beth opened her eyes to find Ryal watching her. When he spoke, she read the words on his lips, rather than heard them.

"And I love you, too," she said.

They sealed what they'd done with a kiss, and then slowly made their way out from under the falls and back across the stream to where they'd left their clothes.

Ryal wrung out the length of Beth's hair as best he could, then dried her off with his shirt before he helped her dress. When he finally put on his own clothes, he hung his shirt on the bushes to dry.

"My feet are too wet to get in my boots," he said.

"We can go barefoot awhile," Beth said, as she crawled up on a flat rock nearby. She eyed the droplets on his thick black hair, and then reached forward and caught a droplet off the ends of his eyelashes before it fell into his eyes. "You are one sexy man, Ryal Walker, but I guess you know that, don't you?"

"You make it happen, Bethie. This part of me has never been for anyone but you. I love you. I never want to spend another day without you."

Beth's heart twisted anxiously. "I hope we can make that happen," she said.

"Don't say that," Ryal cautioned. "I keep telling you this is all going to work out. They'll put that SOB in prison and the world will go on, this time with us in it together, not on opposite sides of the country."

"Promise?" she asked.

"Promise," he said, and took a sandwich out of the sack and handed it to her, then took one for himself, unwrapped it and took a bite.

Beth did the same, eyeing the beauty of the area as she chewed and swallowed. She caught Ryal watching her and almost blushed, still self-conscious about how abandoned their lovemaking had been.

"You're turning me into someone I don't know," she said.

"No, darlin'. I'm not changing anything about you. It's just that when you're with me, the real you comes out."

She knew he was right, but it was still disconcerting to know that this lustful, wanton woman had been inside her all along.

When she didn't answer, he got a little anxious. "Are you okay?"

She glanced back, then smiled shyly. "I'll let you know when my head stops reeling."

He grinned and took another big bite of his sandwich. As long as she was good, he could handle anything.

"I wish I had a sketch pad," Beth said, as she continued to admire their surroundings while they ate. "This place is amazing."

"We'll have to come back here sometime when all this is over. You can take as long as you like to draw it," Ryal said.

Beth smiled. "Really? That would be great!"

"Really," he said, then finished off his sandwich.

She ate most of hers, tossing the remnants into the water to feed the little fish she could see darting in and out along the bottom of the streambed.

"There's a storm coming in," Ryal said, as he pointed up to the building clouds. "We'd better head back to the house."

Beth remembered the last thunderstorm, the constant crash of thunder and the white-hot flares of lightning. That had been the night they'd first made love. It had been great inside the house, but she didn't want to be caught out in anything like it.

She got off the rock, and began to look around for her shoes and socks while Ryal did the same. He folded up the sack and put it in his hip pocket, then held out his hand.

It never crossed Beth's mind to hesitate. Her hands were nearly healed, and after the way they'd just made love, the bond she felt to him was so strong that she wouldn't have rejected his clasp if she'd been openly bleeding.

"If we're lucky, we'll get back to the house before the rain begins," he said, and started walking.

"Don't slow down on my account," she said, and increased her stride to keep up.

Their trip home was less leisurely than the walk up, but it was physically easier, since they were moving downhill. By the time they reached the clearing at the back of the house, the wind was changing.

"Just in time," Ryal said, as they crossed the last twenty yards and hurried onto the back porch. Before they got inside, they heard the sound of an approaching vehicle. "That's probably James with the groceries."

Beth stopped on the porch with Ryal as James's dark truck appeared around the corner of the house and drove all the way up to the steps before he stopped.

"Oh, man, I thought that damn storm would beat me here," he said, as the wind began to whip the tree limbs. "Grab some sacks and let's get all this inside before the rain hits."

They got the groceries inside just ahead of the first drops, and had just begun putting everything up and catching up on news of the family and the mountain, when the front door suddenly flew open with a bang.

Ryal spun toward the sound just as Quinn came striding into the kitchen.

"Sorry about the door. The wind caught it as I was coming in. It also took the tent while I was making sure no one had followed James up here. I found the damn thing but didn't have time to put it back up before the rain started. Decided I was too delicate to stand out in another storm."

Beth put a hand on Quinn's arm. "You're soaked. Ryal has a dry shirt. Go change before you make yourself sick."

Ryal watched surprise come and go on Quinn's face.

"Yes, ma'am, I believe I will," he said quietly, eyeing Ryal to see if there was an objection, then left the room.

"I'll start some coffee. Hopefully it'll get made before the power goes off," Ryal said.

"None for me," James said. "I'd love to stay and visit, but Julie's uneasy when it storms, and I want to get off this slope before the road gets too slick."

"Drive safe," Ryal said. "And thanks for the delivery."

James grinned, then winked at Beth. "Totally my pleasure. Ya'll be careful. Call if you need anything."

"Thanks again," Beth said.

James waved and then ran out the back door, jumped into his truck and took off down the mountain as fast as he dared to go.

Ryal slid the coffee carafe into place and turned on the coffeemaker as Beth walked up behind him and wrapped her arms around his waist.

"I love the Walker brothers."

Ryal laid his hands on hers. "Thank you, baby," he said softly.

Quinn soon joined them, sheltering with them until the worst of the storm had passed. When there was nothing left but a little wind and the rain dripping from the leaves, he got up.

"I need to get back and get set up before dark."

"You didn't get any sleep today, did you?" Beth asked.

"I'm good," Quinn said. "You just worry about my big brother." He smiled to soften his words, and moments later he was gone.

"Do you need to go help him put up the tent?" Beth asked.

"No, and he wouldn't welcome the help anyway, so I'll leave him to it. Let's brown up some of these short ribs and then put them in a stew pot with a can of that beef broth. We need to let them simmer for two or three hours before we add the vegetables, but this feels like a good night for a one-dish meal."

Farther down the mountain, Moe sat in his car, hidden off the road in the cutout behind the trees and bushes, tracking James Walker's progress on his laptop.

When James finally stopped, Moe made a note of the coordinates, then waited to see what happened next. When the truck began moving again, he realized James Walker was heading home. This time, when the truck stopped, Moe knew where he was at. Confident that he also had a good idea of where Beth Venable was hiding, he drove out of his hiding place and carefully made his way off the mountain and back to Mount Sterling.

He rented another room for the night, but in a different motel, then drove down the street to a restaurant. After the day he'd had, he felt like treating himself to a decent meal.

The storm swept through Mount Sterling as he dined, and by the time he'd paid the bill and was ready to go back to his motel, it had passed.

Once inside his room, he got back on the laptop, punched in the coordinates where

James Walker had stopped, then used an overlay of a county map to get an idea of the location. After that, it was a matter of researching land-deed records until he found out who owned that particular plot of land. To his surprise, it had belonged to a man named Elder Foster, who was deceased.

The name didn't mesh with anything he knew, so he began another search on Ryal and James Walker, and found out that their mother's maiden name was Foster. That was when he began to smile. It was all falling into place. Dead granddaddy's house was being used as a hideout. It was the perfect location for staying under the radar.

Moe checked all his notes one last time, then put in a call to Ike Pappas and waited for it to be answered.

Ike's nerves were on edge. He couldn't remember ever feeling this out of control. Adam was MIA, and Valenti had threatened him. The friends he'd called to dine with him had made their excuses and begged off, claiming a sick child. Of course, he knew it was possible that was the truth, but his gut feeling said otherwise. It wasn't that they would have been shocked to learn he'd committed a murder. It was just that they didn't want to be associated with him right now in case of an arrest. He understood that. But it still pissed him off.

Ike's anger kicked in. By God, he wasn't going to let a bunch of pussies run him into a hidey-hole. He called an escort service, made a reservation at one of his favorite restaurants and then booked a suite at a nearby hotel. He was going to eat steak and fuck his brains out, and sleep somewhere other than the guest room in his own damned home.

Tomorrow was always a new opportunity for things to change for the better. God knew they couldn't get much worse.

He was at the restaurant waiting for his "date" to arrive when his cell phone began to vibrate. He started to let it go to voice mail, then checked the caller ID and saw it was from Moe Cavanaugh, so he headed for the men's bathroom. Once inside, he locked the door for privacy and took the call.

"This is Pappas."

"Mr. Pappas. I have some very promising info."

"I don't want promises. I want facts," Ike snapped.

"Then these are my facts. I think I've located her position, but I can't be sure without revealing myself. If that happened,

I think they'd move her again, so I couldn't take the chance."

"Yeah, okay, I see your point. So where's she at?"

"Can I send you all the info in an email?"

"Yes, but not to me. Send it to Kalamata Press dot org. I'll be watching for it. Are you sending it tonight?"

"Yes, sir, and then flying back to L.A. tomorrow."

"As usual, your fee will be paid via direct deposit into your account. Same info as always, I assume?"

"Yes, Mr. Pappas. Same as always."

"Thank you," Ike said. "I hope your work pays off."

"So do I," Moe said. "I'm always at your service."

As soon as Ike hung up, he washed his hands and returned to his table. Within minutes his date arrived. She was a tall, leggy brunette, with boobs the size of water floats and a waist he could span with both hands. Just how he liked a woman to look. This promised to be a good night after all.

Back in Mount Sterling, Moe was hard at work compiling his notes and suggestions. Once he finished, he fired the memo off to the email address Pappas had given him,

313

booked a flight on the first plane out in the morning that was heading to L.A., then set the alarm and went to bed.

Ike wasn't the only Pappas with fucking on his mind that night. But it wasn't a woman Adam wanted to fuck — it was Ike, and not in the literal sense of the word.

He'd been watching the house for hours. When he saw his father leave for the evening, and saw what he was wearing and that he was driving himself instead of using the driver and the family limo, he knew Ike would be in someone else's bed tonight, with a woman for hire playing with his dick. This was better than he'd hoped for. As soon as Ike was out of sight, Adam came out of hiding and drove down the street and onto the estate just as he'd done for the past ten years. When he got to the house, he was met by the housekeeper.

"Mr. Adam. You just missed your father," Beatrice said.

"I didn't come to see him," Adam said. "I came to get some of my fitness gear that I stored in the basement. I'll be down there for a while, sorting through boxes."

"Will you need any help?" she asked.

He frowned. "No. I don't want to be bothered, and as soon as I'm finished, I'll

314

be gone."

"Yes, sir," she said, and eyed him curiously before quickly looking away.

He knew she was thinking about the mess they'd found in Ike's room, but he had no intention of satisfying her curiosity. Without wasting any more time, he headed for the basement door.

Once he'd committed himself to testifying against his father and promised hard copies of documents to back up his claims, he'd known the first place he would look. As he proceeded downstairs, he remembered a night long ago when he was just a kid, and how he'd stayed awake playing with a new toy long after he was supposed to be in bed.

He'd heard his father's voice in the foyer below and run to the landing to meet him. But Ike hadn't come upstairs to bed. He'd gone toward the kitchen. Thinking he would get a midnight treat with his father, Adam had followed on bare feet, only to find the kitchen empty. When he saw the door to the basement slightly ajar, he peeked in and saw the light on downstairs. Curious, he tiptoed quietly down the stairs just in time to see his father walk into a storage room and turn on a light. To Adam's surprise, when his father pressed on the wall, a secret door swung inward.

Adam had gasped, then clasped his hands over his mouth and dashed back up the steps before he could get caught. Even then, he'd known that was a place that was meant only for his father. And while he'd always remembered where it was, he'd never gone in. He'd never had a reason to — until tonight. With no time to waste, he went straight for the storage room, turned on the light and then closed the door behind him before he began to search for the trigger that would open the secret door.

He closed his eyes and thought back to that night, trying to remember where he'd seen his father put his hands, then began his search.

It didn't take long.

When the door swung inward, an odd odor hit him square in the face, making the hair stand up on the back of his neck. It was what death smelled like, and it occurred to him that there could be actual bodies in there as well as documentation of his father's many misdeeds. The thought was disgusting enough to give him pause, but it didn't take him long to get past it. He felt along the inside of the wall until he found a light switch and turned it on. There were no bodies, but even so, the sight was enough to stop him cold. Shelves lined three walls from top to bottom. There were boxes on the shelves, all of them labeled and numbered. A quick search revealed a second set of books for each of the businesses Ike owned, along with what appeared to be info on the men he'd put in charge — info that could be used to blackmail them, if the need arose. There were at least a half-dozen black garbage bags scattered about, but they weren't labeled. Curious, he opened the one with the least dust on it and looked inside.

Almost instantly, he recognized his father's clothing. The Gucci shoes he'd bought in Italy when they'd been on vacation last year, and one of his favorite Calvin Klein suits — the kind he favored for daily office wear.

Upon closer inspection, he realized the suit and shoes had dark, blotchy stains all over them. He rubbed one spot between his fingers, then looked. A dry, powdery substance the color of rust had rubbed off on his skin.

"What the hell?"

Then he suddenly dropped the garments back in the bag and tied it up as he realized what it was. Blood, undoubtedly belonging to someone other than his father, and no doubt the source of the stench that had greeted him. He wondered if — given that he'd opened what seemed to be the most recent bag — he'd just discovered his mother's blood. At that point, his last vestige of regret for what he was doing disappeared.

He began gathering up the bags and carrying them out into the basement. He paused for a moment and looked around, trying to figure out how he would be able to get them out of the house undetected. Then his gaze fell on his luggage, stored off to one side. The two largest bags were wheeled. He opened them, packed the bag he'd checked inside one suitcase, along with as many sets of the cooked books as he could carry, and then packed the other bag with other potentially useful items. The last thing he saw were a couple of handguns lying on a top shelf. No telling who his father had killed with those. He stuffed them inside the last suitcase, too, and then turned out the light, closed the secret door and exited the storage room, making sure that light was off, as well. Now all he had to do was get the two suitcases up the steps and out the door.

He dragged the first one upstairs, then ran back down for the second and pulled it up, as well. Once he had them both in hand, it was simple to wheel them through the kitchen, out into the foyer and then outside, so he could heave them into the trunk of his car.

Beatrice was nowhere in sight when he drove away, which suited him fine. She would tell Ike that he'd been there to get some of his things, and Ike would no doubt assume he'd taken some of his fitness equipment. Ike would see that the suitcases were gone and check out the gym where Adam had spent a lot of his time. Ike never used it, so Adam was banking on the theory that he wouldn't know what had been taken and what had been left behind. It should never occur to him to check his secret room, because Adam wasn't supposed to know it existed.

He drove back up to the lodge, taking care to make sure he hadn't been followed, and then went inside. He would have to wait for morning to finish what he'd started, but he was trusting in God to keep him safe, at least long enough to avenge his mother's murder.

SEVENTEEN

Adam couldn't sleep. He kept seeing the gaping gash in his mother's neck and wondering if she'd tried to scream when it happened. Physically, it would have been impossible, but she wouldn't have known that. She would have opened her mouth — maybe to beg for mercy or at least to scream for help — only there wouldn't have been any sound, just the arterial spray that sent the life gushing from her.

He sat up in bed and scrubbed his hands over his face, trying to rub away the thoughts in his head. His belly growled, reminding him that he hadn't eaten in hours. Too sick at heart to sleep, he threw back the covers and went to the kitchen.

It was so quiet up here. No sirens, no traffic, just acres of space and a beautiful panorama of the San Gabriel Mountains.

He poked around in the fridge before he took out a jar of jelly and a loaf of bread.

He'd purchased a few basics earlier, and now he opted for a peanut-butter-and-jelly sandwich. Simple, filling and easy to prepare, not to mention it exhausted the extent of Adam's culinary skills.

He took his sandwich outside onto the patio and watched the sunrise while he ate. A small ground squirrel popped out of the brush surrounding the lodge and scampered up onto the far end of the patio, then sat watching Adam eat. The intensity of the little creature's gaze made Adam smile.

"You hungry, too, little guy?"

The squirrel didn't answer, but it did take a step closer, then sat up on its hind legs and stared.

Adam tore off a bit of the crust and tossed it across the space between them. The squirrel made a dive for the bread, then took off into the brush with his prize between his teeth.

"Survival of the fittest, even out here," Adam muttered, then swallowed the last of his sandwich and went back inside to dress.

A couple of hours later he was the first one in line at Garcia Storage Rental when it opened. A short while later, after a large amount of cash had changed hands, he had rented a small storage unit under the name Arnold Benedict without showing any identification. For what he'd paid him, the owner wasn't asking questions, nor did he recognize the irony of the name under which Adam had signed. The original Benedict Arnold had died of old age in London after betraying his country. Adam only hoped he could look forward to a similarly long life after turning traitor to the Mob. However, he wouldn't even live to see his next birthday if he didn't have a good exit strategy in place once he ratted on his father and his cronies.

Now that he had the evidence to back up his testimony, along with several bags of clothing that should reveal some interesting DNA, he felt confident that he was on the right track.

Once this was over, if he survived it, his next move was simple. It would involve a different lifestyle — a different identity. One where men didn't covet money but prayed to be absolved of greed, and where God was the first name on the residents' lips. His mother had always wanted a priest in the family.

Ike woke up alone in the hotel, but there was a smile on his face. He'd been in need of a good fuck, and last night he'd gotten one. He'd sent the escort home just before

3:00 a.m., then rolled over in bed and slept like a baby.

It was a new day, and he felt like a new man. If Moe's info was good, his troubles were almost over. Suddenly he couldn't wait to get home and log on to his computer to see what kind of info Moe had sent.

He dressed quickly, opting not to shower or shave, and was out of the hotel without so much as a cup of coffee. When he drove onto his estate, the guard at the gate waved as he drove past. The sun was shining through the branches of the trees along the driveway. It felt like a heavenly spotlight leading him home, and he took it as a sign from God that all was well.

He left the car in the drive, entered through the main entrance and went straight up to his room to shower and change.

To his relief, all signs of the vandalism in his bedroom had been removed. A new and pristine white coverlet was on his oversize bed, and the bloody rug had been cleaned. He stripped as he went, tossed his clothes on a chair and paused in the bathroom to look at himself.

He looked good for a man in his fifties. He wasn't overweight, but he had bulk in his shoulders and arms — a sign of strength, he thought. His face showed very few signs of aging, and since he sported the bald look, there was no gray hair to show his years. He patted his chest in satisfaction and then got in the shower.

By the time he had shaved and dressed in fresh clothes, nearly a half hour had passed. He met his housekeeper in the foyer as he was coming down the stairs.

"Good morning, Beatrice. Tell Cook I want a three-egg omelet with cheese, buttered toast and hash browns, and a pot of black coffee. I'll be in my office. You can serve it in there."

"Yes, sir," she said, and hurried off to deliver the order as Ike moved through the house to his office.

Once inside, he closed the door and logged on to the computer, then did a quick search of his email accounts for Moe Cavanaugh's information. It was there, just as he'd promised.

Ike scanned the message, impressed — as always — by Moe's thoroughness, and then swiveled around from his computer to his desk and reached for his Rolodex. There were no names on the cards, only letters from the Greek alphabet that represented a code Pappas had created years earlier.

He made a call. The phone rang twice before the call was answered.

"Bose Aviation, Kelly speaking."

"Kelly, this is Ike Pappas. I have a job for you."

"Yes, sir, Mr. Pappas. What do you need?"

"I need a location verified and some photos taken, specifically of any people you might see around the house. Only one fly-over. Don't want to alarm anyone, you understand. And I need this stuff by the end of the day. Can you do that?"

"Sure, Mr. Pappas. Just give me the coordinates."

"It's in Kentucky."

There was a momentary pause, and then he heard Kelly clear his throat. "That will up the cost considerably, Mr. Pappas. I hope you understand, but what with the cost of fuel and —"

"I don't care what it costs. Just do it."

"Yes, sir. We'll leave as soon as I fuel up."

"Who's we? I don't want anyone else involved."

"I'll have to use my chopper and fly a little lower to get the photos you want, and I'll need a photographer for that."

"Oh, yeah, right. Whatever. Just remember, whoever you get doesn't know who hired you, or who the pictures are for. Got it?"

"Yes, sir. Definitely, sir."

"I'll be waiting." He disconnected just as there was a knock at the door. "Come in."

It was Beatrice, with his breakfast.

"That smells wonderful," he said, as she sat the tray on a table near the window and then stopped to pour his coffee.

"Thank you, Mr. Ike. I'll tell Cook." She started to leave, and then stopped. "Mr. Adam came by right after you left last night."

Ike frowned. He hated that he'd missed an opportunity to talk to his son. "Did he say anything? Leave a message for me?"

"No, sir. He said he was just stopping by to pick up some of his things from the basement. He wasn't here long."

Ike frowned. "Thank you. Close the door when you leave."

"Yes, sir," she said, and made a quick exit.

Ike's appetite had been somewhat stifled by the news, but as soon as he took the first bite, it returned. The cheesy omelet was cooked just to his taste, the buttered toast was a crisp accompaniment to the creamy eggs and the hash browns were perfection. He soon forgot about his disgruntled son as he continued to make plans to remove what his father used to call "the splinter in his eye," which was how Dimitri Pappas had referred to someone who got in his way.

As soon as he'd eaten his fill and Beatrice had carried away the tray, he was back at his desk pulling up another code and making another call to a mercenary by the name of Silas. Ike couldn't afford to send any of his own people for this job. There could be no trace of a connection between him and the hell he was about to rain down on the woman who held his life in her hands.

The call was answered on the first ring. Silas's voice was deep and raspy, a condition related to a fire that had almost taken his life years earlier.

"Silas, this is Ike Pappas. I have a job for you."

The thunderstorm from the night before had washed everything clean on Rebel Ridge. For the first time since they'd come to the old mountain house, Ryal had left Beth alone long enough to go check on Quinn. When he hadn't come in for breakfast, or at noon, Ryal got worried. When he still hadn't arrived by late in the afternoon, Ryal made a plate of food as an excuse to go talk to him.

Beth opted to stay behind, and Ryal was okay with that. She would be safe for the short time he was gone, and there were no other roads leading to the house other than the one Quinn was watching, so no one could get to her without coming by them first.

Beth was feeling like a champion because she was finally able to do a few simple chores without damaging her healing hands. It felt good to have her hands in the warm, soapy water as she washed the dishes, and it was nice to be useful again.

But there were only so many dishes to wash, and Ryal had already swept the floors. The beds were made, and there was nothing left to do but kill time. Back home, she would have been working, but this mess was getting in the way of her job as well as Ryal's. For safety's sake, since her hands had been in soapy water, she got Aunt Tildy's ointment and went outside to doctor her palms while she sat on the porch swing and watched the squirrels and the birds put on their daily show.

It wasn't the first time she'd marveled at what a treasure trove of subjects she would have here as models. She was also aware that she could do her job just as well long-distance as she had in L.A. Once she got set up with Skype for the occasional one-on-one meeting with a client and had email available, she would be good to go.

Ryal hadn't actually said, "Will you marry

me?" but he'd made his intentions clear in every other way she could imagine, and she felt certain the time would come — and soon — when he would speak the actual words. If it hadn't been for the mess she was in, she would be absolutely giddy.

Once she'd finished doctoring her hands, she laid the jar aside and began to swing. She didn't know what it was about the repetitive rhythm that was so soothing to her, but she loved it almost as much as she loved the solitude and beauty of this place.

She'd been sitting and swinging for at least fifteen minutes when she saw something moving in the grass about twenty yards from the house. She couldn't tell what it was from the porch, but she was curious, and got up and walked to the top of the steps for a better look.

The grass kept moving, back and forth, back and forth. She thought about going out to look but knew there was a good possibility she could walk up on a big snake, so she decided to stay put.

As she watched, she became aware of another sound separate from the constant swishing grass, a sound she hadn't heard since she'd been this far up Rebel Ridge — the sound of a helicopter. She looked up just as it topped the mountain and dipped down toward where she was standing. She shaded her eyes for a better look as the chopper kept coming in her direction, memories flooding back. Watching planes passing over the mountain had always been a favorite childhood pastime. She almost waved as it passed over, just like she'd always done as a child.

Once it passed, she looked toward the meadow again. Whatever had been out there was long gone . . . maybe scared away by the noise.

She started to go back to the porch swing when she heard yet another engine, but this time she recognized it as Ryal's pickup truck. Grateful that he was coming back, she waited for him on the back porch. It wasn't until he was closer that she realized how fast he was driving.

Her heart skipped a beat. What if something had happened to Quinn?

When the truck came around the corner of the house and slid to a stop beneath the trees, she went out to meet him.

"What's wrong? Is Quinn all right?"

His eyes were wide with fright as he grabbed her by the arms.

"That chopper. Were you outside when it went over?"

"Yes, but what —"

"Did they see you?"

"Probably. I was standing on the edge of the —" All of a sudden she felt sick. "Oh, God! I didn't think. I didn't expect —"

There wasn't anything he could say that would change what had happened. He pulled her up against his chest and just held her.

Beth was shaking so hard she felt weak. "What did I do? Do you think it was them? Do you think they've found me?"

"I don't know, Bethie. It's just strange that it came over the back of the mountain, flew directly too damned low over the house and then, once it passed, took a sharp right and flew out of sight."

"Was Quinn there? Did he see the chopper? What did he say about it?"

"He was there. He believes it was searching and that we have less then twenty-four hours before they return with firepower."

"By air? Are you saying they'll come by air?"

"He doesn't think so. He thinks they'll need a positive identification of your body to make sure you've been eliminated as a threat before they quit. That will mean coming up the mountain, either on foot or by vehicle. Either way, he says there will certainly be more than one."

Beth suddenly felt light-headed, and leaned over and grabbed her knees to keep from passing out.

Ryal scooped her up into his arms and carried her into the house to the bedroom they shared, and then laid her on the bed.

He started to get up to get a wet cloth for her face when she grabbed him by the hand.

"You need to get me out of here before someone gets hurt. I won't bring a fight to this mountain. I never should have come. I'm sorry. I'm so sorry."

A muscle jerked at the side of Ryal's jaw — the only sign of his emotional state.

"You're not going anywhere, Beth. You didn't bring anything to Rebel Ridge but yourself. Whatever comes after you is a threat to all of us, not just you, and we protect our own."

"Oh, my God. Oh, my God." She rolled over onto her side and began to weep.

It was just before 9:00 p.m. when Ike's doorbell rang. He was on the phone with an associate in the Virgin Islands when he heard the chime. He heard Beatrice's footsteps going down the hallway toward the door, then the mumbled undertones of an unfamiliar voice before the door went shut.

He paused, absently listening to the man

on the other end of the line while watching the door. There was a knock, and then Beatrice peeked inside.

He motioned her in as he ended the call.

"Who was at the door?"

"A courier, sir. I signed for it." She handed him a large envelope — the kind used for shipping photos — and then paused. "Is there anything I can get for you?"

"No, I'm fine. Thank you, Beatrice. You can retire for the night. I'll be going to bed soon myself."

"Yes, sir," she said, and quietly left the room.

As soon as she was gone, Ike opened the envelope and took out a dozen eight-by-ten black-and-white photographs. All of them were of a small-frame house sitting in the middle of a tiny meadow on the side of a mountain. The first photo had been taken from a distance, and he didn't initially see the figure standing on the porch at the back of the house. But the next six shots had been taken in rapid succession as the chopper flew lower and closer, and it was obvious the figure was that of a young woman. The last four were close-ups, and they were so clear he could see the shadow of her hand on her forehead as she shielded her eyes from the sun.

He looked at that face for several moments, then turned around and went back to his desk and pulled out a folder with the info he'd printed out from the email Moe Cavanaugh had sent him earlier. Inside was a picture of a woman identified as Lilabeth Venable. He held it up next to the photo of the woman on the porch. His eyes narrowed, and then he smiled.

"Gotcha!" he said, and reached for the phone. It was time to let Silas know the hunt was on.

On Rebel Ridge, Quinn was gathering up his own band of warriors. They knew the job that lay ahead, and were willing and able as they gathered with him up at his campsite.

He took them over and over the traps he'd laid, until he was as confident in them as he was in himself that if the opportunity arose, they could lead the intruders right where he and Ryal wanted them.

Back in the cabin, Beth was too afraid to sleep, and Ryal was no longer in her bed helping keep the nightmares at bay. He was standing his own watch inside the house, moving from room to room throughout the night, making sure the only shadows out in the woods were moving on four feet and

keeping their distance from his grand-
father's house.

335

EIGHTEEN

Lou was frying up some leftover mush to
have with her morning coffee. A little fried
mush with some warm honey was a good
way to start a day. As she waited for the
mush to brown, she glanced at the calendar.
It was the first of August. Autumn came fast
up on Rebel Ridge, and winter wouldn't be
far behind. She didn't know how many
winters she had left in her, but she hoped
for at least a few to spend with her prodigal
granddaughter before the Good Lord took
her home.

She was sipping from her coffee while the
last piece of mush was browning when her
phone rang. A call at this early hour of the
morning was never good news. She took the
skillet off the fire and then hurried into the
hall, where she sat down in the chair beside
the phone to answer, unaware her voice was
shaking.

"Hello?"

"Granny Lou, it's me, Beth. I borrowed Ryal's phone. I hope I didn't wake you."

Lou held the phone a little closer to her ear, as if it would bring her son's child that much closer to her heart.

"No, sugar, you didn't wake me. I was up frying me some mush. Wish you were here to have some. I even warmed up a little clover honey to pour on it."

"That sounds so good. I wish I was, too."

Lou could hear the tears in her granddaughter's voice.

"What's wrong, Bethie? And don't fib to me, because I'll know."

Beth pressed her fingers against her lips to quell a sob, then closed her eyes briefly and took a deep breath.

"I just wanted to talk to you again."

"Did they find you, girl? I need to know. If they did, then it's time I got down on my knees in prayer."

"We think so, Granny, but they're not here. At least not yet. You eat your breakfast and drink your coffee before you do any praying. I need you to be at your strongest and pray some really big prayers for us. For all of us."

"I'll do that very thing," Lou said, and Beth could tell she was crying. "I love you,

Bethie, and I have faith that God didn't bring you back into my life just to take you away again, you hear? You have faith, and I'll have faith, and that will make my prayers that much stronger."

Beth swallowed another sob. "I will, Granny Lou. And one other thing before I go. I'm sorry . . . I'm so sorry I didn't come home sooner."

"You're here now, and that's all that counts. Now you let me talk to Ryal. Is he there with you?"

"Yes, ma'am, he's standing right beside me."

Beth handed the phone to Ryal, and then stumbled out of the room so that her grandmother wouldn't hear her cry.

"Mornin', Lou. This is Ryal."

Lou's voice was shaking, but her words were firm. "Son, I need you to take good care of my girl. I don't think I can bury another member of my family and survive."

Ryal was numb to everything but keeping Beth alive. He hadn't allowed himself to go there, but now, hearing Lou's fear for Beth's life brought the danger home to him all over again.

"All I can promise you is that I'll die to keep her safe."

Lou sighed. "Now, don't go and do that,

338

either. I need the both of you in one piece when this is over. How else will I get myself another great-grandbaby if you're dead?"

Ryal managed a smile. "Yes, ma'am, I can see how that could present a problem. We'll certainly do our best to see that we make that happen."

"Thank the Lord. I was hoping isolation would be good for what ailed the both of you. I'm happy to know I was right."

Ryal took a deep breath. "I'm glad you were right, too, Granny Lou. You stay safe, and so will we."

The conversation between them was over. The buzz of the dial tone told him that Lou had hung up. He dropped his phone back in his pocket and went to find Beth.

Silas had already assembled his men a few miles from the mountain the locals called Rebel Ridge. Since it was unfamiliar territory, he'd planned their attack for broad daylight. No sense giving the target an edge and trying it at night, when his quarry's familiarity with the area would provide a distinct advantage.

Silas stopped thinking about the timing of the attack and turned his attention to his team. He'd worked with these six men before. They were mercenaries who'd been with him on desert forays, in the winter months in Afghanistan, even on a couple of jobs down in the tropics to oust a reigning dictator. They were good at their work and had no qualms about killing for money.

Silas had just ended a phone call with Pappas, who'd given him the final go-ahead, as well as firm directions to their target's location, and he entered the coordinates in his GPS.

His men, all ex-military who still maintained their buzz cuts and fitness routines from when they were on active duty, were sitting around the cold camp they'd made last night, awaiting further orders. He eyed them closely, assessing them one by one before they got started.

Warwick was his sharpshooter. If a rocket launcher was ever needed, Farmer was the man for the job. Emerson was his freak. He liked to torture people, even himself, as the scars on his arms testified. Taggert was the oldest and a veteran of two wars. He was also the most savvy and dependable. Bordain was a snake in battle. He could get anywhere in record time, but he drank too much. Mason was his only potential question mark — an ice-head who loved meth more than his mama — and he wouldn't even be here except that the man Silas had wanted was already out of the country on another job.

These were his men. They would be frowned upon in society, but they were choice picks if you were going to war, and in a way this exercise was a little war. No matter. All he needed to do was make sure everyone at their target location died. It should be an easy job that wouldn't take long.

He walked over to where they were sitting, aware that his reputation as a hard-ass always preceded him.

"Listen up," he said shortly. "It's a go. We have our coordinates and strict orders. Take no prisoners and leave nothing behind that says we were there. Is that clear?"

"Clear, sir!" they echoed, and began to clean up the area and load up their gear. By the time they were all inside the two gray SUVs, it was as if they'd never been there.

Silas was driving the lead vehicle, Taggert the second. Both SUVs were loaded with guns, ammo and Farmer's rocket launcher.

There was no talking, no camaraderie. Each man was focused on the task at hand. All they had to do was make sure they were the survivors when the mission was done.

Silas drove just beneath the speed limit so as not to call attention to their little convoy, but they had to pass through Boone's Gap to get to the road that would take them up the mountain, and his fear was that two matching SUVs with strangers inside were more than enough to attract attention.

The only stop sign in town was at the intersection where Frankie's Eats was located, and SueEllen was topping off a customer's coffee cup when she saw two SUVs stop at the sign, then proceed through town without any of the passengers looking right or left.

She didn't know what it meant, but considering everything that was happening, it was strange enough to be worth mentioning. She bolted for the back door with her cell phone in her hand and made a quick call to her grandmother.

After the phone call Lou had received from Beth only an hour earlier, she was still praying as she sat in the darkened hallway by the phone. When it rang, she answered quickly.

"Hello?"

"Granny Lou, this is SueEllen. I'm at work, and I just saw two gray SUVs come through town with a bunch of men inside. I don't know where they're going, but considering what's going on, I thought I should let you know."

"Thank you, sugar. I'll pass it on." Lou hung up, then picked up the receiver again and made a call to Ryal.

"It's me," she said as soon as he answered. "SueEllen just called. Said two gray SUVs just came through Boone's Gap, both full of strangers. It may not mean anything, but I thought you should know."

"Thank you, Lou. I'll tell Quinn."

Satisfied she was doing her part, she disconnected and went back to praying.

Ryal made the call to Quinn and quickly relayed the info.

"I'll spread the word," Quinn said, and then the line went dead in Ryal's ear.

As he pocketed the phone, he heard footsteps behind him. Beth was standing in the doorway. The panic on her face was hard to witness.

"What's happening?" she asked.

"SueEllen just saw two gray SUVs go through Boone's Gap. She didn't recognize the men inside, so she gave us a heads-up, in case it mattered."

"Does it? Matter, I mean."

Ryal could only shrug. "Either way, we're on alert, baby. Come to me. I need a cuddle, even if you don't."

He leaned his rifle against the wall and opened his arms.

Beth walked into them, locked her own arms around his waist and hid her face against his chest.

Ryal held her close, gently rocking her where they stood.

"You are the best thing that's ever happened in my life, and you're crazy if you think I'm gonna let anything happen to you," he said softly.

Beth leaned back so that she could see his face. "I love you, Ryal."

He leaned down and gently brushed a kiss across the surface of her lips. "Love you, too, Lilabeth. You just wait. This is gonna turn into one of those stories we'll be telling our grandchildren one day. And you'll be the heroine."

"That means we'll be making babies," she said.

He grinned. "Well hell, honey, I thought we were already in the process of doing that. Lord knows we're getting in the practice. When this is over, you better be figuring out a date for the wedding. The least we can do for our children is get married before they begin to arrive."

Beth smiled through tears. "You just

proposed to me, didn't you?"

Ryal's eyes widened, and then he laughed. "I guess I did. So will you, Lilabeth? Will you marry me? I promise I'll never make you sorry."

"Yes, yes, a thousand times yes . . . anytime, anywhere."

He cupped her face, kissing each eyelid and then her nose before he paused and looked down.

"Sealed with a kiss," he whispered.

She rose up on tiptoe to meet him, and for a few precious moments the world was theirs for the taking.

Then reality surfaced, and Ryal began double-checking the house and making sure everything they needed was still in place, while Beth disappeared into the bedroom. She had a sudden need to be on her knees and begging God for mercy.

Silas and his men had turned off the main highway and were now headed up the mountain. His gaze was quick and sharp as he took note of everything they passed, from an abandoned shack to a house with more cars in front of it than rooms inside. Dogs barked at the unfamiliar vehicles as they passed. One even chased them a short distance down the road, and he had to warn

Emerson, who was riding with him, not to shoot it just to see it suffer. There would be no gunplay until the target was in sight, and even then, if they were lucky, very little of that.

For now he just followed the road that was winding up Rebel Ridge through trees so tall and thick they looked as if they'd been there for centuries.

A quick glance at his watch told him they'd been on the road for exactly thirty-four minutes when they came around a big curve and he had to suddenly slam on the brakes.

An enormous tree was partially blocking the road. It appeared that it had fallen recently — probably during some recent storm. There were no tire tracks on the road above the dead tree, which told him no one had been in or out since the last rainfall.

He eyed the three men with him. "Emerson, you and Bordain get out and move that off the road so we can pass."

"I'll help," Mason said. "I need to take a piss anyway."

"Tree first," Silas said unsympathetically, then sat in the vehicle with the engine idling, watching as the men got hold of the broken limbs and the trunk, and began dragging the tree off to the edge of the road.

As soon as the way was clear, he saw Mason duck into the trees on the far side.

"What the hell, Mason?" he yelled. "Just piss anywhere!"

Mason stopped and looked back. "Now I gotta take a shit, too. Just wait, damn it. That bitch ain't goin' nowhere."

Silas cursed beneath his breath as he watched Mason disappear into the trees. The other men got back into the truck and closed the doors while they waited for Mason to come back.

Dooley Walker was one of the cousins. He'd been lying in the underbrush, about twenty yards in, ever since he and his brothers had dragged that dead tree onto the road. After that, Mike and Pudge had taken off to their own assigned locations, leaving Dooley at the first roadblock. Pudge had laid spike strips in the road before sunup, and everyone else was on watch.

He'd heard the vehicles before he saw them, and as he watched the men climbing out of the first SUV, strapped with pistols and wearing camo clothing, he knew the bad boys were here. He counted heads and took note of as many types of weapons as he could see, and then lay low, waiting for them to leave.

When he saw one of the men separate from the others, he froze. Then the man headed into the woods in his direction and he tensed, waiting to see what the guy was going to do. The driver of the first vehicle called out his name — Mason — and then Mason yelled back. "That bitch ain't goin' nowhere," he said, and Dooley got pissed. Damn it to hell, that bastard was talking about Beth. Dooley stayed low, watching Mason go farther into the woods before he stopped.

When Dooley saw Mason take down his pants and squat, he smiled grimly. Old Mason was about to have a real shitty day. He rose up, notched an arrow and drew back, letting it fly straight into the side of Mason's neck. It cut off whatever outcry he would have made and broke his neck at the same time. Mason was dead before his shit hit the ground.

Dooley got up in a crouched position. Moving swiftly, he grabbed the dead man under the arms, threw him over his shoulders and carried him deeper into the trees, then rolled his body off the side of a cliff before disappearing.

Back on the road, Silas was fuming. Time was wasting, and he had decided that Mason hadn't really needed to take a crap but was probably getting high instead.

"Emerson, go get Mason, and be quick about it."

"Yes, sir," Emerson said, already jumping out of the vehicle.

He ran off into the trees and quickly found where Mason had squatted, but the man himself was nowhere to be found, only a single set of footprints leading off into the forest. Puzzled, he followed the footsteps for a short distance, until he reached a wide expanse of rock and the footprints disappeared.

He ran back double-time, knowing Silas was going to be pissed.

Silas saw him coming back alone and jumped out, cursing at the top of his voice.

"Where the fucking hell is Mason? I thought I told you to bring him back now!"

"I looked, Silas. I saw where he took a dump, but then he got up and walked off into the woods. His footprints just disappeared."

Silas frowned. He didn't want to think that they were already under attack. More likely the damn ice-head had gotten high and walked off the side of the mountain.

"Fine. Get in the truck. We're leaving. If he wants a ride back, he can track us, or sit on his ass and wait for us to come back down."

Emerson blinked, a little surprised that they were leaving one of their own behind, but he wasn't the one in charge, and he quickly got back inside.

The two-car caravan continued upward, moving past homes that weren't much more than shacks by the side of the road, while other houses, even if not elaborate, seemed well cared for. They passed a large metal sign on the side of the road with an arrow pointing up a track to the left, indicating the way to the Foley Brothers Mining Corporation. The trees grew taller the higher up they went, while the underbrush got thicker and the road rougher. There were potholes and old ruts that hadn't been graded out in years. One stretch of the road appeared to have recently been filled in, but when they drove over it, the drop was so deep that the undersides of the SUVs banged against the ground.

Silas cursed. All he needed was to bust the oil pan, but when he glanced back in the side-view mirror, he didn't see any evidence of leakage or any car parts lying on the ground.

As they topped the next hill and started down, Pudge darted out of the woods behind the SUVs and quickly pulled up the spike strips that had been concealed under a thin layer of sand, then disappeared back in the trees.

Silas kept a close eye on their surroundings the farther up they went, but it didn't appear to him as if anyone lived up here anymore — no one but a fugitive, and they were on her trail.

Just as he started around a sharp curve, his vehicle began to pull hard toward the right. He fought the car back onto the road, his ears registering a regular ka-thump.

In the rearview mirror, he could see that Taggert was experiencing similar difficulty staying on the road. Before he could manage to stop, one of his tires blew out. The sound was startling, and he grabbed the wheel with both hands, fighting to keep the car in the road instead of careening off into the trees.

Silas signaled for a halt, but Taggert had already done that on his own a few yards back. Taggert got out, cursing, then stared at the wheels in disbelief. One tire had blown out and the other three were going flat.

"What the fuck?"

He looked up at Silas's car a few yards ahead. All the tires on that vehicle were going flat, as well. Instinctively, he crouched, his hand on his holster as he scanned the tree line, looking for the enemy.

Silas had come to the same conclusion. He didn't know how it had happened, but this wasn't a coincidence. These yokels had managed to take out both their cars, leaving them afoot.

It was humiliating, and it also explained Mason's sudden disappearance.

Silas was a soldier. He'd fought more wars on foot than any of these men combined, except maybe Taggert, but he'd underestimated the enemy.

"What happened?" Warwick asked, as he got out of the second SUV.

"See for yourself," Taggert said, and pointed to the hatch. "Get the weapons out. We're packing them in on foot."

"How will we get back down?" Farmer asked, as he grabbed his baby, an American rocket launcher that had gone missing from a New Jersey armory five years earlier.

"We'll go back down on rims if we have to," Taggert said. "For now, we've got a job to do."

Silas shouldered his pack, as well as the one Mason would have carried, and waited for Emerson and Bordain to get their own packs strapped on.

"Are you ready?" he asked.

"Ready," they echoed.

"How far are we from the target?" Bordain asked.

Silas scanned the GPS. "About three miles as the crow flies."

"Are we taking the road or the trees?"

"We're done with the fucking road," Silas said. "And if you find yourself a hillbilly hiding in the trees, take him out."

NINETEEN

Nathan Walker was up in one tree about a mile and a half from Grandpa Foster's old house. His brother Moses was in another tree about fifty yards farther up. Their brother Paul was on the ground, covered up in leaves and grass so completely that Nathan was looking at the location where he'd watched Quinn put him and still couldn't see where he was at.

They were the Walkers from the redheaded side of the family, so they were all wearing black or green sock caps to keep their hair from giving them away. It was a common understanding that John Walker's three sons were the best sharpshooters on Rebel Ridge, except for their cousin Quinn.

Nathan shifted slightly, easing an ache in his left leg, and hoped the action started soon. He'd been up this tree so long, he was afraid if he had to come down, he would be too damn stiff to run.

The theory was that the killers' tires should all be flat by now, forcing them to go the rest of the way on foot. And since the cousins could see the road from the treetops, that would give Quinn's little mountain army the opportunity to pick them off one by one before they ever reached the house where Beth was hiding.

A trail of ants kept moving past Nathan's right hand, carrying tiny bits of grass and seeds up the tree. He *would* pick a tree with an ant den inside. Damn but he hated bugs.

All of a sudden he heard movement about a hundred yards down the slope and grew still while his heart began to pound. They were coming, but not by the road. He glanced once in Moses's direction and could tell that Moses had heard them, too.

His rifle was ready, and he knew the drill. Shoot to kill.

The hair on Silas's neck was standing at attention. He felt like a sitting duck, even though they had good cover among the thickly growing trees.

His men were moving in a grid pattern, twenty yards between them as they walked up the mountain. They'd come at least a mile and a half without encountering anyone or anything unusual, but he still felt uneasy. They were making good time, but going in on foot had not been part of the plan, and they were already nearly an hour behind schedule.

Suddenly something dropped to the ground a short distance ahead, and he gave the signal to stop, quickly scanning the area. Taggert signaled, then pointed up at a small squirrel that was jumping from tree to tree above their heads as fast as it could go.

Silas nodded, scanned the area one last time, then gave the signal for them to continue. It was his best guess that they were still about another mile and a half from the target. His plan was to encircle the house so no one could escape, then turn Farmer and his rocket launcher loose to blow the place and everyone in it to kingdom come.

All of a sudden there was a loud crack, like a bolt of lightning striking too close. Bordain was down with a neat round hole in his forehead, the back of his head splattering on the tree behind him as he fell.

Another shot from a different direction knocked Emerson backward so hard the others heard bones break as someone hit the trees behind them.

Silas was shouting orders as they scattered and began to fire, but it soon became apparent that they were just wasting ammunition, because no one was firing back.

Silas was flat on the ground with his rifle still in his hands. He hadn't seen anything to shoot at but trees. He keyed up his walkie and began calling roll.

"Warwick."

"Here!"

"Farmer!"

"Here."

"Taggert!"

"Here."

"Emerson!"

No answer.

"Bordain!"

No answer.

Silas was getting nervous. He was down three men and had yet to see his enemy's face.

After about fifteen minutes without making a move or a sound, they retreated a hundred yards downhill and took another trail, moving on the diagonal toward where they needed to go.

Uncle Fagan's boys had heard the gunfire. It made what they'd set out to do a reality. People could be dying. They hoped to God it wasn't any of them.

Mike notched an arrow and then crouched down in a thicket just off the trail. If they came his way, he would take out the last one in line and then disappear.

If they did what Quinn had predicted, though, they would have shifted their trail again after the gun battle, and that would take them to where Pudge was waiting at his new location.

Pudge took a deep breath, remembering his cousin Beth and how the Feds had nearly gotten her killed, and proceeded to be pissed all over again. That was all it took. He was ready and waiting for whoever came up the deer trail.

Silas wanted to run straight for the target, turn Farmer loose with the rocket launcher and get the hell off this mountain, but they couldn't take a chance on walking into another ambush. However, if they did, at least this time they would be ready with something more than bullets. Grenades weren't particular. They took out anything within the radius of the blast. Fucking hillbillies. They wanted to play war? He would show them what war was all about.

They were less than three-quarters of a mile from their target when Silas heard a grunt, then a thud.

He pivoted in a crouch, saw Warwick on the ground with an arrow sticking out of his back, and pulled the pin on his grenade and flung it as far as it would go.

"Take that, you motherfuckers!" he screamed, as the other men let fly with grenades of their own.

Quinn had set himself up as the last line of defense between Beth and the attack, but when he heard the grenades go off, it sent him right back into a war he thought he'd left behind.

He hit the ground with his rifle in his hands and started to belly-crawl into the hole he'd dug for himself. He flopped down inside, then rose up just enough to aim the rifle over the edge, took a deep breath and blocked out everything but the enemy who was coming closer.

When the first sounds of gunfire erupted, Beth panicked. Like Quinn, the sounds had thrown her back into a mind-set where the only thing she knew how to do was run.

Ryal caught her coming down the hall and spun her up against the wall, his gaze frantic.

"Beth! Stop! All that means is they're out there, not in here. Quinn and the men have them pinned down away from the house. That's what we want, honey. That was the plan, remember?"

Beth was looking at Ryal's face. She saw his lips moving, but she couldn't focus on what he was saying for the sound of gunshots echoing in her head.

Once again Ryal was facing how deeply she'd been traumatized by what happened to her before they got her to Kentucky. Her eyes were wide, her pupils fixed and dilated, and he could feel every muscle in her body trembling. Talking hadn't worked, so he wrapped his arms around her and pulled her close against his chest.

"It's me, Bethie. It's me. You're not in L.A. anymore, you're home with your family and with me, back in Kentucky. Hear me, baby . . . we won't let you get hurt."

He looked over his shoulder and out through the living room window, scanning the clearing for signs of anyone coming close. He was worried about his cousins, and about Quinn. Part of him wished he was out there blasting the bastards to hell for the fear they'd put in Beth's heart, but he wouldn't leave — *couldn't* leave, not and count on her being there when he came back.

"Come with me, love," he urged. "I need to keep watch at the window. You can watch with me. See all that open space between the house and the trees? There's no way they can get here without me taking them out. No one's that fast, okay?"

Still shaking, but reluctant to be alone, she let him lead her into the living room, where they crouched at the window. At his bidding, she dropped to her knees beside him, but she didn't look out. She kept her gaze on Ryal. He was her anchor to sanity, and she had to keep him in sight.

Silas was hunched over and running, with Taggert on his left and Farmer on his right. Farmer was carrying the rocket launcher cradled in one arm and his rifle in the other, while bullets and arrows flew past their heads and into the trees beside them.

The roof of the house was now visible to them. All Silas needed was to get Farmer close enough to take aim, and then the rocket would do the rest. Once that fireball went up, their pursuers wouldn't be interested in taking them out. They would be too busy trying to find survivors.

From the corner of his eye he saw Taggert vault over a downed tree and then suddenly drop out of sight. A second later, Taggert let out a scream that caused Silas to stumble. The scream continued in one long, frenzied breath, until it finally dissolved into a bubbling gurgle and went silent.

Silas's gut roiled. He was beginning to realize he might not live through this foray after all, and it didn't make sense. How could a bunch of mountain men outwit and outfight seasoned soldiers? All of a sudden he and Farmer reached the edge of the forest and got a full view of the house, and he spun and hit the ground on his knees.

"Set up here!" he yelled, as he began shooting into the trees behind them to give Farmer some cover.

Farmer skidded to a halt, loaded the rocket and swung around to take aim.

At that moment Farmer jerked, then screamed, as his leg went out from under him. He fell with the loaded rocket launcher trapped beneath him. He rolled over and tried to stand up, only to see the lower half of his leg lying on the ground beside him. He passed out before the pain reached his brain.

Silas screamed in rage and emptied his automatic into the woods behind him in a sweeping spray of bullets.

Vance Walker was coming up on the right behind Quinn when a bullet caught his shoulder and spun him backward onto the ground.

Nathan had the shooter in his sights and pulled the trigger just as one of Silas's bullets cut through his side. He cried out as he fell, and then belly-crawled back into cover while trying to quell the gush of blood between his fingers.

The bullet Nathan fired missed Silas by a hair, but it amped Silas's need for retribution. His men were down and he might be next, but he wasn't about to kick the bucket alone. He was taking that damn house and its occupants with him.

It didn't take long for Silas to assess the damage. Farmer was unconscious, and from the looks of the blood gushing from his leg, he wasn't going to wake up. He rolled Farmer off the rocket launcher, swung it to his shoulder and took aim. He squeezed the trigger a millisecond before Quinn's bullet went through the back of his head. He was dead before he hit the ground, but the rocket had been launched.

"No, no, no!" Quinn roared, but it was too late.

The rocket was only seconds away from its target as Quinn went running toward the house.

"Get out! Get out!" he kept screaming, and then the house went up in a ball of flame.

Ryal saw two armed strangers pause in the

trees opposite the house, which meant at least two attackers had gotten past Quinn and everyone else.

That wasn't good.

He thrust his rifle out the window and took aim, although he feared he was too far away for a clear shot. Just as he was about to squeeze the trigger, the man dropped to the ground.

Good, Ryal thought, and tried to get a shot off at the other one, but the man was on his knees and the grass between them was too tall.

The gunfire was constant, and he felt helpless so far away, unable to watch his brother's back or aid any of his cousins.

He could feel Beth clutching his leg, but she hadn't made a sound.

All of a sudden he saw the last man bend down, and when he came up standing, he had something big resting on his shoulder. The moment Ryal realized what it was, he grabbed Beth by the arm and yanked her to her feet.

"Run, Bethie! Run with me, and don't look back!"

They flew through the house and out the back door, clearing the steps in one leap. They were less than thirty yards from the house when it went up in a ball of flame.

The impact of the explosion sent them flying, and then burning debris began raining down around them. He heard Beth groan, then saw her starting to move. He shoved her back down and rolled on top of her just before the world went black.

The house was a wall of flames by the time Quinn arrived. His chest was heaving, and there was a bullet wound in his thigh he had yet to acknowledge. He wouldn't let himself believe they were dead. Ryal was smarter than that. He would have seen. They would have run. Surely to God they would have run.

He turned in a circle. His cousins were coming out of the trees and running toward the house. By his count, two were missing. He wouldn't let himself go there. Not yet.

He kept thinking it was a blessing that they'd gotten so much rain or this explosion would have set the mountain ablaze.

He stomped out two small fires in the grass as he circled the burning house, telling himself that any minute now he would see Ryal and Beth coming toward him hand in hand and it would be over. The war on Rebel Ridge would be over.

But when he reached the back of the house, he saw nothing but burning debris.

Tears clogged the back of his throat and blurred his vision when he called out, "Ryal! Beth! Answer me! Where are you?"

The fire was roaring at his back as he walked farther toward the woods.

"Ryal! Beth!"

Then he heard a sound — the sound of someone crying.

"Beth! Bethie! It's me, Quinn! Where are you, honey?"

This time the sound was clearer. It was Beth, and she was calling out for help.

He started running and was almost on them before he saw Ryal's body lying in the tall grass, with Beth's legs caught beneath it.

"I'm here, Beth. I'm here," Quinn said, as he dropped to his knees. He pulled Ryal's motionless body off her and began checking for his pulse.

Beth sat up, sobbing and grabbing at Ryal's shoulder. "Ryal! Can you hear me? Oh, my God, Quinn, is he breathing? Can you feel a pulse? Please, God, don't let him be dead."

Quinn rocked back on his heels. "He has a pulse."

Beth couldn't quit shaking. "We got out before it blew," she said. "But the debris! It was falling and burning, and he rolled on top of me. I felt him jerk, and then he didn't move."

Quinn reached for Ryal's head to check for injuries, and his hand came away covered in blood.

"Shit." Head injuries were the scary ones. Too often you didn't know how bad they were until it was too late.

The moment Beth saw the blood, calm swept through her. She began digging in Ryal's pockets for the keys to his truck, which was only a short distance away. She dropped the keys in Quinn's hand.

"Get the truck. We need to get him to a doctor."

"I'm missing two more," Quinn said. "Let me check on them. We need to take them all in one trip."

"Hurry," Beth said. "And give me your shirt before you go."

Quinn peeled the T-shirt over his head and dropped it into her lap, then took off at a lope as Beth folded the shirt into a thick pad and pressed it against the back of Ryal's head.

The waiting room at St. Benedict Hospital in Mount Sterling was standing-room only, with more than twenty members of the Walker clan and half that many again who were Venables waiting for word of their loved ones. They had gathered silently around Beth, who was visibly shaken, but without pushing her for answers. It was the only way they knew to show their support without sending her over the edge.

What they knew so far was that Vance was out of surgery. The bullet that hit his shoulder had missed the arteries but broken his collarbone and torn some muscle. Still, he would have a complete recovery.

Nathan was still in the E.R. waiting to be taken to surgery. The wound in his side had been a through-and-through and wasn't deemed life-threatening.

Quinn was on an exam table in the E.R., waiting to get the gunshot to his thigh checked out, although he kept insisting it was nothing but a flesh wound.

Ryal was the only one who was still unconscious. He'd been in X-ray for nearly an hour, and Beth was frantic. Every time someone looked at her, she felt the weight of guilt on her shoulders and kept bursting into tears. Despite James's and Granny Lou's best efforts to reassure her that this wasn't her fault, she knew better. None of this would have happened if she hadn't come home.

As a matter of course, the hospital had

reported the gunshot wounds to the police, which had brought a detective named Callaway to the scene.

He began hammering Beth with questions she didn't know how to answer. She was terrified the local newspaper would get wind of the mess and then word would reach the national media, which would be disastrous. When the detective informed Beth that he was taking her down to headquarters for further questioning, she knew she had to explain.

"Wait. I'll tell you, but not here. Somewhere private."

"Want me to go with you?" Lou asked.

"I'm fine, Granny Lou. Just wait here in case we get news about Ryal before I get back."

"Take him to the chapel," Lou said, as she gave the man a warning glare. "It's a few doors down this hall and on your right."

"Yes, ma'am," Beth said, then turned to Callaway. "Will you please hear me out before you do anything else?"

"I'll give you five minutes, and then we're going downtown."

Beth couldn't let that happen. She had to trust this man, even when every instinct she had said not to. As soon as they got inside the chapel, she hurried all the way to the front and sat down.

Callaway followed. "All right. You've got your five minutes. Now talk."

Beth folded her hands in her lap to keep them from shaking, but there was nothing she could do about the tremor in her voice.

"You need to call Special Agent Ames with the FBI. He's in California. They're building a case against a man named Ike Pappas, who's the head of an organized-crime gang out of L.A. I had the misfortune to witness him murder his wife."

Callaway's eyes widened. He clearly hadn't expected anything like this.

"The Los Angeles police and the Feds had me in protective custody, and during that time had to move me to three different safe houses. And every time they moved me, Pappas's men found me and shot up the place, and each time it was a miracle I lived through it. When the third house was breeched, I ran. I couldn't trust the LAPD anymore. I couldn't trust the FBI. Ike Pappas is a very powerful man, with snitches everywhere. There was nowhere to hide and no one to trust, so I came home. My people have been keeping me hidden up on Rebel Ridge until today, when Pappas's hired killers found me again. From what I was told, we nearly had them whipped when one of them pulled out a rocket launcher. After that, everything went up in a ball of fire when they shot the rocket into the house where I'd been hiding. Ryal got me out just in time, or we would have died in the explosion. The seven men who attacked us are all dead, so they can't tell a different story, and I need Pappas to think I died in the fire. I don't have enough luck left to live through a fifth attack. Please, Detective . . . so many people have died or been hurt trying to keep me alive to testify, even my best friend, Sarah. I can't let all that effort be in vain."

Callaway's mouth was open. He had the good sense to close it when she finally stopped talking.

"You're serious, aren't you?" he asked.

Beth sighed, and then looked down at her hands and turned them palm up.

Only the worst of the wounds that she'd suffered were still healing. The rest had already turned into scars.

"This is what happened to me the night I ran. I haven't been able to use them at all until the last couple of days, and as you can see, they're still not healed. Listen to me, please. I have cousins and a fiancé who nearly died trying to keep me safe, and if you take me downtown the media will hear about it. If Pappas finds out I'm still alive, you might as well shoot me yourself and save me some grief. This is my life we're talking about. Just call Ames, but please don't tell him where I'm at. Tell him I'm still alive, but to tell everyone else that I'm dead. I'll still testify, but I'm not coming back until the trial."

Callaway took out his phone and made the call.

TWENTY

Special Agent Ames was on his way to a crime scene when his cell phone rang. Hearing a man identify himself as a homicide detective from Mount Sterling, Kentucky, was surprising, but when he mentioned Beth Venable's name, Ames's heart sank. All he could think was that she was dead. He pulled off to the side of the road to finish the call.

"Yes, I know Beth Venable. Has something happened to her? Is she okay?"

"She's all right," Callaway said. "Although some of her associates were not as fortunate. Is it true that she witnessed a murder? Is she really going to testify for the FBI?"

Ames was stunned. "She told you all that? Why?"

"Because seven men tried to kill her today and they're all dead. The state police are in the process of recovering the bodies as we speak. One was in a ravine off the side of a mountain with an arrow in his neck. One was pulled out of a pit lined with stakes, and the others were shot, some with arrows. Real crazy shit. Four of her family members are in the hospital being treated for gunshot wounds. The hospital called the police, which, of course, is protocol in gunshot victims. That's how I got mixed up in this mess."

Ames was impressed by the ingenuity of the people who'd been protecting Beth. "The men who attacked her . . . I don't suppose you know who they were?"

"She says they were sent by a man named Ike —"

"Pappas," Ames said, finishing the sentence. "We're building a case against him, and she's our prime witness. Can I talk to her? Is she there?"

Callaway held out the phone to Beth. "He wants to talk to you."

Beth didn't want to talk. She wanted to get back to the family and find out if Ryal was going to be okay. But just as it had been since this madness began, no one in authority much cared what she wanted. She took the phone.

"I'll make this brief. Seven men tried to kill me today, and they're dead — all of them — because my family saved me. Four of my people were hurt, one has yet to wake up, and if anything happens to him, I'm coming back to L.A. and killing Ike Pappas myself. If you want this trial to happen, then you tell the world we're all dead. Tell them thieves broke into the house and caused the explosion that killed us all. Then, when the trial is set to begin, you call Detective Callaway, because I'm not talking to you again. He'll get word to me, and I'll be there. I have to go now."

She handed the phone to Callaway and walked out of the chapel. Callaway started to call her back, then let her go and started finalizing details with Ames.

When Beth got back to the waiting room, her grandmother saw her and hurried over to her.

"Glad you're back, sugar. Ryal woke up. He's asking for you, and they can't calm him down."

Beth raced down the hall, and even before she got to the E.R., she could hear the panic in Ryal's voice. She hurried past the nurses' desk and over to the examining room, then pulled back the curtain. Ryal was pushing an orderly away while a male nurse was trying to restrain him.

"Ryal Walker, you stop that this instant," Beth said, as she pushed the two men aside, then softened her words by putting her arms around his neck. "I'm right here, my sweet man. I'm right here."

"I'll be back," the nurse said, as Ryal made a frantic grab for Beth's shoulders, then held her close.

"Oh, my God, Beth. I thought you were dead and they just wouldn't tell me."

The kiss they shared was poignantly brief — a brush of lips, a sigh of relief. Then Beth took charge.

"Lie back down. You have six stitches in the back of your head, and you've been unconscious for almost two hours. I'm the one who's been in a panic thinking I'd gotten you killed."

Ryal lay back against the pillow but kept a grip on her hand.

"I have a hard head," he said.

Beth sighed. "That's what the doctor told us after he'd seen your X-rays. Quinn said he could vouch for that."

Ryal's eyes darkened. "Quinn's all right?"

"He will be. He took a bullet in his right thigh, but it was just a flesh wound. Vance was shot in the shoulder. It broke his collarbone, but he's out of surgery and expected to recover just fine. Nathan was shot in the side, but the bullet didn't hit anything vital."

"Thank God," Ryal said.

Beth thought of the prayers Granny Lou had sent up and held Ryal's hand a little tighter.

"Yes, we can all thank Him," she said. "Now be still and be well. The sooner we can get away from here without causing any more scenes, the better."

More than twenty-four hours had passed since Ike had spoken to Silas. He kept waiting for the phone to ring to tell him the job was finished, but with every passing hour he feared the worst.

It wasn't until bedtime the next night, when he caught the national news on CNN, that he learned what had happened.

They were broadcasting a story about five members of a family who'd all died in an explosion in rural Kentucky. He fumbled for the remote and quickly upped the volume, listening intently as the details were revealed.

"*. . . tragedy on a mountain called Rebel Ridge in rural Kentucky. Five members of the Venable family, people local to the area, were all killed by an explosion as thieves invaded their home. The thieves were caught in the* *explosion that they triggered and perished along with the family. Identifications of the perpetrators are still pending. The Venable family has announced that there will be no funeral services, but that sometime later a memorial service will be held."*

Ike leaned against the headboard and grinned. A huge weight had just been lifted off his shoulders. Let the cops try to pin Lorena's murder on him now.

He still hadn't heard from Adam, and the urge to talk to him again was overwhelming. It was almost midnight, but what the hell, Ike thought. Adam was like his old man — both were night owls. Maybe this time when he called, his son would answer.

Adam wasn't awake. In fact he'd been in bed and asleep since a little after 10:00 p.m., and when his cell started ringing, he woke abruptly. Without thinking, he almost answered it then roused enough to check the caller ID. When he saw who was calling, he let it ring and was about to go back to sleep when a shadow in the corner of the room suddenly moved and came toward him.

He reached for his gun, but it was too late. The room was flooded in lights, revealing Amato and Staley, two lieutenants from his father's syndicate. He'd known something like this might happen, but it didn't change his decision about what he'd done. He sat up in bed and lifted his chin in a defiant gesture.

"So, is this a social call or a cleanup operation? I ask because I need to pee. If you're here to talk, I'm gonna take a piss. If you came to shoot me, get it over with and I'll just pee the bed when I die."

Amato's eyes narrowed as he waved Adam toward the adjoining bathroom. "Just leave the door open."

Adam threw back the covers and got up, sporting an impressive erection he was about to pee off. He walked across the room without a hint of reluctance to be naked in front of two men. As soon as he was finished, he washed and came back, picked up a pair of sweatpants and pulled them on, then sat down on the side of the bed. It was their party, so he waited for them to start talking.

Amato was a short, heavyset man who'd worked his way up through the organization the hard way. Staley's old man had been a bagman and then a cleanup man before he was killed.

Amato didn't know Adam all that well, but he knew what he'd done. They all knew, and he and Staley had been the ones chosen to sort it out.

"You went to the Feds," Amato said.

Adam's eyes narrowed. "I don't know why it surprises me that you know, but it doesn't matter. You would have found out soon enough anyway."

"Why turn on your own kind?" Staley asked.

Adam's face underwent a dark transformation as he stood abruptly, his hands curled into fists. His nostrils flared as a dark flush spread beneath the skin.

"Because my kind turned first, goddamn it!"

Amato nodded slowly. "So it is about your mother's murder."

"Hell yes, it's about my mother's murder. My father . . . my own fucking father cut her throat and left her to bleed out on the living room rug, then lied about it to my face. If that's the kind of people I belong to, then I just abdicated the fucking throne. She was my mother, for God's sake. My *mother!*"

He was so angry his whole body was shaking. The urge to hit something or someone was overwhelming.

Amato held up his hand in a calming gesture. "We're not saying it was right. What we want to know is how much are you going to tell the Feds in return for a conviction in Lorena's death?"

Adam moved closer until he could feel Amato's breath on his face. "I'm gonna tell them whatever the fuck they want to know, so if you boys have any exit strategies planned, you better take them. And just so you know, even if you kill me tonight, it won't stop what's already happening. They have hard evidence," he lied. "I expected this to happen, so I made sure they'd have what they needed."

Staley sighed. "It's a damn shame you turned rat on us. You're focused and hard-nosed . . . as hard-nosed as they come, to turn on one of your own. You would have been a good man to run the organization."

"Yeah, like father like son, right?" Adam said. "We're all about betrayal and deception. So do whatever my father told you to do or get the hell out of my house."

"Just so you know, your father had nothing to do with this visit. When we took a vote, it wasn't you we wanted to eliminate, it was your old man. He crossed a line and put us all in jeopardy."

"So there's a hit out on him and not me?"

Staley smiled. "Weird how that happens sometimes, isn't it? We just needed to know where you stood. Now we know — and thanks for the heads-up. We'll let ourselves out," he added, and as they left the room, they turned out the lights, leaving him standing in the dark.

Adam heard the front door slam, then the sound of a car engine firing. He walked to the window and watched until the taillights were no longer visible, then sat down on the side of the bed and began to shake.

It was just after 10:00 a.m. when Special Agent Ames and Federal Prosecutor Ashton Caine walked into LAPD headquarters. Ames flashed his badge, informing the desk sergeant that Captain Tatum in Homicide was expecting them, at which time they were promptly escorted to the captain's office.

Tatum was still smarting from the Feds taking over their murder case, so his greeting was somewhat clipped when he offered them a seat.

Ames sat. "I'll get straight to the point. The FBI no longer wishes to be in charge of Lorena Pappas's murder. We're turning all the evidence and authority back over to you. We're asking you to issue a warrant for Ike Pappas's arrest, and then to proceed with a trial as soon as possible. A judge will be made available ASAP, so tell your D.A. to get it in gear before everything goes sour."

Tatum was stunned. "What's going on? First you usurp our jurisdiction in the case, and now you dump it back in our lap when everything's gone cold and the witness is missing? I don't think so."

Ames glanced at the prosecutor.

Ashton Caine nodded and took it from there.

"Nothing is cold. The case is airtight, despite what you believe. Bring the charges. We need him convicted. It's part of a deal we've made with someone who's going to turn state's evidence on Pappas and his entire organization. We have the opportunity to take down at least a half dozen of Pappas's lieutenants, maybe more, and put them away for life. But we need to distance ourselves from this crime, so that it's prosecuted first."

Tatum was speechless. "Then use your witness and forget trying to prosecute for the ex-wife's murder. He'll still be behind bars, which is what's most important, don't you think?"

Caine shrugged, as if to say this part was out of his hands. "We can't. If there's no conviction for Lorena Pappas's murder, our deal with the witness goes south. Justice for the dead woman nets justice for the country."

"How do you expect us to make that stick? You know as well as I do that a good lawyer can take the DNA we found and come up with any number of reasons as to how it got there. And there's still no plausible explanation for why he'd want her dead. They seemed to have a good relationship."

Caine glanced at Ames, who hesitated, then gave him a nod.

Caine continued to explain. "*Seemed* is the operative word here. There's something we know about Lorena Pappas that you don't. She learned he'd brought their son into the organization, something he'd promised her years ago that he would never do. When she found out, she was shocked, hurt, then furious. So angry, in fact, that she agreed to testify against him, even with the understanding that her son would be indicted, too, to get even for what he'd done. We think he found out about it, and that was his motive for murder."

"You *think?* Damn it, Caine. You know as well as I do that won't fly. Without the witness —"

Ames interrupted. "Just file the damn charges and bring him to trial. You'll have your witness. But if I hear one word of what we've said here today from anyone else's lips, then I'll know you talked. And if that happens, I'll kill you myself."

Caine looked startled.

Tatum was furious. "How dare you threaten my life?"

Ames slapped the desk. "I dare because someone in your organization was feeding info to Ike Pappas and nearly got the witness killed. Yes, I know we had the same problem, but I've made it my personal business to make sure I'm the only one in the FBI who knows anything about her now, and I'm damn sure not talking. For all I know it was you who leaked the info about her in the first place. I didn't want to come to you with any of this, but Mr. Caine was presented with a deal he wouldn't refuse, only it's tricky, and that leaves me following orders, which are to inform you that you still have a witness. Leave her name on the records so the defense can't say we pulled a fast one and slipped in a witness they didn't know about. Don't worry. They won't argue, because they think they know something we don't. Now file your damned charges, and file them fast."

Ike was getting out of the shower when he heard a loud, constant knocking at his bedroom door. He grabbed a towel, wrapping it around his waist as he strode to the door.

"Damn it, Beatrice, can't a man —"

It wasn't Beatrice. It was the LAPD.

"Get dressed, Pappas," the detective said, as he grabbed the towel from around Ike's waist and walked him back into the room with four other officers following.

"What the hell's going on?" Ike yelled. "You have no right to —"

"Ike Pappas, you're under arrest for the murder of Lorena Pappas. You have the right to remain silent. Anything you say can and will be held against —"

Ike's thoughts were in free fall. What the hell was happening here? There was no way this charge would stick. Not now, with Beth Venable dead.

"I thought the FBI was in charge of that case," he said.

"They gave it back," the detective said. "Lucky us. Now get some clothes on or we'll take you in as is."

Ike was furious as he yanked on clothes. He was about to put his cell phone in his pocket when the detective took it out of his hands.

"You get one call after you're booked. You can call your lawyer from jail, just like everyone else."

Ryal had been home for nearly three days and still woke up with a sense of wonder that he was alive and Beth was sleeping at his side. The worst of his concussion had passed, leaving him with little more than a lingering headache. The stitches in his head were sore but healing, as were the multitude of bruises on his back and legs caused by the falling debris.

He was still under doctor's orders to take it easy, so he was on forced hiatus from the woodworking shop, even though it felt so good to be home. Beth was a quiet but persistent presence in the house. Callaway had called her that morning to inform them that Ike Pappas was in custody. It was the best news they'd had in days.

Something had changed in her after the explosion, and he couldn't quite put his finger on it. She didn't cry as much anymore, and she seemed more at peace with what still lay ahead.

At her insistence, Quinn had come home with them, too, and was sleeping in Ryal's extra bedroom.

He'd let her believe he was there because he needed to be babied until his leg healed, but in truth he had no intention of moving out until the trial, which was scheduled to begin in two weeks, was over. Even if Pappas had finally been arrested, that didn't mean all was well.

Ryal's family, as well as the Venables, made all kinds of excuses to stop by and check on the men, but it was evident every time they came that a good portion of their concern was for Beth.

All of the Venable cousins she used to play with as a child had come together, and officially welcomed her back with open arms and a vow of secrecy as to where she was that she knew they would not break. He could tell that it had been a life-altering moment she wouldn't forget.

But he also knew that her entire focus was on the approaching trial, where she would soon come face-to-face with the man who'd tried so hard to kill her.

TWENTY-ONE

The Criminal Justice Courthouse in L.A. was the site of a media frenzy. Not since the O. J. Simpson trial had so many news crews been in one place at one time. Yesterday had been opening statements in the Ike Pappas murder trial. When all the talk was over and the lawyers had played all the games possible with the laws of the land, Ike would face a jury of his peers for the murder of his ex-wife.

Cameras were not allowed in the courtroom, which was good news as far as Beth was concerned. She'd arrived in Los Angeles last night after dark and had been taken to the courthouse the next morning, then sequestered in a small room near the courtroom with four federal agents as guards.

But it wasn't the presence of the agents that gave her a sense of security. That was thanks to Ryal and Quinn and Uncle Will, who were gathered around her. Those were the men who'd already proven their worth and devotion.

Quinn's leg was healed, except for a faint limp when he was tired, and Ryal would bear a scar on the back of his head for the rest of his life.

The moment Will had learned she'd been attacked on Rebel Ridge, he'd driven back to Kentucky, parked his semi down in Boone's Gap and come home to stay with his mother, Lou, and be nearby in case Beth was in need.

Like the Walker brothers, Will's life had been put on hold for Beth until this trial was over and they knew for certain she would finally be safe.

Ryal kept watching Beth's face, looking for signs of an emotional breakdown, but she seemed calm. Almost too calm. He put his arm around her and pulled her close.

"How are you feeling, honey?"

"I'm okay. I'm ready for this to be over, though."

"We will be right there in the room with you when you're testifying," Will said. "The prosecution allowed your request that we come in with you and take seats he's providing at the back of the room."

"Good. I want to know my cheering section is nearby."

Ryal's eyes narrowed. "I feel like more than your cheering section. I'm still locked in protection mode. What I wouldn't give to get my hands around that son of a bitch Pappas's neck and give it a quick twist."

Quinn smiled briefly. "Dang, brother. That sounds like something I would have said." He winked at Beth. "You've turned him into a real butt-buster."

Ryal snorted softly.

Beth grinned.

And then the door opened and a bailiff stepped into the room. "Beth Venable?"

"I'm here," she said.

"They're ready for you, ma'am."

Assistant D.A. Benton Frame represented the prosecution and he was ready to get the show started. He knew what he was about to do was going to start a verbal riot, but he was prepared.

He stood and addressed the court. "Your Honor, we call our first witness, Lilabeth Venable, to the stand."

The doors at the back of the room swung inward. Two federal agents walked in, then stepped aside, leaving the aisle open as Will and Quinn entered, then moved off to their seats at the back of the room. Ryal walked in beside Beth and then joined her family, leaving the other two federal agents to follow her down the aisle.

As soon as she reached the stand to be sworn in, they took positions against the walls near the front of the courtroom. The judge was well aware of what it had taken to ensure this woman's presence in the courtroom today and was bending some of his normal rules by even letting this showy arrival occur.

Ike's heart had stopped the minute he'd heard her name, and he leaned in head to head with his lawyer, Sal Moreno.

The minute she was sworn in and took a seat, Moreno stood up.

"Your Honor, I object! We had no knowledge of —"

Frame was waiting for that. "On the contrary, Your Honor. Her name has always been on the witness list."

"But we thought —" Moreno stopped without finishing the sentence, but he'd introduced the notion.

"Thought what? That she was dead?" Frame fired back. "That's what your client intended to happen when he put a hit out on her life. That's what he thought had finally happened when he blew up the house she was in!"

The judge was pounding his gavel sharply

against his desk.

"Order in the court! I will have order in the court! Gentlemen, approach the bench. *Now.*"

Moreno glanced over his shoulder at Ike, who was visibly pale. His mind was racing as he began sorting through his options before this trial went any further.

As soon as they reached the bench, the judge covered the microphone and leaned over.

"Mr. Moreno, was the witness's name on the list provided by the prosecution?"

"Yes, Your Honor, but —"

The judge stopped him with a look.

"Mr. Frame, do you have any other surprises up your sleeve of which the defense is unaware?"

"No, Your Honor."

"Then we will proceed. Return to your tables. Mr. Frame, you may begin questioning."

"Thank you, Your Honor," Frame said, and then walked over to the witness box where Beth was sitting.

This was the first time he'd seen or spoken to Beth Venable, and his whole case hinged upon whether or not she fingered Pappas. He was ticked about the rules he'd been given by the federal prosecutor's office.

After all, it was his career that would tank, not theirs, if Beth Venable got scared and reneged on what she claimed to have seen.

Then he looked into her eyes, and what he saw reassured him as he took a deep breath and began the routine of establishing name, location, why she'd been there and the time at which she'd witnessed the crime.

Beth answered each question with a clear voice and a calm demeanor, but he knew she was nervous because her hands were shaking in her lap. That was when his estimation of her fortitude hitched up another notch.

"Now to the question on everyone's mind," Frame said. "Miss Venable, do you recognize anyone in the courtroom as the person you saw murder Lorena Pappas?"

Beth turned her head. It was the first time she'd allowed herself to look at the man sitting at the defense table, but she recognized him instantly. There was a moment when their eyes met, and she saw the fire and anger on Ike Pappas's face. Even now he was trying to intimidate her into changing her story.

She looked back at Benton Frame and then answered. "Yes, I do." She pointed at Ike. "It's the baldheaded man sitting beside the defense attorney."

"Are you referring to Ike Pappas, the man on trial?"

"Yes. I saw them fighting. I saw her slap him. I saw him shove her back. She yelled, and then he slit her throat so fast I didn't know what had happened until I saw the arterial blood spray hit the window."

The room erupted into shouting and arguing, and the guards started escorting people out of the room, while one federal agent took a stance beside the judge and another by her.

All the while Ike sat silently, his stare fixed on Beth's face.

Then, all of a sudden, she turned and faced him again, and lifted her chin, as if to say, *I beat you after all.*

It was Ike who finally looked away.

That night Ryal made love to Beth in the Wilshire Hotel while sirens sounded and horns honked and lights were flashing from the streets down below.

It was the kind of slow, gentle sex that comes from familiarity — a bonding that had little to do with passion and more to do with gratitude for still being alive.

When it was over, Beth refused to turn him loose, wrapping her arms around Ryal's neck. "I love you, my sweet man. Rest well. Tomorrow will be the first day of the rest of our lives."

Ryal kissed the hollow at the base of her throat. "Ah, Bethie, I love you, too. You always did take my breath away."

"I want to go home tomorrow."

"Home as in your apartment here in L.A.?"

"No. Home as in Rebel Ridge — with you. I've already hired a moving company to pack up my things and ship them to Kentucky. My landlord let me out of my lease, and I'm sure I have the FBI to thank for that. After the quiet nights of our mountain home, I feel assaulted by all this noise."

"*You* feel assaulted? I feel like I'm living in the middle of a *Star Wars* movie. I don't know how in hell people live and sleep in this mess, but I'm forever grateful I do not."

Beth held him tighter, pulled him closer, remembering when she thought he'd died protecting her from the blast.

Ryal propped himself up on his elbow. "Are you sure you know what you're doing? Life isn't fancy where we come from. Life is hard. Money is even harder to come by."

Beth put a finger on his lips, as if to hush his concerns. "Life couldn't have been any harder here, and money isn't everything. I have my work. You have yours. We'll be fine."

"Then all we have to do when we get back is plan a wedding."

"Pretty much," she said, and then closed her eyes. "Good night, sweet man. See you in the morning."

Ryal fell asleep smiling.

The verdict in Ike Pappas's trial came in early the next morning, and he was brought back to court to hear it read.

As early as it was, the room was packed. All eyes were on the door through which the judge would enter. Ike wasn't expecting any miracles. The best Moreno could hope for was a conviction for manslaughter rather than premeditated murder.

And then the door opened.

"All rise for the Honorable Judge Collins."

Ike became acutely aware of everything around him — the shuffling of feet as people stood, a whispered aside, the faint scream of a siren somewhere off in the distance. Someone coughed. Someone else blew their nose. It was as if time was passing in slow motion.

Then he heard the judge direct him and his lawyer to stand. A bead of sweat ran out from behind his ear and into the collar of his shirt as the foreman of the jury stood up and read the verdict aloud.

All he heard was ". . . find Ike Pappas guilty of first-degree murder," and then sound ended, as if someone had turned off a switch.

Ike shuddered. He didn't want to die behind bars.

Moments later he was handcuffed, then led by two armed policemen out of the courtroom through a side door into a hallway. So he was off to jail. The sentencing phase would be next. He was trying to figure out how that would play out when two men in suits appeared out of nowhere and took control. They introduced themselves as federal agents and waved an arrest warrant under his nose, and then one grabbed his right arm and the other grabbed his left.

"What the hell's going on?" Ike spluttered. "The trial is over."

"That trial was for the murder of your ex-wife. The federal government wants a piece of your ass, too. Ike Pappas, you are under arrest for the murders of Antonio Melani, Mario Cruz, Harold White, Angus Moran, Wanda Henderson and Thomas Elliot. You are also charged with one hundred and twenty-seven counts of fraud, seven counts of interstate wiretapping, ten counts of forced prostitution, fifteen counts of illegal gambling —"

Ike felt the blood draining out of his head and for a moment thought he would faint. He stumbled, then stopped. "What the fuck's going on here?"

The agents yanked him off balance, forcing him to keep walking as they continued to rattle off the charges against him, but he wouldn't listen.

"You're crazy. I don't know what you're talking about, and you can't prove any —"

He caught movement from the corner of his eye and turned in time to see his son step out into the hall. He hadn't seen him in weeks, and he didn't immediately tie his unexpected presence to what was happening.

"Adam! Did they arrest you, too?"

"No. I won't be arrested. That was part of the deal."

Ike frowned. "I don't get it. Part of what —" Then he froze. "You turned me in?"

Adam shrugged. "Just finishing what my mother started."

Ike struggled to draw breath. "The syndicate will kill you, you know."

"No. In fact, we've already had that conversation. Truth is, they're more pissed at you than they are at me. I'd watch my back in prison if I were you."

It was the disdain in Adam's voice that yanked Ike out of his state of shock.

"I don't fucking believe you!" he screamed.

Adam's voice rose louder and higher. "Then believe this, you sorry son of a bitch! You better say your prayers and make nice with God . . . if you still believe in Him, that is."

Ike felt as if his head was going to explode. He wanted to squeeze Adam's neck until his eyes bugged out and his breath stopped.

"You can't prove anything. They won't believe you. They'll think you're just lying to get back at me for Lorena's death."

"No, they'll believe me, Daddy. In fact, they already do. I gave them hard evidence. Lots of it. It was all over the place in your little secret room down in the basement. The extra sets of books, the records of hits with dates and times and why they happened, the garbage bags with all that damning DNA. All I did was gather it up. I handed it over this morning, along with information as to how to get the rest of it, since I couldn't carry it all. I just took the best to get things started."

Ike lunged at Adam, but the agents' grips were firm. He was yanked back so hard he practically got whiplash.

"Goddamn you!" Ike yelled, as they began leading him away. "You're a traitor. A turncoat. All you worked for, and you tossed it away as if it was nothing! You don't deserve to draw another breath. I gave you everything, and this is how you repay me? You go to hell!"

Adam followed as the agents dragged Ike toward the elevator.

"I don't want a life doing what you did. I regret I even share your DNA. But I *will* draw breath. I am going to live for a long, long time and do everything I can to live my life completely opposite to the way I was raised. You're the one going to hell, Daddy, and the Devil already knows you're on your way."

By then they had reached the elevator, and Adam watched as the doors opened and the agents pulled his father inside.

Ike turned, staring at Adam with a malevolent intensity.

Adam looked back as calmly as if he were eyeing a bug on the wall.

The doors slid shut, and just like that, Ike Pappas was no longer a part of his life.

Adam walked away. His debt to his mother had been paid.

The sun was shining when Will Venable

headed up Rebel Ridge. The limbs on the trees shading both sides of the road seemed to be reaching out to each other, sheltering their passing.

Quinn was sitting in the seat beside him — more legroom up front for his wounded leg.

"It is good to be home," he said, and caught a glimpse of a raccoon just before it waddled off into the underbrush.

"I hear you," Will said, but his mind was already on the trip he would start tonight.

He had to be in Birmingham by morning. He'd done longer trips in shorter time. It would be a piece of cake.

Ryal was in the back with Beth, who'd stretched out on the seat and fallen asleep with her head in his lap. The past weeks had been rough, but he would do it all again just to have Beth back in his life where she belonged.

The car hit a bump just hard enough to rouse Beth from her sleep.

"What happened?" she said, as she pushed herself up.

"Your uncle can't drive," Ryal drawled.

Will cursed.

Beth laughed.

Even Quinn managed to crack a smile.

"Sorry-ass roads," Will muttered. "Don't

they ever patch the damn blacktop?"

No one answered; it was understood that the question was rhetorical. Nothing got patched on Rebel Ridge except the occasional heart.

"I am sleeping in my own bed tonight," Quinn announced. He didn't want to fight with Beth, but he'd had all the fussing he could handle.

"I'll be on the road," Will said.

"I'll be in my own bed tonight, too," Ryal said.

"And I'll be with you," Beth said, poking Ryal in the ribs and making him smile.

"I notice neither one of you mentioned sleep," Quinn drawled.

Laughter ensued.

Much later, after Will was gone and they'd delivered Quinn to his home, and Ryal and Beth were finishing their supper dishes, Ryal's cell phone rang.

"Would you get that, Beth? My hands are still soapy," he said.

She nodded and picked it up, noticing it was her grandmother.

"Hello, Granny Lou."

"Hello, Lilabeth. I was just making sure you're settling in all right. Will left here around three o'clock, and I've been busy washing up his bedclothes and such."

"Yes, ma'am, I'm doing fine. I was sure glad Uncle Will was with us in L.A. I know you're sorry to have him gone so much."

"It's all right. Will always did have a Gypsy foot. He wouldn't be happy up here like the rest of us."

"Yes, I know that's so."

Lou paused, then blurted out the fear that was on her mind.

"You're happy here, too, aren't you, girl? I mean, you don't have any plans to go back to California or anything like that?"

Beth turned to look at her gorgeous man with his hands in the dishwater.

"No, ma'am. I don't intend to go back to California or anywhere else unless Ryal Walker is going, too."

Lou smiled. "Well, I didn't mean to be nosy, but I'm glad to hear that. So, now that's settled, have you two set a date for your marryin'? You *are* gettin' married, right?"

Beth grinned. "Yes, ma'am. We're getting married, but we haven't set a date as yet."

"Good. I wouldn't like it known that one of my grandchildren was livin' in sin, especially since she's plannin' on having babies."

"Oh, we're having babies?" Beth said.

Ryal turned around, and the look on his face was priceless. He turned pink; then he rolled his eyes and threw soapsuds in her direction.

"Yes, Ryal promised me you were trying."

Beth laughed out loud. "He promised we were trying? Really?"

"Tell your granny good-night," Ryal said.

Beth was still grinning. "Granny, Ryal says to tell you good-night, so I guess we're going to bed soon and make you that baby you're wanting to play with."

"Oh, my God," Ryal muttered.

Lou laughed in satisfaction. "That's all I wanted to know. See you soon, Bethie."

"Okay, Granny Lou. I love you."

The line went dead in her ear.

She laid down the phone, then folded her hands in front of her like a little girl who was about to recite her memory verse for church and waited for his reaction.

Ryal growled beneath his breath. "How do you suppose I'm supposed to get all interested in making love now, when you and Granny Lou have been talking about this as if it was a recipe you were trying to get right?"

Beth pulled her T-shirt over her head and undid her bra. Her breasts rested heavy against her body as she waited for his re-action.

She didn't have long to wait.

"That'll work," Ryal said, and swooped her off her feet and into his arms.

He carried her back to the bedroom and then proceeded to strip her naked before he undressed himself. Then he crawled into bed, parted her legs and settled into the valley between them with the head of his erection almost there — but not quite.

"So, if we're making a baby tonight, are we making a boy, or are we making a girl?"

Beth frowned. "You can't make that choice. You have to take what God gives you and be happy."

Ryal leaned down and brushed her lips with a kiss.

"I knew that. I was making sure you did, too."

"So what are you waiting for?" Beth whispered.

"A sign from God," Ryal said, and then all of a sudden he was inside her, but still he stayed motionless.

Beth moaned. He was hard and pulsing, and she wanted him to move, but he'd pinned her so hard against the bed she couldn't move for him.

"Ryal . . ."

"What, honey? Is there something I can do for you?"

Beth groaned and then wrapped her legs around his waist the minute he shifted his weight enough to free her.

"Ryal!"

"I'm sorry. I didn't hear you," he said, and then took one of her nipples into his mouth and sucked until it was a hard, achy peak.

"Oh, my Lord." Beth sighed. "Read my mind, you fool, before we both die of want."

Ryal laughed, but the dance had begun, which meant he'd definitely read her mind.

Eleven months and a wedding later, Lilabeth Walker gave birth to a bouncing baby girl.

They named her Sarah, after the Sarah from Beth's past who would live on in Beth's memories and this blessed little child.

The employees of Thorndike Press hope you have enjoyed this Large Print book. All our Thorndike, Wheeler, and Kennebec Large Print titles are designed for easy reading, and all our books are made to last. Other Thorndike Press Large Print books are available at your library, through selected bookstores, or directly from us.

For information about titles, please call:
(800) 223-1244

or visit our Web site at:
http://gale.cengage.com/thorndike

To share your comments, please write:
Publisher
Thorndike Press
10 Water St., Suite 310
Waterville, ME 04901